WHITHER
THOU GOEST
I WILL GO

WHITHER THOU GOEST I WILL GO

NAOMI DATHAN

KIRKDALE PRESS

To Don, of course.

For your wisdom, faith, support, humor, strength,
and most of all, your unfailing love.

Whither Thou Goest, I Will Go

Kirkdale Press, 1313 Commercial St., Bellingham, WA 98225
Visit us at KirkdalePress.com or follow us on Twitter at @KirkdalePress

Print ISBN 9781577996873
Digital ISBN 9781577997313

Kirkdale Editorial Team: Lynnea Fraser, Elizabeth Vince
Typesetting: ProjectLuz.com

NOTE TO READERS

Life for settlers on the Great Plains was never easy, but the winter of 1887–1888 was particularly tough. After fighting tough sod, drought, and prairie fires all summer, an arctic cold front moved across the center of the United States—and stayed. Pioneers huddled next to their stoves, burned braided straw and buffalo chips, and waited for a break in the –30 degree temperatures.

That break came on January 12, 1888. For the first time in weeks, the temperature rose above freezing. Relieved settlers left the warmth of their fires to go to town for supplies, tend to their livestock, or just walk and breathe the balmy air. Children hurried to school to see their friends.

No one was prepared when the storm hit.

Some people saw the cloud coming and had time to run for their shanties or sod houses. Some didn't suspect anything—until the sky went dark and the 45 mph winds screamed to life around them. The temperature plummeted from 9 degrees Fahrenheit to 30 below. The whirling ice—ground to flour-sized particles by the wind—reduced visibility to inches.

Historians estimate that a thousand or more people may have spent the night on the prairie, wandering lost in the storm, burrowing into haystacks, or huddling in the thin outerwear they'd donned that morning. Somewhere between 100 to 400 people perished in the storm.

Most of them were children.

For a true-life account of this storm, read *The Children's Blizzard* by David Laskin. I read this book with a pounding heart. Then I read it again. And then, again. Finally, I was inspired to write the fictional story of Seth, Jem, and Charley, and how they fared on that cold, dreadful night.

CHAPTER ONE

JANUARY 12, 1888

At midnight, Charley woke shivering in his trundle bed. "Ma?"

He rose, but couldn't see his mother's form in the faltering lamplight. "Ma? Mom-mom?"

Still no answer. The cast iron stove was dark and silent. The wind outside howled like a wolf and caught at the door of the sod house, swinging it open and shut.

Where was Ma? Why wasn't she making the stove hot or snuggling him warm under the covers? Was she outside with the wind-wolf?

Charley went toward the door. Ice blew into his eyes, making them water. But he wasn't crying. Not yet. Warmth brushed his legs and a wetness caressed his cheek. The big dog, Zeke, curled his shaggy body against Charley, pushing him backward—away from the open door.

Charley pushed back and shook his finger at him. "No! Bad."

Zeke whined and pressed harder. Charley fell, landing on something warm and solid. It didn't hurt, but he set to wailing anyway, protesting his alone state, his empty belly, and the bitter cold that bit at his eyes and ears and nostrils like fierce ants.

No one came to comfort him, so his cries soon dried up. He scuttled across the still form on the floor, pausing at a tinkling sound. "Ging," he said, remembering. "Ging, ging, ging."

The bell. Pa had rung the bell today. Ding, ding, ding. He'd stoked the fire high and hot, gave Charley cold mash to eat, and clung to the doorframe, ringing and ringing the bell. Once, Pa had fallen to the dirt floor, but after a long while, he pushed himself upright, clutched the doorframe, and rang the bell again.

Now Pa was on the floor again, unmoving.

Charley stepped on Pa's head as he went to look outside "Ma!" The storm sucked his voice away so fast that he didn't even hear himself. The winds answered in high voices, scared and scary at the same time. Was Ma out there in the black with the wind voices?

At last, Charley made up his mind. With Zeke making little worried sounds close beside him, Charley stepped out into the blizzard to find Ma.

AUGUST 14, 1886 (Seventeen months before)

The Reynolds' tea was well attended, but the August heat oppressed the guests, subduing the conversation to a languid pace. Servants discreetly watered—and even fanned— the profusion of roses arranged in vases throughout the room. Ladies and gentlemen sipped English tea and nibbled at scones and trifles to be polite, waiting for the blessed moment when they could return home, untie their cravats and corsets, and have a cool bath.

Jem Perkins had nothing but sympathy for the wilting flowers. She sank onto a thickly upholstered chair next to her sister and fanned herself.

"Can we go home now?" she whispered.

"Hush!" Sally hissed, shooting a worried glance toward their hosts. "Mrs. Reynolds has been planning this tea for weeks. And we haven't even greeted the guest of honor yet."

Hiding behind her fan, Jem peeked at Mrs. Ashley Grayson seated near the window. She couldn't hear what Mrs. Grayson said, but it drew appreciative laughter from the surrounding crowd. Jem smiled at her sister with her eyes. "She sure feeds off the adoration, doesn't she?"

Sally frowned. "Oh, Jem, I'm sure that's not fair. Mrs. Grayson deserves credit for starting the Children's Board."

"Of course she does! But don't you think she has a bit of the look a cat gets when he's found a sunny spot on the windowsill?"

Sally pursed her lips. "You could have worked with her, Jem. I know she asked you to. Then you'd be right up there beside her."

Wasn't that just like Sally to make out that Jem was jealous. What had she to be jealous of?

Jem fanned herself again, waiting until her irritation ebbed before answering. After all, it wouldn't do for Jem—the married woman—to engage in sibling squabbling with her poor spinster sister. Once satisfied that there would be only kindness in her voice, she answered. "I was hardly in a position to take on an outside project right then, was I? A woman's first responsibility is to her family. Perhaps you'll understand … one day."

Sally's cheeks went pink as the arrow found its mark. She was Jem's elder by three years, poor thing, and she didn't even have a serious beau. She sniffed. "I'm sure that was it. I'm sure it wasn't because you discovered that setting up a charitable foundation actually requires a great deal of work."

That stung. Jem lowered her fan. "Now you're just being cruel. You know I work very hard, Sally. Look at how many hours I put into the flower garden last year."

"And then you lost interest and Rogers had to take it over."

"And think of all the poetry I've written. You've never written a poem in your life!"

"And I'm better off for it."

"At least I'm trying things. Maybe I haven't found my true calling yet, but you shouldn't fault me for trying."

Sally opened her mouth, but then shut it again, holding up a restraining palm. "Oh, we're quarreling like children." She sighed. "I apologize. I'm sure you have found your true calling, Jem. I'm sure your true calling is motherhood. You're wonderful with Charley, and what's more important than raising a happy, healthy child?"

Jem settled back in her seat, buying herself a minute by sipping her iced tea. Sally would never have apologized a year ago and would certainly have never offered a compliment. It was disconcerting really. "It is hot," she offered.

Seeing Sally relax, she did too, leaning forward to whisper to her. "And *boring.* I know Mrs. Grayson deserves all of our admiration. I do, truly. But I'm so tired of seeing all the same people and having all the same conversations day after day. This city is chockfull of people, but you couldn't tell by us."

"There's the doorbell," Sally said. "I'm sure it will be someone fascinating."

"Like Mark Twain?"

"That's right. Or Buffalo Bill."

Jem giggled. "How about Jesse James?"

"I think he's dead. Wasn't he killed? Oh—" Her tone changed abruptly. "Look. It *is* someone new."

Jem looked. Her fan froze. The tall man stood in the entry to the parlor, his bearing military even out of uniform. He bowed slightly to Mr. and Mrs. Reynolds, shook Mr. Reynolds' hand, and exchanged greetings with the surrounding guests. Feminine eyes followed his progress as he strode in, but he didn't seem to notice. His pewter gray eyes scanned the crowd and landed on Jem.

She returned his gaze, then lowered her attention to her skirts. "Well, now. The new guest is dashing, wouldn't you say, Sally?"

Sally made a haughty *harrumph.* "Oh, Sister, he looks to be a bit of a ruffian to me. Like someone who spends time in the Wild West. You'd do well to stay away from him, I think."

Jem murmured her agreement and peeked at the man over her fan again. His eyes were still on her. "I believe I'll have some refreshment."

She approached the buffet table, turning her back on the man. Her sister was at her elbows, but when she felt Sally withdraw, she knew the man was approaching. She peeked at him over her shoulder while she ladled pink punch into a glass. He removed his derby and offered a slight bow.

"Ma'am."

"Lieutenant."

His lips twitched at her return address, or perhaps at the Virginia drawl that had crept into the single word. "I wonder if I might join you for a beverage."

"Why, sir, as a guest of this tea party, you are as welcome as anyone to partake, I daresay." Yes, the drawl of her childhood was definitely back, sliding through her words like sugarcane molasses.

"Indeed," the man said. He poured himself punch and downed it in a single motion. The glass looked ridiculous in his large hand, like a child's play teacup. "I have to say, ma'am, that the scenery in St. Paul has certainly improved since my departure to Washington. I don't remember such fine, dainty creatures as yourself frequenting the Reynolds' teas in the past."

Jem smiled at that but flushed a little too. "Perhaps, sir, you are mistaking me for one of the young ladies playing Botticelli in the next room. I'm afraid I don't particularly"—she took her time with the word, savoring each syllable as she hadn't in years—"qualify as dainty anymore."

He imitated her accent, exaggerating it into a parody of a Virginia gentleman. "Why, ma'am, you are very mistaken, I'm sure. Why, you are the ... the *epitome* of feminine beauty and delicacy. Your eyes are as blue as cornflowers. Your lips, well, they're two precious little, uh, roses. In fact, I wonder if we could step out into the gardens and take a stroll together? Just the two of us?"

"Why, sir! Surely you don't expect me to leave this tea with you unchaparoned. Think of the scandal."

He pressed his hand to his chest and gave her moon eyes. "Nothing of the sort, ma'am. I cherish your reputation as I would cherish, well, the soundness of my horse's legs. I would die before compromising your honor. In fact, in order to protect your good name, I am willing to go this far: I will tell these people that we are married."

Jem started to giggle; she couldn't help it. He grinned back at her, and the game was up. She threw her arms around his neck, in spite of all the company around. "Oh, Seth. I'm so glad you're home. I thought you wouldn't be back for two more weeks."

"Jem." He put his arms around her waist and let out a long breath, letting his rigid stance relax. "This was long enough. I missed you. Can we break away from this tea? How is the baby?"

"Oh, I hated to leave him. I think he might be getting diphtheria."

"Diphtheria?" He didn't sound worried. In fact, he sounded a little amused. She backed out of his arms a little to frown at him.

"Diphtheria is very serious."

"You've had the doctor by, I take it?"

"Of course. Twice now."

"And he said?"

"Oh, you know how Dr. Hollister is. You'd have to lay an egg for him to agree you have chicken pox."

Seth took her elbow lightly and led her through the parlor, nodding to the ladies and offering greetings to a few of the men. "Jemima, I'm sure Dr. Hollister would know if Charley had diphtheria. It's very distinct."

"You know I worry. He coughs continually—all night long. And his nose is running."

"Darling, it sounds like he has a cold." He led her to the front door, where they made their apologies to the Reynolds. "Come," he said as he led her to the carriage. "I'll have a look. I certainly know what diphtheria looks like."

Before they'd stepped through the French doors of their home, they could hear Charley's outraged screams ringing through the house. Jem dropped Seth's arm and ran up the long, curving staircase. "Charley! Oh, dear, what's happened?"

She stopped when she entered the nursery. Her boy was upright, clutching the bars of his crib with chubby fingers, red-faced and tearful, but otherwise apparently fine. "Oh, dear." She hurried to lift him and snuggled him against her bosom. "What's the matter, you poor little boy? Are you hurt?"

Charley's cries subsided. He rested his nearly bald head against her, coughing.

"Poor boy," Jem crooned. "Mama's here now. Where's Nursie, hmm? Didn't she hear you cry?"

"He has grown." Seth's voice came from the doorway. "Was he standing? When did he start doing that?"

"Last week." She smiled up at him, keeping her cheek pressed against the peach fuzz of Charley's warm head. "I wrote to you about it, but I suppose you didn't get the letter."

"No, but I haven't stayed in one place for more than a night." He sighed and came and wrapped his arms around Jem, enveloping her and the baby in a hug. "My family."

"Oh, no, ma'am!" Sophie's voice was sharp. "He's supposed to be napping."

Jem and Seth turned to look at the nurse. Her hands were closed into tight fists pressed against her stout body as if she were restraining herself from snatching the child and putting him back in his crib.

"Oh, but he was crying so hard. Poor boy."

"Good afternoon, Lieutenant. Welcome home," Sophie said, then firmed her voice to Jem. "No, ma'am. Colonel Wilkinson was clear on that. The boy must stay in his crib for his nap. The colonel don't want him spoiled."

Seth's voice was pleasant. "Sophie, I believe you work for me, not Colonel Wilkinson."

"No, no." Jem hurried to the crib. "It's fine, Seth. Really. My father is right—you know I'll spoil him."

She peeled Charley off her chest and set him in the crib. His screams renewed, broken by sobs. He rolled and pulled himself back up to his feet. Seth picked him up. Charley reached for his mother, but Seth didn't hand him over.

"Oh, Seth, really. My father is right."

"I haven't seen my son in two months. I believe he and I will take a walk around the nursery."

Sophie gave Seth a long, tight-lipped look and retreated from the room.

"Oh, my," Jem said. "She'll let my father know. She always does."

"Darling, this isn't your father's child. It's ours. Why should he have anything to say about when we hold him?"

"You know how he worries. He wants the best for his only grandson."

Charley stopped reaching for his mother and stared up into Seth's face.

"Look, he remembers you."

Seth made a scoffing sound, but Jem saw he looked pleased. "He's far too young. I'm glad he's letting me hold him though. So other than this dire illness that has him at death's door, he appears to be thriving."

Jem sighed. "You shouldn't tease me, Seth. Ima Caldwell—do you remember her? She said her sister's husband's niece lost both of her little boys last winter—one to diphtheria and the other to pneumonia. And Amy Wiley's whole family is ill."

Seth sobered and kissed Charley's head, holding him a little closer. "It's terrible. I can't imagine what they've suffered. But Charley is healthy. God has blessed us. Let's thank him for it instead of borrowing trouble."

"Y—yes. I do, of course."

She shook her head. It was the sort of comment Sally had been prone to make lately. Seth had been no believer when they met; he'd gone to church only to please Jem and her family. But something had changed over the last year. Seth had changed.

When he was home, he attended church on Sundays as well as a Bible study on Wednesday. He led prayer at mealtimes, even if it was only the two of them sitting at the long polished dining table. She tried to act like it was normal behavior—after all, she was the one who had been brought up in the faith—but it was really rather embarrassing.

"There, you see, Jem? He just needed a little walk." Charley was settled against his father's chest. His face had relaxed and his eyes closed in sleep.

Jem plucked a cloth from the chest of drawers and swiped at the path of drool running down the baby's chin. "You do remember about this part, don't you?"

Seth gave her a wry smile. "I tried to forget. I go through fewer shirts riding on top of the stage coach. Well, I suppose I should put him down."

Jem arranged the soft blankets in the crib. After Seth laid Charley on them, they stood side by side, admiring their little boy. "Isn't he beautiful? I think he's the prettiest baby in St. Paul."

Seth slid his arm around her waist. "By far the handsomest, anyway." He sighed then. "Is your father at home today? I need to discuss some things with him. I didn't see him at the Reynolds' tea."

"He said he had business to attend to today. I'm not sure whether he's at home or at the office. But, Seth, can't it wait? You've just gotten home. Can't we spend the rest of the afternoon together?"

She looked up at him as she finished the question and was surprised to see the grim expression on his face.

"I'm afraid not, Jem," he said. "I'm sorry; I know I just got home, but I have to handle some business."

She gave him a quick pout, making sure to smile with her eyes so he knew she was teasing. "It's a shame when a man would rather spend his homecoming with his father-in-law than with his wife."

Seth didn't smile back, but he kissed her on the forehead. "I'll be home in a couple of hours. We'll have dinner together—just the two of us, all right?"

Jem wrapped her arms around his waist and accepted his embrace. "Hurry back. I'm sure my father will be glad to see you, anyway."

CHAPTER TWO

Jem's father, John Wilkinson, lived on Summit Avenue, only a mile from his daughter but in a much more fashionable section of town. Seth found him in his library. It was one of the finest in the St. Paul area. The fireplace on one end of the well-appointed room drew out the scent of leather from the floor to ceiling tomes and comfortable arm chairs. A tapestry spread across the wall, with a faded fox hunt woven into the fabric. The room smelled of male satisfaction.

John sat behind his broad, gleaming desk, but he rose when Seth was ushered in.

They shook hands across the desk. "Mr. Wilkinson."

"My boy, how are you? How was your trip? You're home earlier than anticipated, I see. I hope my silly daughter was at home to receive you instead of flitting about."

"We have been reunited, sir. I'm sorry to trouble you on a Sunday, but I'm afraid this business can't wait."

"Come, sit." The older man urged him toward a facing chair. "I'll call the girl to bring refreshments."

"Not for me, sir. Thank you."

John Wilkinson leaned back in his own chair and studied Seth's face. "What's happening out in Kansas, son? There's trouble?"

"Here and there. Some of the signals observers want nothing more than to track the weather. Others, unfortunately, want nothing more than to fish."

"To fish?"

"I'm afraid so. One fellow wrote his observations a full week ahead, dropped them off at the telegraph office, and went on a fishing trip. He would've gotten away with it too, if the operator hadn't been taken with the ague. The replacement operator saw the stack of telegrams and sent them all at once. Chicago was surprised to hear that there had been fresh to high winds that gradually became northerly—next week."

The tension in the room lightened with their laughter, but Seth soon sobered. "I wasn't able to finish my inspection tour. I got called back to Washington."

John's posture was relaxed, but his blue eyes were alert. "Washington? I'd heard talk that something was stirring."

"Yes, sir. When the new signal chief took over, he ordered an audit going back five years. The corps is missing somewhere in the range of $150,000." He hesitated. "Your name came up."

"Mine? Why, I resigned my commission over two years ago. They've got nothing to do with me."

"The money disappeared over two years ago. Colonel, if you're found to be responsible for that money, they may prosecute you criminally."

John leaned toward Seth, his eyes narrowed. "What did you tell them?"

"There was nothing I could tell them, sir. I was here in St. Paul when the money went missing. The chief asked me to talk to you informally, before they start any kind of process. Senator Allison—"

"Senator Allison is not a friend of the Signal Corps."

"No, sir, he isn't. He feels very strongly that weather predictions belong with the Department of Agriculture."

"Indications is an army pursuit. Always has been. Who has more at stake than the army when it comes to the weather?"

"Well, the farmers, perhaps. But if this scandal breaks, it surely won't strengthen your argument. That's why the colonel sent me to talk to you."

John met Seth's gaze. The smile had left his eyes. "And say what, boy?"

"Colonel, if you have any knowledge of the whereabouts of the money, or if, er, you check your books and realize that you made a calculation error, the chief would gladly allow you to simply reimburse the corps."

John leaned back in his seat. "I see. So, they've determined that I've stolen this money from the corps?"

"Not necessarily, sir. Naturally, they have to exhaust every avenue of information before reporting the problem."

John stretched his lips in a smile. "I see. And are you headed back to Washington to report on this conversation?"

"I—I'm to report back there before resuming my inspection tour. The chief hoped that—since we're family—you and I might be able to quietly resolve the matter."

"I see," John said again. He drummed his thick fingers on the polished surface of the desk. "Well, you go on back to the chief and tell him that I know nothing of any missing money. I served my time honorably as Assistant Signals Chief, and I resigned my commission without a speck of question as to my conduct."

"Rather abruptly, though, Colonel," Seth said, then wanted to bite his tongue. He had no problem confronting a man who might have dishonored the army. It was a ticklish situation though when the man was his father-in-law.

"For personal reasons."

"So, that's all? You just want me to tell them that you resigned for personal reasons, and you don't know anything about the missing money?"

"Correct." John clapped his hands lightly, business completed. "Now, then, what did you think of that handsome boy of ours? Has he grown much since you saw him?"

That night, Seth and Jem had a lovely dinner in the dining room. Seth was at his best—handsome in his uniform, attentive. Sometimes getting him to talk was like pulling hen's teeth, but not this night. He told Jem stories of his adventures out West. When he told her about a signals officer who had used the weather station to take indecent photographs of a woman, she blushed, but she couldn't help laughing a little too.

A thought struck her. "Did you see her? The woman?"

Seth's cheeks went ruddy. "No. Really, Jemima, don't ask me questions like that."

"But ... how did you know? How did you catch him?"

He sighed, fidgeted in his chair, then laughed. "I saw a photo. Just one. But there had been reports. Anyway, let's talk about something else. I saw William while I was in Kansas."

"You did? How is he? And his wife—what's her name?"

"Susan. They're fine. They're looking forward to meeting you one day. They were hoping to come east for a visit this winter, but they had a bad year."

Jem shuddered. "Every year is a bad year on the frontier. I read where grasshoppers can just devour every green thing on a farm out there. And the Indians! Why don't people stay in civilization?"

Seth took a final bite of duck and dabbed at his mouth with the linen napkin. "A new life in a new land. Opportunity. Adventure. That doesn't tempt you?"

She shook her finger playfully at him. "Don't you think about it, mister. St. Paul is primitive enough for me, after being reared in Virginia."

He smiled, but it didn't carry to his eyes. "Well, we'll see."

She felt her own smile fade. "What do you mean? Seth, surely you're not thinking of moving us. My father is here—my sister. This is where we belong."

"I ... I am thinking about making a change."

Sudden energy propelled her to her feet, rattling dishes on the big table. "What? Surely not! Surely you're not thinking of moving us out West! Why—you aren't taking me to some godforsaken land to live in primitive conditions while the army sends you all over the country!"

"Let's not start the histrionics."

"You might as well murder me right here where I stand!" She gestured toward a knife on the table and threw her head back to expose her throat. "Do it! Just kill me right now! Surely that's more merciful than putting me on a homestead to starve. To watch my baby starve! Oh!" She jerked her head back down to stare at him. "The baby! You'd do this to our Charley—place him in this kind of jeopardy?"

"Jemima, my dear, I don't intend to put you or the baby in danger. The West has become quite civilized. Before you know it, homesteading will be a gentleman's pursuit."

"A gentleman's pursuit! A gentleman's pursuit!" Outrage had her pacing the length of the room. "Why, a woman in Kansas could be scalped as easily as ... as ..."

She halted, searching for an apt phrase. Seth watched her from his seat at the table, too patiently for her taste.

She gave up on her metaphor—she'd work on it for next time—and addressed his argument. "No *gentleman* would drag his wife and baby into the wilderness, where they might be killed by Indians one day and die of drought the very next!" She finished with triumph.

Seth sighed. "Jemima, you're really getting too worked up over—"

"Worked up?" Her voice grew shrill enough that he winced. Well deserved, but—remembering the servants—she lowered it. No need for her father to hear that they had an argument Seth's first night home. "Of course I'm worked up. As you should be, at the very thought of this, this *exflunctication.*"

His brows shot up. "Where did you learn that word?"

She placed her hand on her heart and worked up a couple of tears. "I," she said, her voice quavering, "am a delicate woman. You know, I barely survived my … my confinement … with Charley. Why, if we were in the wilderness, I wouldn't dare to have another child. We would just have to cease all …"

Seth laughed at that. "Pulling out the great guns, eh, Jem?"

"This isn't funny, Seth."

He rose then, put his hands on her shoulders. "Jem, I've run into some complications that may force me to make some difficult decisions."

"What kind of complications?"

"You don't have to worry about that. But I promise you this: My first commitment is to ensure that you and Charley are safe and provided for."

"You're having problems with the army? Is that what you mean?"

He hesitated, appeared to be considering for a minute, but then shook his head. "Darling, you don't need to be burdened with all of that. Do you suppose Charley's in bed already? Let's take him for a stroll."

"Oh, we can't. The night air is bad for him. He'll get colic."

"Nonsense. Come along." He extended his elbow and she took it, pleased to present a harmonious picture to the servants as they headed toward the staircase. She smiled at him as they ascended, and spoke low enough that only he could hear.

"We're not through discussing this. If you think I'm going west, you're much mistaken."

He smiled back and patted her hand. "You'll go where I go, my love."

"Unless you go west," she murmured. "In which case, Charley and I will be staying with my father."

"I'll expect you to keep your promise," Seth answered, then nodded to the elderly man at the top of the stairs. "Good evening, Rogers."

"Good evening, sir. Welcome home."

"Thank you. I'm certainly glad to be home."

Jem nodded to Rogers as well. "It's a beautiful night, isn't it? Quite comfortable after such a dreadfully warm day."

Rogers made his way down the steps, keeping his gnarled hand wrapped securely around the polished handrail. When he was out of earshot, Jem cocked her head at Seth. "What promise do you mean, darling?"

Seth led her forward toward Charley's room. "Why, my love, I'm referring to the promise you made on our wedding day."

She spun on him. "I never promised to go to Kansas with you. I never would have said that!"

"Softly, darling."

She huffed and spoke through gritted teeth. "I never would have said that."

"Whither thou goest, I will go ..."

Jem pressed her lips together and released Seth's arm to walk into the nursery alone. Had she said that? Was that one of their wedding vows? She strained to remember. *To have, to hold, to ... well, obey.*

"Whither thou goest," she muttered. She'd definitely heard that before. Had she promised him that? Maybe, but even so it didn't necessarily include Kansas.

Sophie was in the rocking chair holding Charlie. He'd already had his bath; he was dressed in his cotton nightgown, and his cheeks glowed pink. He squealed when she entered and climbed to a standing position on Sophie's ample lap.

Sophie caught him around the waist and handed him to her, smiling. "There's mother, just in time to say goodnight. We had a fine dinner, didn't we, Charley? And a nice bath."

Jem heard Seth come in behind her but kept her back to him, kissing the baby's chubby fingers and cheeks.

The warmth left Sophie's voice. "Good evening, Lieutenant Perkins."

"Sophie." His voice was pleasant enough, but Jem had to wonder whether he cared for Charley's nurse. "Charley, old fellow. How's business?"

Charley leaned back from Jem to see his father. Jem turned to accommodate him and was startled when the boy pushed off of her to reach for him. "My goodness! He certainly has adapted to your return."

"Not to worry, darling. He and I have some business to discuss, but he's hardly lost interest in his main source of sustenance."

Jem gasped and Sophie clucked.

Charley commented in baby gurgle and slapped his palm on his father's face in a friendly greeting. Seth caught his wrist. "Easy, there, old boy. I'll want that cheek later." He plucked a blanket out of the crib and started out of the room. "Have you done any reading lately?"

"Gah."

"Exactly what I said. So much chaff, it's difficult to find the wheat. Have you read the piece by Stevenson?"

"Gh—gh."

"No, I can't recommend it. A fellow in the capital had a copy, and he shared it with me for a night. He was very excited; called it revolutionary, actually. Something about the duality of man. Not at all to my taste."

Charley burbled another response. Left with no alternative, Jem started to follow, but Sophie's sharp voice stopped her.

"Mrs. Perkins, where is he taking that baby at this hour?"

"Apparently, we're going for a walk." She hurried out before Sophie had a chance to respond.

CHAPTER THREE

The day Seth departed for the West, Jem left the baby with the nurse and walked to her father's house. It was only a mile, but that was enough of a walk on such a warm day.

Jem adored Summit Avenue. The houses were all bigger than the one they'd had back home in Virginia, and each one was adorned with details that made it unique—carvings over the doors, fancy flower beds, brickwork. Father's house wasn't as large or elaborate as, say, Mr. Hill's 35,000 square foot monstrosity. But his Queen Anne style home, with striking brown accents on white, was very distinctive and as large as some of the newer places that were being built.

Sally was strolling the grounds but rushed to Jem when she saw her. "Oh, my goodness! Did you walk the whole way in this heat? It must be 80 degrees out!"

Jem dabbed at her face with her handkerchief. "I am very warm. I suppose I should have come in the carriage, but it seemed foolish for such a short distance."

Sally led her to the wrought iron bench placed near the rose garden and thrust her own fan into Jem's hand. "Sit." She waved at the gardener, who went to alert the housekeeper to bring refreshments. "I didn't expect to see you today. Didn't Seth just leave?"

"He did. I wanted to talk to Father. Is he home?"

"Yes, but you'd better hurry. I know he's got a meeting this afternoon. His attorney."

"His attorney?"

Sally shrugged. "About an investment, maybe? Anyway, here comes Maude with some lemonade. You can have her let Father know you're here."

Father was in the foyer, his hat already on, by the time Jem went inside. His hair had thinned to soft gray tufts on either side of his head, and since his departure from the army, his belly had grown over his belt. The additional bulk only added to his aura of success. "No time today, Jemima. I have business to attend to."

"Please, Father. Just a minute or two. This is so important."

He harrumphed. "If you need some pin money, I'll arrange for it when I return. I must go."

"No ... Father. This is about Seth."

He hesitated. "What about Seth?"

She glanced around. There was no one in sight, but that didn't mean they wouldn't be overheard. Father saw the look and led her to the library. He didn't sit down and didn't invite her to.

"Now, what's this all about? Seth sent you to put the pressure on me?"

"I—what? No, sir. Seth doesn't know I'm talking to you. I wondered if ... if he's mentioned Kansas to you."

"Kansas?" His rigid expression relaxed into something like relief ... but what had he to be relieved about? "What about Kansas?"

"Oh, I'm sure he was just tired. Or exasperated with the army. He's been traveling so much. But he mentioned—*hinted,* really—that he's considering homesteading."

"Homesteading? He's talking of farming? You silly girl, I'm sure you misunderstood. Seth's an army man through and through. And he has a fine life here. Homesteading is for desperate hopefuls that have no other prospects."

"Yes, that's what I said. But he just seemed so serious for a minute. And when I said I wouldn't go—of course I wouldn't move away from you and Sally—he said ... he said *whither thou goest.*"

Her father frowned. "What does that mean?"

"I think it's a wedding vow. He meant that because I'm his wife, I have to go where he goes."

Father's interest in her worries had waned. He patted her arm and checked his pocket watch. "My dear, your Seth would no more become a farmer than you would wear trousers. I'm sure he was just talking to talk. After all, he's a man of science, not a plow pusher."

That was certainly true. Seth loved reading of new scientific advancements. He was always going on about hydraulics and electricity and microscopes. He'd even done some experiments in their basement. Once he'd made her look at one of them, something he'd called an electric motor. He'd wasted quite a lot of time building it and missed a luncheon that she'd wanted to attend, but she'd tried to seem interested.

"But, what if—?"

"If he does go off on a wild hair, you'll stay here, of course. You have the house, and if you're more comfortable, you can move yourself and Charley back home."

"But you don't think he will?"

"Of course not. Don't worry your foolish little head about it. No daughter of mine will be braving the wilds of the frontier."

Jem waited for a feeling of relief, but instead her anxiety deepened, taking on a heavy feel. She forced herself to smile. "Thank you, Father. I—I'm sorry I kept you."

He felt his head, found his hat still in place, and nodded. "You know I always have time if you or Sally have a problem. But I do have to go. Investment meeting, you know. You two cost me quite a pretty penny, I tell you. Have to stay on top of things."

"Well, really, Father. I cost *Seth* the pretty penny these days."

"Well." Her father harrumphed.

"Not that I'm forgetting about the house," she hurried to add. "It was a lovely wedding gift. But Seth feels very strongly that we need to live on his money—his salary and what his father left him."

"A pittance. Be sure to come to me when your expenses outweigh his bank account, as they no doubt soon will. You didn't bring the boy?"

"No, I thought the walk in the heat would be too much. He's still coughing at night."

"Best keep him indoors then."

"I thought so." Thinking of Charley, her smile felt more natural. "I think he's saying 'Mama.' He says 'muh.' "

"Very good. But the true sign of genius will be when he says 'grandfather.' " He extended his elbow and led her back to Sally on the lawn before going to his carriage.

As August moved into September, the weather cooled to a pleasant warmth. Jem, who had been assigned the modest task of making the flower decorations for the Women's League Autumn Luncheon, decided to match them to the dazzling golds, reds, and yellows of the trees on Summit Avenue.

She bought the tissue paper and—on the Wednesday before the luncheon—conscripted her sister to help her fold.

They'd accumulated a small stack in the center of the work table when Rogers tapped on the doorframe of her sitting room. "You have a letter, Mrs. Perkins."

"Bring it in, Rogers. It's just us."

She scanned it, closed it and set it aside. "Will you hand me more wire, Sally?"

Sally pursed her lips and studied Jem's face as she handed it over.

Jem took it and aimed to create a distraction. "Mr. Reynolds mentioned that Sergei Markov will be arriving in town soon."

Sure enough, Sally looked away from the folded paper and back down at her flower, pink creeping up her cheeks.

"That's no interest of mine."

"Mr. Reynolds said he'd asked after you."

Sally jerked her gold tissue paper into shape. When it tore, she dropped it to the surface of the work table, muttering, "Bother!" She left it and aimed for a distraction of her own. "What are you wearing to the luncheon? I have my green lawn, but I don't want to wear it if you're wearing your green dress."

"I ... may not be attending."

That got her attention—she goggled at Jem.

"But, of course you're attending!" Sally picked up her half-made flower and shook it at her. "We're not making all of these dreadful decorations so you can stay home and lounge about. You're going to come and make up compliments to say to Mrs. Reynolds, and pretend to admire Susie Gorham's new dress, and act like you don't know that Irma Reece is smitten with your husband. You're going to go and suffer, just like me!"

Jem giggled. "There is that. Luckily, my husband has no interest in women twice his age. And size."

Sally frowned. "Don't say that. You know better than to say unkind things about people. I—I shouldn't have brought her up either. Irma Reece doesn't have a mean or ... cunning ... bone in her body. And after three children, she's bound to—well—bound *not* to have the same figure she had before."

Jem raised her palm. "I'm just playing, Sally! Truly!"

"Irma would never hurt anyone."

"No, she wouldn't." Jem started winding paper again, giving Sally a minute to calm down. "I vow you're a puzzle to me. You're really very sweet under all that fire and temper."

"I don't have a temper!"

Jem responded by pushing the sleeve of her dress up and pointing solemnly to a thread of raised flesh, nearly two inches long, arcing over her forearm.

Sally blushed. "You were being cruel to that cat."

"I was tying—*trying* to tie, at any rate—a firecracker to its tail. A time-honored tradition among the youth in our part of Virginia. And thanks to you and your sewing needle, I lost the dare and had to kiss Johnny Quinn."

Sally laughed. "You did not!"

"Well ... I would have. But when he saw the blood and heard how hard I was crying, he released me from my commitment. And gave me halvsies on his turnover."

"You see, it all worked to your benefit in the end." Sally's smile faded suddenly. "It always does."

Jem eyed her. "Is there a problem?"

"No." She set her handful of wires and tissues down, rose to look out the window. "No. There's not."

Jem wondered if she should go to her. "Are you tired of making flowers? Maybe we should take a break. It's pretty out—do you want to take a stroll?"

Sally turned and forced a smile. "I'm fine, Jem. Really." She returned to the table, lifted her half-completed flower, and twisted it idly between her fingertips. "Why did you say you aren't going to the luncheon?"

Jem drew in a deep breath. "Kate Baker's little girl, Belle, is ill. Do you remember Kate?"

"You were in school together." Then Sally remembered. "Oh."

"Exactly."

"I thought you'd stopped communicating with her. Father said—"

"I know what father said. But Kate's been my friend practically since we were in diapers. I couldn't disdain her because of something she had no control over. She's asked me to come by on Saturday, and I shall. If I get back in time, I'll go to the luncheon."

"Father will hear if you miss it."

"I don't care." Jem made her voice breezy and ignored the tightening in her chest.

The two women worked in silence for a while, stacking colorful yellow and orange flowers on one another.

Jem folded her paper into an accordion shape, thinking about Kate. Poor Kate who'd been banned from polite society at 12, after her mother ran away with a gambler. Poor Kate who'd married a sincere boy who died of pneumonia the very next winter, leaving her alone with a little girl and no means of support.

Sally gave her yellow tissue a final light tug and held the flower in front of her to examine it with a critical eye. "I'll send a basket with you for Kate—sewing things, and I have some lovely yellow calico."

"Oh." Jem lowered her own flower. "Thank you, Sally."

"And you should take some apples. We have so many growing in the back. And have Cook make some of her sweet rolls."

Her sister's gifts and her own filled two large baskets. Jem had Rogers drive her to the ratty side of town and help carry the baskets to the chipped door of the small, wounded house. She knocked lightly, then pounded the knocker and nearly gave up when the handle finally turned and the door opened.

Kate was a tall woman, naturally thin, with black hair so curly it wouldn't stay properly restrained. Jem loved her for her wide smile and merry ways, but the Kate who answered the door today seemed lifeless. Her skin was pale and her brown eyes were dull and blank.

"Jem," she said, but didn't smile, didn't move back to allow her in. "You're here."

"Kate." Jem hesitated. "May I come in?"

"Oh." Kate's voice was hollow. She stepped back and nodded to Rogers. "Please."

Belle? Was Belle ... Surely not. Surely Kate was just exhausted from caring for a sick child while trying to keep body and soul together. And no wonder! Jem looked around the place—a single, musty-smelling room. But ragged curtains prevented much light from entering through the soiled windows. Kate lowered herself to a chair, and Jem sat across from her.

"Kate," Jem said. "What—?"

"She died, Jem. She drowned."

"Drowned! I thought she was ill."

"She drowned." Kate's eerie calm frightened her. "The water was inside her. You couldn't see it. But I saw my pa drown kittens before, and I know what a drowning looks like. Belle drowned."

"Oh, Kate! Oh ... oh, I don't know what to say. Is she—when did it happen?"

"Right after I wrote to you." Kate plucked at the fabric of her faded skirt, staring toward Jem without seeming to see her. "She died."

"Is there ... a funeral?"

"She's buried already. They took her. I tried to find the grave—they say there are number markings. But no one would help me find it."

"Oh, Kate." Jem felt tears pressing the back of her eyes but didn't dare release them—not when Kate was so dry-eyed and stunned. She glanced at the baskets stacked on the floor by the front door, then back at her friend. "You must come and stay with me. Seth's traveling again, and when he returns, he'll be glad to have you."

But Kate didn't move. "No. No ... I'll just stay here."

"Oh, Kate you mustn't! You can't stay here alone. Oh, I should have had you and Belle staying with us all along."

"Your father—"

"Blast my father!" The shocking words rang in the little room. Another wriggle of tension jiggled through Jem's belly. If she succeeded in persuading Kate, her father would be furious. He wanted no connection between his respectable family and Kate's broken one. But she couldn't leave her friend here like this. Jem rose.

"Come, let's get you packed."

But Kate remained where she was. "Thank you. Thank you, Jem. But I'll stay here. I'll just stay here."

"Kate, please." Jem's tears were getting away from her, in spite of herself. "Please. Oh, this is just awful. Awful!"

Kate patted her, almost absentmindedly. "It will be fine. It will all be fine. Thank you for coming."

"Oh ... I brought you ... some things. But, Kate, please. Come and stay with me. We have plenty of room."

But Kate refused. In the end, Jem did what she could: She made Kate some tea, tidied up the place, and slipped money into Kate's handbag before leaving her with a hug. Over the next few days, Jem couldn't stop thinking about her. By Wednesday morning, she'd made up her mind.

"I'll insist," she told Rogers. "She has to come stay with me. She can't be alone."

"Your father's not going to like that, Mrs. Perkins."

She waved her hand at him. "I'm a grown married woman. I don't need his help choosing my friends."

Rogers drove her back to the pitiful little house. But this time no one answered, no matter how hard Jem knocked. Rogers booted the door open, and they found the place empty but for dust. Kate was gone.

Two days later, Rogers brought Jem another letter from Kate. Their eyes met as he handed it to her. She saw sympathy in his eyes … and something else. Accusation?

She used her thumbnail to open the envelope and read.

> *Dear Jem,*
> *You have always been a good friend to me, so I don't want you to worry that I've left. There was nothing to keep me here any longer, so I've gone out West. I know it sounds like I've lost my mind. Maybe I have—I just can't tell anymore. But I answered an ad from a homesteader. He has four children and needs a wife. It will be a while until I can write again, I imagine, but I will always be*
>
> *Your friend,*
> *Kate*

Seth did not expect this meeting to go well.

He'd chosen his location carefully—the park. Quiet, neutral, and fairly private on this drizzly October day. He made sure he had his thoughts in order, his stream of logic intact, even though he knew logic wouldn't help him today.

He was dealing with his wife.

"Jem," he began.

Her hand was tucked into his elbow. She'd been smiling, chattering about Charley's first steps and first words, but he'd seen the glittering suspicion in her eyes. She knew he had something to say, and she knew she wasn't going to like it.

"Darling," he began again.

"Yes, dear?"

"Some things have come up."

"What do you mean, dear?"

He wanted to shudder at her false brightness. He'd seen storm clouds gather on the prairie that had less potential for destruction contained in them. "Darling, I'm afraid that my career in the army has ... taken a turn for the worse."

"Oh!" Her face cleared—the sun shining through the clouds. "Your career? Have they moved you out of indications? I know how you enjoyed that."

"I've resigned my commission."

She stopped walking and chewed her bottom lip, considering this. "So you aren't in the army anymore?"

"No."

"Oh, but Seth, that's wonderful! You won't have to travel so much. I've wished—a thousand times, I've wished—that we could be together more, be a true team, making decisions and building our life."

That startled him. "You have?"

"Oh, of course! I'm not the sort of woman who wants to sit back and let life pass me by. I want to accomplish things. And I want to do it with you! Look how Mr. and Mrs. Reynolds have worked together to perform so many good works. And how Mrs. Grayson helped research Mr. Grayson's book about Africa. We could do something like that. Well, not a book about Africa. I don't care for travel books, do you?"

"N—no. So, Jem, you'd like us to be partners?"

"Oh, yes!" She spun to hug him. "Oh, I'm sorry! I know you must be sad about the army, but it's hard for me to be sad about this."

"Jem, there's more. I—hmm. Where do I begin?"

Jem smiled at him, released his arm to spin in a happy circle, and turned her face up to let rain drops fall on it. "What else? What shall you do? Write a book?"

"No, Jem. I'm afraid we've had some financial reversals."

Her smile faltered. "What sort of financial reversals?"

"Well, of course, we're losing my income from the army. We are also … losing the house."

She tipped her head in the manner of a curious little bird eyeing an intruder. "Losing the house? How can that be? My father gave us the house."

"That's … how it can be. We have to give the house back to your father. He … owes some money. It's difficult to explain."

Jem tucked her hand back into his arm. "Oh, you're just being silly. My father has plenty of money. Look at the house he's in. Why, it's twice as big as ours."

She started to walk, but Seth turned her to face him. "Listen, you need to understand. I no longer have a salary. As of the first of the year, we no longer have a house."

"But, I love our house!"

"I'm sorry. I truly am."

"Well," she forced a brave smile, "I'm sure we're going to be just fine."

Seth felt a little release of tension in his chest. He shouldn't have underestimated her. Certainly, Jem was opinionated, perhaps even a tad spoiled, but she would stand by him through thick and thin. Why, she'd make a fine frontier woman!

Jem drew in a bracing breath and managed an even better smile. "After all, my father's house is very large. There's plenty of room for all of us."

Seth closed his eyes. "No, my love. We won't be staying with your father."

"Why? Of course we will, Seth! He wouldn't have it any other way."

"Jem, we won't be staying with your father. For one thing, I don't believe he'll be keeping his house either. For another ... we just aren't, that's all. We're a separate family. We need to make a life for ourselves. Just like you were talking about, remember? Working together, setting goals together—remember?"

Jem took her time reading his expression. He tried to maintain the impression of strength and confidence. They could do this. They could embark on a wonderful new life together. They would be happy and successful.

But when she spoke again, there was no warmth in her voice. "What, exactly, did you have in mind?"

Seth drew in a deep breath. "Jem, I've bought a farm."

Her voice went to shrill. "In Kansas?"

"No. No, not in Kansas."

Jem raised her palms up and closed her eyes briefly. "Not in Kansas. Not in Kansas." She nodded. "Very well. Farming. Not my cup of tea, but ..."

She stepped away from him, pacing, thinking. "A farm." She nodded again. "That could be very nice."

"It could?"

"Yes. A country place. I think I'd enjoy that. Rogers could manage the help, don't you think? He's never run a farm before, but he's very capable. He did a wonderful job with my little garden." Her smile was returning. "Seth, this could be marvelous. I think Charley will be happy on a farm. We'll get him a pony when he's bigger. Sally can come visit—we'll have plenty of room, won't we? A big farmhouse! She'll be so jealous! There's nothing finer than acres of rolling green hills, with pastures of beautiful horses. And sheep. Shall we have sheep? They're so adorable and fluffy. I'm very fond of sheep."

She clasped his hands in hers. "Oh, Seth, I was so worried. I shouldn't have doubted you. We'll have a happy life in … where did you say the farm is? I hope it's not too far away. I do like to see Sally every day. Is it near here?"

"Jemima," Seth said. For once she waited patiently for him to go on. He didn't want to, but he did. "Darling, I bought a homestead. In Nebraska."

Jem's expression went blank.

The drizzle had subsided, allowing the sun to break through the clouds. Birds—cheered by the sight—began to sing harmony to the melody of the rustle of the trees' damp leaves. Seth had one minute—just one minute—to enjoy the sound. And then the howling winds of Jem's temper blew in.

CHAPTER FOUR

Jem didn't know what she was doing here, and couldn't believe that she was here. But—soon, certainly—Seth would realize his mistake and take them home. She'd be glad to ride the immigrant train again—suffer bouncing on the hard wood bench on her sore bottom, inhale dust and the pungent smell of cow manure and urine—if it meant going home.

Seth and another man hunched over the table by the stove in the drafty, one-room shanty, figuring on paper and muttering to each other. The oldest of four gaunt children held Charley, chucking him under the chin so he giggled and grabbed her fingers. Susan, the mother of the four children, kneaded dough at the far end of the table from the men. She didn't glance at them or speak.

Jem shifted on the seat of the rocker and adjusted the quilt over her lap. It was only November, but the wind howled through the cracks of the shanty walls like a living thing, biting hard enough to leave marks on exposed skin. Winter was no stranger to her; St. Paul hadn't been a tropical paradise, and over her three years as a resident, she'd grown accustomed to the harsh weather. She'd take walks when other women wouldn't and considered herself quite hardy and brave for it.

She realized now, with some embarrassment, that it was fine and dandy to go walking in bitter cold when you always had the option to step back into your warm home and have your cook bring you hot tea to warm your insides. It was quite another to be sitting idle by the fire and still have fingers numb from the chill.

Susan slapped the bread dough on the table hard enough to rock it. Her husband, William, lifted his pen and looked at her, but didn't say anything. When she divided the dough into loaf pans, William resumed making notes.

"Diversify," William said.

"Diversify," Seth agreed. "I'm telling you, raising a single crop out here is suicide. Conditions are too unpredictable."

William raised his palm. "Unpredictable? Fires took nearly all of my crops last year, and grasshoppers took it all the year before. Diversify all you want, brother. The grasshoppers don't care."

"It's a tough country."

William glanced at his wife. "It is," he said. "And I tell you, we'd be gone from here, had we anywhere else to go."

The words were like nails being hammered into Jem's flesh. Could Seth not see? Could he not see what an awful decision he'd made? Seth looked up and their eyes met over William's bent head. Jem let her anger burn through her. Seth didn't flinch. The connection was broken by a metallic clang as Susan slammed the lid on the big pot. William started and then got to his feet.

"Let me help you," he said quietly. He went and helped her lift the black kettle onto the surface of the cook stove. She offered him a tight-lipped smile.

Susan had seemed friendly enough when they'd arrived last week. In fact, Jem had actually been embarrassed by the effusive welcome. Susan had clutched her hand in both of hers. "I'm so glad to meet you—so glad you're finally here. How was the train—was it awful? William said you rode the immigrant car. Oh, you must be so exhausted! And freezing! My, the cold has really set in, hasn't it?"

William had practically pried his wife away. "Come, love, let's invite them inside the house. You'll have plenty of time to get to know one another."

Susan ushered her into a shed of all places. But when Jem's eyes adjusted to the light, she saw a table, chairs, and a bed. Four children sat lined up on a bench with slates in hand. They stared at her with unnaturally large eyes, like startled night animals.

"Look, children!" Susan cried. "Our guests have finally arrived."

Jem barely had time to realize that the shed was a house before Susan was guiding her toward a wall below a hole in the ceiling. Short planks were nailed at intervals on the wall. "We set you a bed upstairs. It's not quite as big as the one down here—no room. But William thought you'd like the privacy more than the space. And it won't hurt the girls to stay down here on the floor, not a bit. Why, we'll just make them a nice nest of quilts by the stove, and they'll be as happy as little birds."

Jem glanced at the children, still staring, and thought— happy as owls, perhaps. Susan gave her a gentle push. "Go on, have a look. We've worked all week getting it ready."

"U—up here? Climb up here?"

"That's right."

"Oh, but—" Jem looked around the room, casting about for some alternative. She was expected to climb into the attic? To *sleep* in the attic of this dark little shed? Seth was still outside, so she couldn't glare at him. Then again, she'd glared at him so much recently that he probably wouldn't have taken notice.

"Oh, don't worry. Your husband's still holding the baby. When he brings him in, my Lilly will look after him. Go ahead."

Jem tried to hold the boards loosely as she climbed up, fearful of splinters. When her head rose above the attic's floor level, she paused to look around. Sure enough, crates of supplies were shoved tightly to one side of the attic to make room for the bed. Ropes had been strung across the end of the room, forming a bed which looked hardly large enough for one person. A Joseph's Coat quilt was spread over the top. The red and blue calico fabrics were the only bright colors in the room.

They would be staying here until spring? In this dim and dismal room in this shabby little house with its drafty walls and children who looked like street urchins?

Jem couldn't contain her cry of despair.

"What's wrong?" Susan's voice, sharp with alarm, came from below her.

"Oh. Oh, dear, the ... quilt. It's the quilt. It's so beautiful."

"You like it? Truly?"

"Oh, I do!" Jem was glad that she had that single positive thing to say, but Susan seemed gratified.

"Go on up. In fact, stay up there for a minute, and I'll start handing your things up. I see your man coming now. He's bringing in your bags and your baby."

Jem had no choice but to stand in the chilly room, right in the center so she didn't bump her head on the slanted ceiling. Seth was so tall he could practically reach to put the crates and bags right on the attic floor. All Jem had to do was shift them off of his hands and onto the plank floor, then scoot them to one side. Down below, she could hear Susan making much of Charley and Charley babbling his happy response.

Her heart clenched, hearing his happy sounds. Poor boy— brought into the wilderness of the Kansas prairie through no fault of his own. Would he grow to look like William and Susan's children—hollow eyed, with a quiet kind of desperation? Charley would likely perish here, of cold or starvation, long before spring. He'd never even suffer the final leg of their journey, through Kansas into Nebraska. He'd never see the homestead Seth had selected and purchased sight unseen.

Seth's head appeared beside her ankles. "That's the last of 'em." He climbed the rest of the way up. "Well, look at these fine accommodations." He bent to talk through the hole in the floor. "William, you've outdone yourself. It's more than we deserve, having a room of our own, when you're all bursting at the seams as it is."

"We're just glad to have you here."

Seth stood again and looked around. He went to the bed, bent and slid a flat wooden box with low sides out from under. It was made up to be a bed, with a child-sized mate of the Joseph's Coat quilt. Seth made a pleased sound. "Trundle bed."

"What ... what is that?"

"That's where Charley will sleep. Pulls right out from under at night. Pretty handy, eh?"

Jem couldn't stop herself from hissing. "My baby is *not* sleeping in that."

Seth frowned at her and moved close so he could speak into her ear. "Jemina, you will not offend my friends. They have gone through so much trouble for us."

She compressed her yell into a whisper. "You cannot expect our baby to sleep in a box on the floor like so much— like so much—potatoes."

"Potatoes come in bags."

"Fine, then," she snapped. "Like so many apples! He needs a proper crib in a proper room. One where there isn't a hole in the floor designed to lure him to a tragic death by plummeting. One where he won't catch pneumonia and die the first week. Look at those walls, Seth! You can see sunlight through them!"

"Shh!" He glanced down toward the first floor, holding her elbows so she faced him. "Now, Jem, we'll make sure that—"

Her tears started without forethought. Seth's eyes rolled up to the ceiling, but Jem grabbed the front of his shirt. "Seth, please. Take us home. Please. I'll work; I'll take in sewing. I'll do anything you want. I don't mind living in a smaller house. I don't mind losing Rogers or the other help. But, please, take us home!"

Seth gently removed her hands. "We've already discussed this."

"Yes, we have. And, I admit, I didn't believe you. I thought … well, I thought you were trying to teach me a lesson."

His forehead creased. "For what?"

"Well, I know I didn't always appreciate everything you did, and I know you were upset that … that I sometimes give too much weight to my father's desires."

"You certainly do, but that—"

"I certainly didn't think you were going to bring us out here to the Wild and Wooly West—not really. I didn't think you would! And when you did, when you put us on that train, why, I've just been praying that God would help you see what a dreadful mistake you're making."

"Jemima, you have to accept this. This is our new life now."

"But I've been praying! I've been praying and praying, and I've been reading the Bible every night. God's going to answer my prayer, Seth. He's going to help you see that we have to go home."

Seth ran his hands up her arms—trying to comfort her, she knew, but it just irritated her.

"Darling," he said. "Why don't you pray for our success at our new adventure? Remember how you talked about us being a team? Farming is the only way for a husband and wife to work side by side. You know that."

"Farming, yes! Fine—I'll farm. Take me to a farm! A real farm." More tears rolled down her cheeks, feeling warm against her chilled skin. "A real farm with pigs and chickens and hired help to milk the cows. And a big white farmhouse. Does the homestead have a big white farmhouse, Seth?"

He rocked his head in a noncommittal way. "It ... will."

"It will?"

"Yes, darling. We'll build it together, side by side, working as a—"

"Quit that!"

"Quit what?"

"Using my words against me!" She pulled away and stalked the short distance to the bed and back. "Anyway, if we were truly a team, you would have consulted me before buying the homestead. You wouldn't have just hauled me out here to this frozen wasteland without my consent."

Seth walked to the bed also, but sat down. The ropes creaked softly under his weight. His shoulders slumped a little forward; he'd lost some of his military bearing in recent weeks. His voice had a note of resignation she hadn't heard before. "Jem, if I had ... if I'd consulted you about what to do, what would you have said?"

The question made her pause. "Why, I ... well, I would have said to buy a proper farm. If you wanted to farm, I would have said to buy a nice, established place near St. Paul."

"With what money?"

The question frustrated her. Her arms went up, starting to wave, but she lowered them. There was hope. If she could give a reasonable answer and show Seth that she could be his partner in making a reasonable decision—one that didn't involve grasshoppers and prairie fires—perhaps he would book a fare back home yet. "Well, my father gave us that house for our wedding and it's in a very fashionable part of St. Paul. Surely it's worth even more now. How much money did we get from that?"

"None."

"None?"

"No. I told you, Jem. Your father owed some money. I signed the house over to him so he could pay it back."

"B—but, it was ours. It was our house. He should pay his debts with his own money. He has plenty! He has investments."

"He made those investments with the money in question. Did you never wonder why your circumstances were so much better after he left the army? He has no money besides that. He'll have to cash out all of those investments—as well as the proceeds from the sale of both of our houses—just to temporarily satisfy the … his debtors. And he still owes more."

Jem sighed sharply. "Then you shouldn't have given him the house. If he still owes more anyway, what difference would it have made if he owed that much more?" She sat beside him, lowering herself carefully, hoping the ropes could bear both their weights. "See? If we'd talked about this before, I could have told you that in time."

"And then your father would be in jail."

"Oh." She made a scoffing sound. "So, this is about the army thing. Really, Seth, don't be dramatic. My father told me there was a misunderstanding—some sort of budget-line-item-deficit allocation didn't tally up properly. Why don't we go home and stay with him? Then, once that gets sorted out, he can give us our money back and we'll decide what to do."

"We're not taking any more money from your father!"

"Well, all right! You don't have to bark at me."

"I'm sorry, darling. I apologize. But, from now on, we use our own money. So we know where it came from."

"Do we have any money?"

"Not much."

"Oh, for mercy's sake!" She couldn't help throwing her hands up once, but then she forced them back into ladylike repose on her lap. "And what money we had, you threw away on this mythical homestead."

"And, I ask again, what would you have done?"

"We could have rented a house in the city. Mrs. Mason's nephew's place is empty. And that's a lovely home. You know the one I mean? I would like to live there."

Seth raised his brows. "I'm sure you would. It's nearly twice as large as the one we had."

"Yes, but it has that awful yellow color. We would have to paint. Do you think he'd mind? Do you think it's still available? We could send a telegraph and ask."

"Jem, we can't afford a single month's rent of that house. We could rent, perhaps, a little house in the *un*fashionable part of town, and we could have managed for a year or so. But then what? What is our future? A gradual descent into permanent poverty."

"Oh, I don't understand! I don't understand this. Why did you quit the army? At least with that we had a small amount coming in. That would have tided us over until my father got back on his feet."

Seth's voice took on an edge. "Stop thinking your father is going to rescue you. He'll be lucky if he stays out of jail, Jemima. That wasn't just a line-item error or however you described it. I didn't want to say this, but you're leaving me no choice: Your father stole that money! He stole $150,000 from the Indications Department. He will have to sell the houses and cash everything in so he could pay as much back as possible, but it's not even half of what he owes."

"Oh, Seth, don't be ridiculous. My father didn't steal anything. He told me you'd come up with some kind of wild accusation like that."

"He did?"

"Yes. He said you'd have to, to justify bringing the baby and me into one of your mad experiments."

"This hardly equates to taking weather readings on the roof of our house or trying to make one of Mr. Edison's carbon electric lights."

"Yes, it hardly does. This makes your previous experiments look almost rational."

"Jem, farming is science in action. Farming is the *point* of science, or, at least, one of the points. Farmers don't have to rely on luck and weather anymore. They can benefit from the knowledge of men who have figured out the best methods, the best ..."

He trailed off, seeing, she supposed, that he'd lost her interest. "Anyway," he said. "Since you've had no helpful ideas, you might as well accept that—"

A wail from below had her jumping to her feet. "Oh, the baby! You shouldn't have left him down there."

She hurried to the makeshift ladder and stepped down onto the first rung, ruffling her skirts around her so they would precede her downward and not expose her in some shocking way. This wouldn't do. These accommodations simply would not do. If Seth refused to book fare on the next train back to St. Paul, he would at least have to arrange for them to stay in a pleasant hotel until spring came and they left for their new home in the wilderness.

But there were no hotels nor inns nor even well-appointed boarding houses in this part of the world. And Seth wouldn't have moved them anyway, because they were paying for their room and board in goods and food that William's family very badly needed and wouldn't have taken as charity. As the weeks passed, Jem grew ever more unhappy with their situation.

Charley was in perpetual danger; she couldn't take her eyes off of him for a minute. If he wasn't trying to touch the stove, he was picking up some dirty thing off the floor and popping it in his mouth. Seth slid her trunk over the hole in the attic floor at night, but Jem still couldn't rest easy for fear he would wake and find something deadly in the attic to play with or somehow move the trunk and fall. Susan's girls were anxious to play with him, but Jem worried that they would make him sick. Their hands were usually grimy from tending the single cow and few chickens. Since she'd begun sleeping on the floor, the smallest one—Dahlia, Jem thought her name was—suffered from a constantly running nose. She carried no handkerchief but used her sleeve or the back of her hand to clear her face.

Susan's warm welcome had cooled into frigid courtesy after a day or two. Today though, as she wordlessly slammed pots and pans in the corner of the shanty that served as the kitchen, her chill seemed to have re-heated into outright hostility. Susan wasn't family, nor even a friend, really. Still, it was distressing to live in the same house with someone who seemed to have only unreasonable hatred for her.

Jem pushed herself out of the rocker, letting the quilt slide to the floor. Cold air slapped against her through her dress, but she suffered it and went to Charley's trundle bed that set against the wall by the cook stove. It was near enough to gather some heat but far enough that no sparks from the fire could reach it. Charley was still napping, curled on his side in the box, his mouth closed around his thumb. It was one of many battles she'd lost—her baby slept in a box. He loved his little bed, which was some consolation.

Seth carried it downstairs during the day for naps, but Charley often climbed into it to play or hear Lilly read *Alice in Wonderland* from her treasured volume.

"Jem?" Seth's voice was soft behind her.

She turned and felt an impulse to smile a greeting. He was so handsome; her heart still fluttered when he came unexpectedly into view. But she caught it just in time. She couldn't afford to seem content here or Seth would never agree to take them home. "Yes?"

"Darling, I want you to take over in the kitchen for today."

Jem blinked. "I beg your pardon?"

"I want you to take over in the kitchen for the rest of today. Dinner is mostly prepared, I believe. You can just finish it up, churn the butter, and prepare supper."

Now she did smile. "Seth, you know I don't know my way around a kitchen, not even one as small as this. Why, I wouldn't know how to boil water."

Seth didn't smile in return. "You put the pot full of water on the stove and stoke up the fire. When bubbles appear over the surface of the water, it is boiling."

"It was a figure of speech," Jem said, but she tested his description against her meager smattering of knowledge and decided it was worth storing in her memory, just in case. "Anyway, Susan is doing a fine job. It's not what we're used to, but it's filling. Far better than what I could prepare."

"Susan is feeling … under the weather. You need to step in and help."

Jem frowned and looked over at Susan. The woman's thin shoulders were bowed, her hands covered her face. William stood with his arms wrapped around her, rocking her slightly and murmuring. Jem felt a pang at the sight—jealousy? What could that woman have that Jem would want? William was half the man Seth was—shorter, barrel-chested, and eyes such a light blue they looked like they'd been left out in the sun for a summer. "That's so ... vulgar. Them embracing like that, with us right in the house. Seth, go and remind them that we're still here."

Seth's intense gaze never left her. "Jem, Susan is tired. We've added three people for her to cook and clean for."

Seeing the cool anger in his eyes, Jem remembered to speak softly. "And we paid for that service, didn't we? How many crates of supplies did we give them? How many bags of potatoes and onions?"

"We didn't *give* them anything; we used the goods as payment for our room and board. Our arrangement is more than fair to us, believe me." He paused. "More than I would have imagined."

"What does that mean?"

"It means you are being a very unpleasant houseguest."

Jem gasped. "Unpleasant? Unpleasant! Well, I like that! I'm thrown into this ... this *pit* of dirt and disease, forced to suffer constant cold and the most bland food I could have ever imagined and no conversation to speak of, and you call me unpleasant?"

Seth ground her name through gritted teeth: "*Jem.*"

She realized that her voice had risen after all and that Susan had lifted her face from her husband's arms to look at her. Her ruddy cheeks were damp from tears. When Jem's eyes met hers, Susan's face crumpled. William wrapped her up again, muffling her sobs.

"Well," Jem said. She looked at Seth. "What's happened to her? Did she burn herself?"

Seth took a menacing step toward her. "Go over to the *lean-to*, get the pail of *milk*, put it into the *churn*, and make the *butter*."

"For heaven's sake, Seth." Jem inched toward the door. "You don't have to speak to me like that. I'm your wife, not a mongrel dog."

Seth's upper body leaned in an aggressive stance, pivoting to follow her progress. She snatched her shawl off the hook by the door, and scooted out to the lean-to. Snowflakes drifted onto her hair and face. She brushed them off, grabbed the handle of the pail, and jerked upward. It stayed firmly planted on the frozen dirt floor. Heavy. She rubbed the muscle she'd just wrenched. "Seth?"

"What?" His voice came through the thin wall between the house and the lean-to. He bit off the word like it was a piece of stringy meat.

"Um … nothing. Nevermind." She braced her legs and lifted slowly, anticipating the weight this time. "Goodness!" The pail rocked on the handle. Precious drops of the creamy liquid splashed onto the ground, forming dark spots. Jem peeked toward the house. If anyone suspected, no one called an objection. She used the toe of her boot to rub the spot out and lugged the milk inside.

Then she stopped. Seth, William, and the four girls stared at her. "W—where's Susan?"

"She's gone upstairs to lie down," Seth said. "William and I have traded beds."

That took her aback. "So where shall I sleep?"

Seth glared at her. "With me, obviously, Jemina! We will sleep down here from now on. We'll have the bigger bed—that will give you one less thing to complain about."

He made it sound like she complained all the time. She opened her mouth to object, but thought better of it. Instead, she gestured toward the bucket on the floor by her feet. "I brought the milk in."

"Put it by the fire to warm. Then you can wash up the dishes until Susan comes back down."

Jem warmed the wash water over the stove as she'd seen Susan do. She washed the dishes and scrubbed burned grease off a skillet. The harsh lye soap first warmed, then burned, the tender skin of her hands. She considered pointing this out to Seth—surely he didn't want her to have rough skin like a washer woman. But his expression was still hard and tight. She kept scrubbing.

William led Susan downstairs a while later. Her face was pale but her expression was just as hard as Seth's. She barely looked at Jem. "Skim the cream off the milk and put it in the churn."

She didn't even say please, let alone ask Jem whether she was really comfortable with this turn of events. Jem went to the pail of milk, then hesitated. After a long, embarrassing moment, Susan lifted her arm and pointed toward the overly tall wooden bucket in the corner. Jem had seen Susan spend hours with that thing, raising and lowering the paddle with monotonous repetition as she heard her children recite their lessons.

So. She'd been churning butter when she did that.

"Right," she said. "There's the churn. I'll just ... I'll just ladle the cream into it, shall I?" She dragged the pail over and pretended to fuss with the dasher until Seth spoke from across the room.

"You were going to take the lid off, right?"

"Of course, Seth! I'm not stupid!" She studied the bucket until she saw how to take the lid off. She'd seen Susan skim the cream before, and after a minute of debate, she identified the cream skimming spoon. After some experimentation, she managed to scoop the cream and drop it into the churn with a wet plopping sound. Susan showed her how to add warm water to the cream and wrap a rag around the dasher to keep the cream from splashing. "Now, lift. Now, lower. Like that. Again. Again."

Jem gasped. "How many times do I do this?"

"Till there's butter."

CHAPTER FIVE

Seth and William went out to the barn to tend to the stock, so Jem was left alone with Susan and the children to churn the butter—lifting then lowering the paddle that grew ever heavier. Her shoulders and back ached, and the tender flesh of her palms was rubbed raw.

"I'm not doing this again," she muttered. "We don't need butter this badly."

"Beg your pardon?" Susan said from her rocking chair.

Jem didn't answer. She opened the lid of the churn and peeked in. Soft chunks of cream had solidified and floated to the top. Butter. It gave her an odd thrill. She had made butter.

Well, the beginnings of butter. She replaced the lid and resumed churning.

Shortly after the men came in, Jem peeked again. "I've made butter," she announced.

Susan got up and came over to look. "That's fine," she said. Her voice was flat. "You can go. I'll finish it up."

"Susan," William said. "A word."

He took Susan aside. When she came back, she glared at Jem. "Take the butter out and rinse it."

"Oh. I ... thought you were going to do it."

Seth stepped forward. "Finish the butter, Jem." She'd never seen him angry before. Not like this, at least. Not this white-faced, clench-jawed anger where every word was a bullet finding its mark.

It made her hands tremble as she rinsed the butter, kneaded it, and rinsed it again until the water ran clear. She put it in the mold, and stared with wonder when a perfect pat of butter dropped onto the dish.

"My goodness!"

"What's wrong?" Seth asked, his voice sharp.

"I made butter!" She looked at him expectantly, but his face was still taut and pale. "Seth, why are you still angry at me? I did it! I made butter. I did exactly what Susan told me to do—and it wasn't easy. My back may never be the same."

"Jemima, William and I discussed this problem."

"What problem? There's no problem. I made butter. Oh, think! Now Susan doesn't have to do it. She must be so grateful! Butter churning is actually quite a lot of work. I'll never see butter the same way again." She laughed nervously. But the laugh died when he just stared at her.

"The problem is that you've been here for over a month, and you haven't lifted a finger to help."

"But—" She pointed to the butter, but he shook his head.

"Susan is tired and ... unwell. That poor woman has worked herself to the bone trying to care for three extra people when she already had a family to care for. And now that—" Seth halted and blushed. "Well, William and I have decided that you're going to take over her duties for the rest of our time here."

"I ... what? Seth, I don't know the first thing about keeping house. Not like this! And, anyway, this is Susan's house. We're her guests. I'm sure she would be offended if I took over."

"We are not her guests! They are being kind enough to allow us to share their home when we have nowhere else to go."

"Oh, for heaven's sake. You make it sound like we're indigent."

"Well, we're far from wealthy. And the money we do have left has to be put into the farm. At any rate, you have to learn to manage a household, and Susan needs the help. So Susan will continue to tend her children, and she'll give you instructions. But you'll do the actual cooking, cleaning, and baking. Whatever needs to be done."

Jem shook her head. "I can't possibly do that. I can't possibly take all that over. And I shouldn't have to."

It seemed impossible, but Seth's face grew tighter, his tone colder. "And why shouldn't you have to?"

"Because …" Jem knew she was right about this, but it was difficult to put it into words that didn't sound … pretentious. "We paid to be here," she said at last. "With the goods we brought. I shouldn't have to work as … as domestic help as well."

"Those goods purchased us space in this home—shelter for the winter so we could get to our farm as early as possible in the spring. They did not purchase us a slave."

"A slave? What are you talking about?"

Seth's lip curled. "I'm talking about Susan. She isn't here to wait on you, to fix your food, wash your clothes, and tend to your child."

"I tend to my own child, thank you!"

"When you are inclined. And when you aren't, you hand him off to Lilly or Susan as if you still had Sophie waiting at your elbow."

"Seth," Jem said, forcing patience into her voice.

"Yes?"

"Seth."

He crossed his arms. "What?"

"You don't understand. You can't seriously expect me to just—to just *watch* him every minute. It's just not possible. He's too little to have any judgment, and this is hardly a safe or ideal situation for such a little boy."

"I believe he's your child."

"Well, of course. You know I'm devoted to him. But, you can't think that I—" Again, the words sounded wrong in her head. She cut them off until she could sort them out properly, later. For now, she tried a different tack. "Susan is so good at all of this. She's—why—she's quite a good cook, really, considering what she has to work with. And she just has eyes in the back of her head when it comes to Charley's shenanigans. I don't know what I would do if she weren't here to help me."

It was a good moment to work up a tear or two, but Seth snarled. He actually snarled! "If you cry, I'll throw you out in the snow."

Her jaw dropped open, and she nearly choked on her gasp. She forgot to finish crying.

"Jemima, Susan will tell you what to do, and you will do it."

She crossed her own arms. "And if I don't?"

There was a long moment of silence. Jem wanted to believe that Seth was trying to think of a suitable threat, but the look on his face spoke not of indecision but of the moment before the point of no return. He already had a threat in mind.

"Then I'll take you back to St. Paul on the first possible train."

It was what she'd been praying for, but the way he said it made fear crawl through her. "W—what do you mean?"

"You can live with your father and sister in whatever sort of home he can provide—assuming he's not in jail. You can write to me out here if you have problems. And if I'm in a position to help, I will."

"You're not coming back here! Surely, you're not saying you'd abandon us? What if my father did g—go to jail? Charley and I would be completely unprotected!"

"No," said Seth. "Charley stays with me."

The little house seemed to rock sideways, but she caught herself against the table. She sucked for air but couldn't catch her breath. "W—what? Charley?"

When Seth went on, he no longer sounded angry, but stiff, as if he were addressing a stranger in an awkward social situation. "I'm not trying to be unkind. I know you love Charley. But you can't care for him—not if you refuse to work. So I will have to. You don't seem to understand that your circumstances have changed. I can't pay for servants to take care of you and neither can your father."

Jem lowered herself into a chair and put her head in her hands. "I just don't understand. I just don't understand any of this. Seth ... tell me this is a joke. A prank."

She thought that he must have walked away, he took so long to answer. At last, he cleared his throat. "I'd like for us to be a family. I hope that's what you decide."

And then he did walk away, the heels of his boots making muted clicks on the wooden floor.

⌒

JANUARY 1, 1887

> *Dear Father and Sally:*
> *Well I'm sure you've been wondering how we're faring out here in the Wild and Wooly West. We are all fine I'm happy to say. Charley suffered from a dreadful cold and cough for weeks, poor thing. How I worried*

and begged Seth to send for a doctor, but he said there's not one for 50 miles, and none due to arrive in this part of the world until the spring. Still, he's finally clearing up but coughs some at night.

We are still staying with William and Susan Caldwell—nine people in this little one room shanty. Quite a crunch, I can tell you, and one more on the way (not mine!). I've learned to churn butter, make biscuits and Johnny cakes, and picked up sewing like I haven't done since I was eight and Aunt Mincy got that burr in her bonnet that we should be making samplers. Do you remember how cross she was about it, Sally? Susan has been fine about teaching me to be a real pioneer housewife. You can imagine she's glad to have another pair of hands.

Charley is growing like a weed—I can't keep him in clothes, which is why I've taken to sewing. He's going to be tall like his papa, I'd say. And he's talking all the time, but we can't make out most of what he says— only 'Ma-ma,' 'Pa-pa,' 'Auntie' (that's Susan), and 'Lee' (which is Lilly, but he calls all four of the girls 'Lee').

It's been an awful harsh winter for people and livestock both. William lost everything but two horses and his single milch cow and she's about gone dry. About 15 miles from here, a homesteader with seven little ones went tracking after his herd when they got lost in a storm. He fell through the ice and was lost for two days. His brother found him, carted him back to the house, and put him by the fire. What they say around here is, "You're not dead until you're warm and dead." I guess there have been some pretty miraculous recoveries when people have thawed out and their hearts were beating. But in the case of that man, he was dead when he was cold and then, when he was warm, he was still dead. Other than that, people have been sick and I heard of one woman who got lost in a storm and lost some toes, but most of the casualties have been cattle—hundreds and thousands of cattle. But they say it's not this bad every year, or, at least, every year is bad in a different way.

Already 1887, can you believe it? Why, we're living in the future, or perhaps the end times as they say— which you would believe if you saw the blizzards they have here. They just keeping coming and coming and piling one on the other until you have to dig a tunnel to go anywhere, and I'm not exaggerating! The higher snow is nice though, because it cuts the wind into the place—and it is chill in this house I assure you.

I wonder what kind of house we'll have on our homestead. Seth doesn't even know, if you can believe it. He bought the place on the reputation of its land, and he says whatever kind of house there is will be nothing fancy. But we'll build as soon as we get a good crop in and sell it. He's reading and reading about farming—I didn't know how many books and periodicals he brought in his trunk, and more always are shipped when the train comes. He's set to make a go of this prairie life, though William tells him that this land was meant by God to be wild, not farmed. But Seth is always the one to experiment. He says this time his experiments will be real life ones on real land with real crops. He's set to find a way, and I sure hope he does, because he's bound to stay here and don't think I didn't try to turn him around.

But he never turns easily, as you know, so here we are, and in only three months (as soon as the roads are passable) we'll go on to Nebraska to begin our merry adventure. I can only pray that we'll be more successful than some of the people around here.

Well, I want this letter to go out while this weather is clear, so I'll close here. Father, I hope you got your line-item-allocation problem sorted out and that your fortunes have turned back to the good ones that you deserve. Sally, I got your letter and am interested to know why you brushed off the Markov man when I got the impression he was interested in calling on you. I hate to say this but you're not getting younger, and he comes from a perfectly respectful family—even if he is foreign. Also, thank you for praying for us, and I pray for you every night. And I know you must think I'm a shallow, silly woman most of the time and maybe I am, but prayers do take on a different feel when the wind is screaming like an angry haunt outdoors and the bags of flour dwindle a bit more with every passing day. So I welcome your prayers and ask for more and return them with my own for you.

All my very deepest love, and I hope to have a letter from you both soon,

Your loving daughter/sister, Jem

CHAPTER SIX

Jem dried the last dish from breakfast and added it to the stack in the cupboard—a crate nailed to the wall. As soon as she finished, Susan looked up from the pale blue blanket she was knitting for her coming baby.

"Put the beans on to soak," she said, her face unsmiling. "Then you can put the iron on the fire. Go ahead, Daisy," she said to her daughter. "But, thou, O Lord ..."

Daisy, only six, contorted her face as she tried to remember. "But, thou, O Lord, art a shield for me. I cried—"

"My glory, and ..."

Daisy's face brightened, and she went on in a rush, "But, thou, O Lord, art a shield for me; my glory, and the lifter up of mine head. *Now* it goes, 'I cried,' right?"

"Right." Susan looked away from Daisy to stare at Jem. "Yes?"

Jem shook her head. "Nothing. She's doing very well."

Susan's face closed like a shutter on a stormy day. She turned back to her daughter. "I cried ..."

Jem sighed and got her wrap from the hook. The beans were in the lean-to, and no matter that they were in the middle of what might be the worst blizzard yet this year.

The beans must be got, and they must be rinsed and soaked and boiled. She wrapped herself up, drew a deep breath, and stepped out into the screaming wind. She grabbed for the rope attached to the door frame, just as Seth had reminded her that morning, and trailed it through her hands as she rounded the corner to the lean-to.

Perhaps his reminder meant that he still had some feeling for her. Or perhaps it was only that he dreaded the idea of trying to find her if she got lost in the storm. Or that he didn't want to chisel a grave for an adult woman under the snow covering this frozen land. How did homesteaders bury their loved ones in the wintertime, anyway?

The wind came from the north today. Some days it wouldn't allow her to open the lean-to door—pushed against it with all of its impressive might. Other days, like today, it snatched the door from her hands and threw it open for her, threatening to pull it off the hinges. The wind yanked at the plank door hard enough to hurt her hands even through her thick mittens, but she held fast. She stepped inside out of the wind and stood still, panting. She hadn't realized she'd been holding her breath, but she wasn't surprised. The air outside was so fiercely cold that it felt like sharp blades cutting her airways. She never breathed it in if she could help it.

She found the beans and scooped them into the pot she carried. Yielding to temptation, she tugged her mitten off and shoved her fingers into the perfectly cold, perfectly smooth beans in the burlap bag, letting them run through her fingers. When the cold became too painful, she put her mitten back on and stepped outside. Had the wind softened? Perhaps just a little. Perhaps the storm was finally relenting. She paused and took a cautious breath. A shock of cold entered her system, but, yes, she thought the temperature was rising.

She tried to read the weather in the clouds, but the sky was shrouded in the blacks and grays of deep mourning. She stared upward for a minute anyway, blinking as snowflakes scattered onto her face.

Are you up there? Are you up there, God? Do you see what's happening down here? The blizzards? The suffering?

She listened to the wind screech its ugly, tuneless song. The cold was already penetrating her cloak, but she tried one more time.

I know you have other people to take care of. People whose problems are much worse than mine. Why, Mrs. Hastings, south of here—her husband is dying, and she has six children! And those Morris sisters—what will become of them? But I ... She hesitated. She wanted to do this right. *Please, help them. First. And then, for me ...* She brushed stray strands of hair out of her face. *Well, never mind. I—I guess I'll go iron.*

She pulled the door of the little house open through the resistance of the wind and entered, trying to ignore the rock of dread that lived in her belly all the time now.

Jem was frightened. No one—*no one*—had ever stopped loving her. But now, it appeared that everyone hated her.

She was the youngest daughter—petted, adored, and loved back home in Virginia. And she was the life of the party in St. Paul. Older men and women found her to be charming. Her friends thought she was witty and generous. If her father scowled at her, she cried or showed her dimples, and he forgave her. When she'd screamed and kicked to have her own way, her family had been frustrated and angry, but they eventually gave way, coddling her until her tears stopped and her place in the world was restored. No one had ever stopped loving her.

She simply hadn't known it was possible.

But now, William looked at her as if she were road apples on a garden path—unpleasant, but hardly worth bothering.

Seth spoke to her with cool disdain, if he bothered to speak to her at all. Susan looked through her rather than at her—even when issuing orders. And how Susan did issue orders!

"Fill the kettle with snow and put it on the stove. It's wash day."

"Get the mending basket—you can work on that while you wait for the bread to bake."

"Go build up the starter—we've got baking today."

Jem had learned there was a sort of system: wash on Monday, iron on Tuesday, mend on Wednesday, churn on Thursday, clean on Friday, bake on Saturday, and rest on Sunday. That was all *after* the daily chores, of course. And as quickly as she finished that day's work, it was time to begin evening chores. On Thursdays—since the cow had gone dry—she didn't have to churn. Instead, she did extra cleaning or sewing.

So Jem rose at dawn each day when Susan called her. She fried corn dodgers, tended the fire, scraped clothes on the washboard until her fingers bled, and tended the sourdough starter like it was the most important child in the household.

Her back hurt and her hands were chapped and bleeding. Her skin dried to cracking, and by noon her hair knot disintegrated to scraggly strands hanging in her face. She was embarrassed to have Seth see her working like a servant girl. Then, she was more embarrassed when Susan yelled at her for doing it wrong.

She considered quitting, or at least staging a strike until Seth saw reason. But then she would get a glimpse of Charley and clamp her mouth shut against her complaints. She wasn't going back to St. Paul—not without her husband and child.

At first, the work pounded her body into numb exhaustion. But, as she became accustomed to the routine, she started to dream, to hope that Seth would start to love her again. She started to pray, as she had never prayed before. *Lord, I'm sorry I was selfish. I know you'll forgive me, but will you help Seth to forgive me too?*

But, as the weeks passed with no change, she lost hope that her life would include anything but endless work and a loveless marriage. She could only hope that if she and Seth worked hard, they could provide a happy life for Charley.

The wind grabbed for the shanty door, but she wrestled her way inside. Charley ran to greet her, wrapping his pudgy little arms around her legs. "Ma!" He, at least, was glad to see her.

She set the pot of beans on the table and scooped him up for a hug. "Hello, my little man."

He pushed away from her and shivered. "Brr!"

"It's like hugging a snowdrift, isn't it?" She put him down and peeled off her cloak. Seth and William weren't in view; they must have been out tending the stock. Susan was still knitting and hearing lessons. Now it was Zinnia's turn to recite.

Jem hung up her wraps and ladled water into the bean pot. They'd have bean soup tomorrow and baked beans and cornbread for dinner the next night. But, first ... She took the iron off the low shelf and set it on the stove.

A rush of cold air announced the arrival of the men from the barn. The children ran to greet them and squealed at the cold hands that patted their cheeks.

"Brr," Charley said.

"Cold," Seth agreed. "Brr!"

"Brr!"

"We're not going back out tonight," William told Susan. "We bedded the cow down for the night."

"Good. It'll be fine to have everyone safe inside." Susan's face had relaxed into a smile. "No need to get yourself lost in a blizzard this late in the season, when spring is around the corner."

Seth slung Charley onto his waist and came to Jem. "Why is your hair wet?"

She didn't meet his eyes. "I went to the lean-to. The snow soaked right through my scarf."

"Don't go back out tonight."

That made her look up in surprise. "Oh! It didn't seem as cold when I was out. I thought we were nearing the end of the storm."

He nodded. "We are. But there's another one on its heels."

"You think it will be bad?"

"It will. Worse than this one."

He didn't elaborate, but he'd been an indications man in the army for 10 years. She guessed he could tell—maybe by the look of the clouds or the feel of the wind.

She sighed. "I'd hoped we'd get a break in the weather. Actually, I'd hoped that spring was near."

Seth raised his brows. "If you're thinking of catching a train back east, you shouldn't wait until spring. Not if you expect me to travel with you, at any rate. I won't leave once it's time to plant."

His words coiled through her chest like curdled milk. To give herself time to choose her words, she covered the table with the ironing cloth and spread the first garment over it—one of the girls' dresses. Pansy's, perhaps. She matched his calm voice, as if she were discussing the benefits of one kind of corn crop over another. "If I were planning on going back east, would I be ironing right now? I've done everything you asked, Seth. I've done everything Susan has asked. Whither thou goest ... I'll go whither too."

That didn't sound quite right, but fumbling for better grammar would have ruined the effect. She flicked water on the iron. When it sizzled, she moved it slowly over the bodice. She could feel Seth's eyes on her, but she kept her eyes on the dress, making sure she didn't iron in new wrinkles instead of eliminating old ones. She didn't look at him or say anything else, and eventually he left her to her task.

The blizzard raged for four days. The wind tried to muscle the men away from the rope leading to the barn, so they threw a loop over the line and tied it around their waists. They cleaned the stalls and gave the stock enough food and water so they only had to go out once a day, but that one time took hours. Jem took care of her duties, but a knot of unhappy tension fluttered in her stomach until the banging and thumping on the door told her that Seth was safe back at the shanty.

Jem had guessed that the stores they'd brought would have lasted a year or more, but the bags of flour and beans started to sag like dresses on a frontier woman after a winter of narrow rations. She cut her pieces of bread smaller, reasoning that Charley couldn't grow properly without enough nutrition, and Seth's chores were more physically taxing than hers.

She noticed that Susan was doing the same and watched for opportunities at dinner when all of the adults were distracted. Susan's daughters saw Jem tilting her beans and cornbread onto Susan's plate, but—while they looked at her with wondering eyes—they kept quiet.

On the fifth morning, Jem jerked awake in bed, sitting straight up. "What is it? What do I hear?"

The rope bed creaked as Seth twisted to look at her. "It's early, yet. You can sleep another hour."

She looked around, straining her eyes to make out the cook stove and table, illuminated by the faint red light of dying coals in the stove. "I—I thought I heard something. It woke me up."

"Do you still hear it?" There was a thread of amusement on Seth's sleepy voice.

"I hear … nothing. Oh! Nothing! The wind has stopped. The blizzard's finally over."

"Sounds pretty good, for nothing, eh?"

Jem released a breath and dropped back into bed, pulling the quilt so Seth's warmth curled around her. "Yes. Nothing is very nice, for a change."

She started when Seth's arm curled around her. "Brr," he said and then chuckled. "As Charley would say."

"Mm-hm." Jem smiled in the dark. It was like old days, having him touch her so naturally. "I'll be glad when he has reason to learn words like 'hot' and 'sunshine.'"

"Won't be long," he said. "Spring can't be held back forever." She felt a tickle, and realized Seth was nuzzling her hair. "So you're awake early."

Jem rolled over to look at his face in the dim light. "Didn't we already have this conversation?"

She saw the white flash of his grin in the darkness. "So," he said. "You're awake early."

She laughed, and he shushed her, putting his finger over her mouth. And, then, his lips.

CHAPTER SEVEN

The winter held out longer than their supplies did. On the first fine day in March, Seth and William finished their barn chores, then left for town. They walked the four miles, so as to spare the half-starved horses.

Jem and Susan went about their duties quietly, watching the sky. But it stayed clear and white. They didn't expect their husbands back before dusk, but just an hour after dinner, Daisy squealed. "Pa's coming! His wagon is coming."

"That's not your pa, then," Susan said. "He didn't take the wagon."

"But—," Daisy started, then closed her lips and sighed. Jem felt for her—it was difficult to be sure of something, but have to hold it inside. She went to the window herself.

"That's odd. Susan, are you sure they didn't take the wagon?"

Susan hefted herself out of her rocker and came beside her to look out. "They're riding with someone. I don't recognize them."

It sure did look like Seth and William riding in the back of the weathered wagon. Jem didn't recognize the tall, muscled man who drew the matched team of horses to a halt.

But when he jumped to the ground, Jem saw the woman who rode beside him.

"Kate!" Jem flew out the door, leaving Susan's sound of confusion behind her.

The man swung Kate to the ground just in time for Jem to grab her in a giant embrace. "Kate! Oh, my goodness, I've worried about you!"

Kate hugged her back, a shy smile spreading across her thin face. "I told you not to worry. You didn't get my letter?"

"Of course I did! But it didn't stop my worrying! How in the world did you end up here in the middle of nowhere? Come inside, and we'll have a chat."

Jem hooked her arm into Kate's elbow, then spotted Seth, leaning on the wagon with his thumbs in his belt loops. "Oh, Seth! How did you find Kate? You knew how worried I was!" He grinned. "I scoured the countryside, searching in every little town and village. No, wait … it wasn't quite like that. I saw Kate at the depot. This is her husband, Nat Fletcher."

Jem detached from Kate to shake his hand. "Mr. Fletcher, I'm so pleased to meet you. I hope you're taking good care of Kate. She's one of my dearest friends, and she deserves all the finest things life has to offer."

Mr. Fletcher tipped his hat but didn't smile. "Ma'am."

"But, where are your children? Didn't Kate write me that you have children?"

The man's eyes slid to Kate briefly before returning to Jem. "No, ma'am. I don't have children."

"Oh, but I'm sure Kate said—"

"Jemima," Seth interrupted. "Why don't you show Kate inside? I'm sure she's worn out from the trip."

"Oh." Jem looked at him, then at Kate, who stood with flushed cheeks, eyes downcast. "Well, of course. Of course!" She took Kate's arm again. "Come, you must be hungry.

Would you like some fresh bread?" She paused for effect. "That *I* made?"

Kate giggled. "That you made? Oh, dear. I'm not sure I'm at all hungry, actually."

"I haven't killed anyone yet," Jem assured her. "Although I suppose it's just a matter of time. I'm a genuine frontier wife now though, so I'm as likely to shoot someone as poison him."

Kate gave her a look of pretend horror, while Seth made a scoffing sound behind her. Jem laughed and led the way inside.

Kate looked healthy, so that was one thing. She'd gained weight since the fall, and her eyes looked clear. But there was no hint of affection between Kate and Mr. Fletcher. Kate barely looked at the man; she spoke to him only when necessary. He seemed almost unaware of his wife, but settled around the table to talk farming with Seth and William.

Was Mr. Fletcher the homesteader that Kate had written about? Where were the four children? The pair had been married as strangers, certainly, but shouldn't they have some sort of intimacy by now, some way of interacting that showed them to be a couple?

Jem was dying to ask, to turn the conversation toward Kate's recent life. But she bit back her questions. If her friend wanted to confide in her, she would. Kate didn't seem afraid of her husband, Jem admitted, with a tiny bit of evil regret. Not that she wanted Kate to be afraid, but if she were—why— Jem would have to ask questions. A friend could do no less!

But she chatted about farm life, butter making, and blizzards. Kate admired Charley for his walking and words and sturdy legs. They worked together to put on dinner, reminiscing about their school days together and pranks that they'd—well, Jem, actually—had pulled on teachers and classmates.

Susan tended to her daughters and Charley from her rocking chair while Jem and Kate put on baked beans, corn bread spread with salt pork drippings, and fried potatoes. The house was so little that they waited to eat themselves, feeding the men at the table and allowing the children to sit on the floor to eat.

Mr. Fletcher pushed away from the table and offered Jem a polite nod. "Fine dinner, ma'am. Thank you."

Jem smiled at him, then shot a quick look at Seth to see if he'd heard the compliment. He had and was smiling at her too.

"Well," Seth said to Mr. Fletcher. "If you're bound to leave today, we'd better get our supplies out of your wagon and get your team ready to go."

"Oh, do you have to leave tonight? Kate and I have hardly had a chance to catch up."

"Jem," said Seth, and she realized that she'd just invited guests to William and Susan's home. She felt her face go hot. But Susan rose from her rocker—pushing herself up against the arms of the chair—and set Charley on the floor.

"I wish you'd stay," she said. "You'll have better travel starting with a full day ahead of you."

"Thank you, Ma'am," said Mr. Fletcher. Jem had to wonder if the man ever smiled, but at least he was polite. "We have to be along though. Thank you for your hospitality."

"You ladies can relax and eat," Seth said. "We'll take our time." He winked at Jem and they went out.

Susan began to gather the dirty dishes from the table.

"Oh, I'll clean that up," Kate cried. But Susan waved her off.

"You two sit and I'll serve you. This is your last chance to visit before you leave. A friendship like yours is something to cherish."

Something about the way she said it reminded Jem of Susan's eagerness when she and Seth had first arrived. She made up her mind before she'd even quite realized what she was debating. She took the dishes right out of Susan's hands and looked into the other woman's blue eyes.

"We are lucky, aren't we," Jem said, not making it a question. "Or—at least—I am, to have two such friends. Come, we'll eat off the pans so we can visit while we can."

Susan choked on a laugh. "We can't eat out of the serving dishes!"

"Well, we have no more plates. And we'd be squandering a blessing to waste time washing them now."

So the three sat together at the table, spooning baked beans and potatoes right from the pans, sipping tea, and sharing their stories about their lives on the prairie so far.

Too soon, Mr. Fletcher called his wife to go, and Jem nearly wept as she hugged her goodbye. But then she turned back toward the house. Susan stood at the door, looking uncertain and somehow small, even with her belly jutting out before her. Jem went to stand beside her, and they waved at the departing wagon together.

After they were no more than a speck in the late afternoon landscape, Susan sighed.

"It was nice of you to include me."

Jem laughed, surprising even herself. "You're much too nice." Without explaining herself, she hugged her new friend, and then went inside to wash all the dishes in the place.

CHAPTER EIGHT

Seth stood idle, taking in William's cultivated fields, the distant, broad expanse of green land, the sweep of stunning blue sky above it, the smell of grasses and sage and wildflowers. It was beautiful in a primitive and wild way. For that one minute, he understood what William had been telling him. The prairie was untamed, too full of the fundamental forces of nature to ever be tamed by a mere man.

"Quite a sight, eh?" William sauntered up to stand beside him. He crouched to break a piece of grass and chewed on it.

"I could wish it was in Nebraska."

"I could wish you'd bought in Kansas."

Seth shrugged. "That was my plan."

Seth had wanted to farm near his friend, but his inspection tours had sent him all over the West. By the time he'd decided to adopt the life, he knew what he wanted in his land, and he'd searched until he found it. He'd seen too many farmers try to scratch out a living on inferior land. Most of the best homesteads had been snatched up early—only the remote, waterless plots waited to be claimed. He'd nearly lost hope, until he met a man whose health was forcing him to sell the land he'd farmed for nearly 15 years. Seth couldn't take the time to ride out and see it, but he talked to people he trusted and decided to make an offer. It wasn't until this past week that—leaving Jem and Charley with William and Susan—he'd taken the journey north and finally seen what he'd purchased.

"You say it's good land?" William asked.

"Three hundred twenty acres," Seth told him. "The owner and his brother both filed claims, and later he bought his brother's. Treeless, except by the river that runs along the east border. The river is full. Panfish, pike, buffalo fish."

"And water."

"And water," Seth agreed. "We won't lose our crops to drought."

"Does Jemima know about the house?"

"I believe I failed to mention it. Besides, it's so difficult to explain the idea of a sod house. Best if I just show her when we get there."

"Right. Also, best if she murders you on your own land. I really don't care for burying people." William tossed the piece of chewed grass aside and raised his arms above his head in an elaborate stretch. "Ah, I have to say, this sunshine sure feels good. So, will you have to bust a lot of sod? How many acres are broken?"

"Not much, considering he's been there so long. Troubles plagued him from the beginning—grasshoppers, fires. His wife had some kind of long illness, and scarlet fever blinded one of his sons. He never was able to get on his feet. Now his children are grown, and he wants to go live with his daughter in Pennsylvania."

"But you think you'll fare better."

Seth slapped his hand on his friend's shoulder. "We'll both fare better than he did. It's our grand experiment. It'll take time, but we'll make it work."

William rocked his head in amused wonder. "You really think all your reading will make the difference?

"Of course!" Seth grinned, feeling—for that moment—like they were young comrades in the army again, joshing each other around a campfire. "We've learned from the experiences of others."

"And what have you learned of grasshoppers? How will we keep them from descending every few years and eating everything from corn husks to hoe handles?"

Seth's grin faded. "I haven't found anything about that. Yet. We'll have to do well enough in the other years to make up for the years the grasshoppers come. That's all I can figure. And I trust God to see us through. Think of all the times we should have been gut shot or dead from dysentery, and God got us through all of it. What are grasshoppers to the Lord of all?"

"You can't imagine, man. They're like the plagues in the Bible. They come in as a cloud—darken the whole sky like a blizzard. And when they let loose ..." William shuddered. "I'll never forget what it's like. I have nightmares about it. Susan has dreams where she twitches and tries to brush them off her."

A happy squeal drew their attention to the house. Jem had brought Charley outside to see the new chicks. Seth had bought 24 in all—12 for him and 12 for William.

"Thanks for those." William shifted his feet.

"It was the deal. We paid you for our room and board with goods and livestock."

"You overpaid. I should have refused. I should have, but—" He cleared his throat. "You can't imagine how I feel when my little girls cry for food and I have nothing to give them. Susan—she got so peaked. I was certain she wouldn't live through the winter. I was for *sure* certain that she would lose this baby like the others."

Jem released Charley's hand and crouched to set a tray of mash on the ground. The chicks gathered around it, fluffy bits of yellow pollen, blown into a corner drift by a spring breeze. "They're peeps, Charley. Baby chickens," they heard her say.

"Peep!" Charley yelled. "Peep!"

Seth turned away a little and smiled. "I underpaid."

"She would have learned. We all do—or starve to death."

"I'm afraid her father spoiled her."

William blinked at him. "You don't say? I certainly never detected it."

Seth shoved his shoulder and they both laughed softly. "At any rate, I'm grateful. She hasn't been easy to live with, particularly for Susan."

"The hardest thing for Susan was being ... unfriendly. She wasn't angry for long—you know how she is. She wants to make everyone feel happy. She could hardly bear it when Jemima cried. She would have done anything to make her feel better."

"I had hoped they would be friends, but if Susan had been friendly, Jem would have charmed her into doing everything for her," Seth said. "She would have been lost on our own place."

William grew serious. "She still will be, Seth. This untamed land breaks men's backs. But it breaks women's hearts. The work, the lack of doctors, the loneliness."

Charley wailed suddenly, holding up his finger for Jem to kiss it—he'd gotten himself pecked. Jem's high laugh danced over the breeze. Seth watched as she kissed Charley's finger, then his cheek. She scooped him up, stepped away from the peeps and their breakfast, and spun the boy around until he giggled. Both of their heads were thrown back so the sunlight illuminated their laughing faces.

"When shall you leave?" William asked.

"I'm nearly ready," Seth said. "Cyril Hawkins will sell me his team of oxen, and we'll be set."

"God be with you, then."

Seth looked at his wife and son, collapsed in a merry pile on the sage grass. Then he looked back over the wild land and nodded slowly.

"God be with all of us."

On their last Sunday in the Caldwell home, Jem and Seth went to church with William and Susan. Jem stole looks at Seth throughout the sermon—his strong jawline, the tiny bit of stubble he'd missed in his haste to get ready after chores, the peaceful expression on his face as his eyes closed in concentration.

She felt a flutter and rush—he was so handsome. The first time she'd met him, she'd thought of a picture she'd seen in a book; a statue of a roman soldier. Seth was a warrior—but an intelligent warrior. A gentle man, but one that would raise arms to stand for what was right.

She wished he would open his eyes and look at her. She had a need to tell him that she loved him, to mouth the words silently and watch the tenderness come into his gray eyes. Emotion swelled into her chest, and for a minute she thought she might start to weep. Instead, she lowered her head to pray.

Father, how I love him! I forgive him for bringing us to the wilderness. I know that I made a vow that whither he would go, I would go also. So that's what I intend to do. If you want us to live in Nebraska, so be it. Please bless us, keep us healthy—especially keep Charley healthy. And please continue to provide us with everything we need.

She paused, thinking. Nebraska. The word still sent a spear of fear through her. Tomorrow they would start for their new home. Well. She drew in a deep, sustaining breath.

She could be a frontier wife. She already was a frontier wife, actually. Surely, it would be no more difficult in Nebraska than it had been in Kansas.

Father, I'm not going to ask you anymore to help Seth change his mind. For one thing, I think it's not going to happen. Maybe he just doesn't listen to you. Or, maybe ...

A new thought struck her. *I guess—maybe—you said no. Just because I ask for something, doesn't mean you're going to do it. I'm not in charge. You are.*

She raised her head, then hastily lowered it again. *Amen.*

She hadn't been exaggerating when she'd written to Sally that her prayers had changed since coming to Kansas. She was ashamed of her prayers—they were nothing like the profound expressions of reverence that the clergy voiced on Sundays. Nor were they like Seth's somber, heartfelt worship.

She had taken to praying as if she were having a conversation with God. It had to be wrong—she was certain of that. But it brought her a kind of comfort she'd never felt when praying with traditional words or memorized phrases. And, somehow, she'd started to feel ...

A presence?

She shook her head. No, that made it sound like God was a ghost. Perhaps—if she dared—she would say that she sensed that God was listening. And, more, that he felt affection for her, as if he found fatherly amusement in her wandering treatises that passed as prayer.

She took another look at Seth and realized that he was looking at her. She smiled at him and felt a blush rise on her cheeks. She supposed he would be appalled if he knew how she prayed. But he smiled back at her now and warmth filled her.

Things were finally better between them. That was what she needed to pray about. She needed to thank God for that. She would happily go to Nebraska, be a farm wife, churn butter until her hands turned black and fell off, if Seth loved her again.

Her attention was drawn to the sermon. The pastor had said something, used a familiar phrase or name, that jangled in her mind.

"Brothers and sisters, what's the lesson we find here? What did Boaz say when he met Ruth? 'I've heard of your great beauty?' No. 'I heard about your amazing intellect?' No. He talked about her character." The pastor paused, running his eyes over the congregation, seeming to make eye contact with each person. Jem dreaded the moment when he got to her. But when he did, she felt understanding rather than condemnation.

She glanced at Seth again. He had his head bowed, but for some reason, his eyes were squeezed tightly shut and his face was twisted as if were fighting a laugh, or perhaps a grimace of fear. She elbowed him so he'd look up and let her know what the problem was, but he didn't.

"Character, my dear friends," the pastor went on, "is what will both follow you and precede you. Had Boaz commented on Ruth's beauty, that's no compliment; God either makes one beautiful or he doesn't. He took note of her character—the fact that she'd left her home and family to come to a land where she knew no one. Why? Out of loyalty. Out of faithfulness to her widowed mother-in-law who had no one else to care for her. When Ruth had a choice to make, she didn't turn tail and run for home. No. She said, 'whither thou goest, I will go.' "

Jem gasped. Beside her, Seth's body began to shake in silent laughter. Susan and William, seated on the far side of him, stared at them both. When the pastor began the benediction, Jem lowered her head, waiting for the moment when she got her husband alone.

The wagon was packed and loaded before the sun came up Monday morning. Jem and Susan shivered side by side in the darkness, watching the men tug ropes, jiggle crates to check for soundness.

Susan held Charley, who slept soundly in a thick cocoon of quilts. She nuzzled his head and sighed. "I'm going to miss this little fellow."

Jem put her hand on Susan's arm. "He's going to miss you. His auntie. Shall I take him? He's so heavy now."

"No. Give me just another minute."

"You'll have another little one of your own before you know it."

Susan smiled. "You can't exchange one for another."

"No." Jem hesitated. "Susan, I just have to say, I'm so sorry. I treated you badly. I—I see now how unfair I was. And I'm ashamed of myself."

"No. It's awful hard, learning to live out here."

"Well, that doesn't excuse meanness."

"No," Susan said again. "You mustn't—" But Jem tightened her grip a little and shook Susan's arm.

"Let me apologize. And thank you for showing me everything. How to cook and churn and—"

"Stop," said Susan, and Jem heard the tears in her voice.

She tried to go on, but her own throat clogged. She gave up, and suddenly they were embracing, awkwardly, with both Charley and Susan's baby between them.

Jem felt a hand on her shoulder.

"We have to go," Seth said. "We have a long day before us."

"Oh!" Susan clung tighter. "Oh, Nebraska is so far away!"

"Not so far," William said. He patted her rapidly, as if to hurry his comfort. "It's not so far. We'll surely be able to visit back and forth. Come, Susan. Come, now." He tugged her gently backward.

Seth took Charley from Susan's arms.

"Wait," Susan said, her voice damp and wobbling. "Oh, I almost forgot. Just wait!" She ran back to the house.

"I've set up a bed for Charley," Seth said, starting for the wagon. "He can sleep back there until he wakes up."

Jem hurried after him. "Oh, no, Seth, I don't think he should." She shuddered at the thought of Charley alone in the wagon bed. "What if I don't hear him? What if he wakes and falls out the back? What if something falls on him?"

"He'll be three feet away from you, darling. I promise he'll be fine. And we'll tie up the canvas tight in the back. He's not going anywhere."

Susan rushed to Jem and thrust a large, tissue-wrapped package into her arms. "This is for you."

"Oh! I don't have anything for you!" Jem felt her tears start to flow again. She knew they were partly for the time she had wasted before getting to know this kind woman.

"No, don't be silly. Anyway, the one thing was your wedding present. I'd intended to send it long before you arrived, and I never got it done. And the other—why—my grandmother gave it to me, and now I'm giving it to you. So it's not new."

They hugged one final time. Seth helped Jem onto the wagon seat and walked around one more time, tightening the canvas in back.

He climbed into the wagon next to her. As the first meadowlark of the morning began its song, he clicked at the horses, and they started toward their new life.

CHAPTER NINE

In her dream, Jem thought bugs were crawling on her—over her head, through her hair, and onto her face. She jerked awake, blinked as she looked around, and then screamed. Seth bolted upright beside her.

"What? What is it?"

"Mud!" Jem yelled. She hit him in the chest with the side of her hand. "Mud, Seth! All over me! All over everything!"

Her yells woke Charley in his trundle bed. He began to wail—loud outraged shrieks.

"Jem," Seth yelled over the noise. "Settle down!"

"Settle down! You want me to settle down? You bring me to Nebraska to live like a mole in the ground, and you want me to settle down?" She bounded out of bed to pace the tiny dirt floor of the sod house. Water sloshed over her feet and mud oozed between her toes, making her shriek again. "Mud!"

Seth got out of bed, and she nearly ran into him. "Jemima—"

"Don't *Jemima* me!" She swiped her hand across her cheek and thrust it at him. "Look at this! Do you see this?"

"It's rather dark in here—"

Charley was still crying, so she scooped him up, careful not to swing him too high—the ceiling in the sod house was barely higher than Seth's head.

"Rather dark?" She spat his words back at him. "Perhaps that's because we live underground like moles! Like snakes! Like worms! Do you think I'm a worm, Seth? Is that what you think?"

"Now, Jemima ..."

"Stop, Charley." Jem patted his little back mechanically. "Just stop, now. Mama will get the mud off of you." She glowered at Seth, knowing he probably couldn't see it but hoping he felt it all the same.

"Jemima." Seth was just a shadow in the darkness. He was using his reasonable voice, as if he were intentionally trying to infuriate her more. "Jemima, you knew that this house might be less ... elegant than what you're used to."

"Elegant?" she screeched. "You say this is less elegant? Well, I think it's just fine! Just fine, indeed, if I were a—a ..." Mole? No, she'd used that one. Worm? No. What else lived underground? "If I were a prairie dog!" She finished at last.

Then she paused. "They do live underground, don't they?"

"I believe so. Jem, I know it's upsetting to wake up with mud on you."

Reminded of the main topic, she drew in her breath to begin again.

"Wait!" Seth said. "Just wait, darling. Please. Please. We're upsetting Charley. Let's just calm down."

Charley—either comforted by his mother's weak attempts or simply accustomed to her histrionics—had already stopped crying. He wriggled in Jem's arms, but she held him fast.

"I can't put you down, Charley. You'll get all muddy."

Seth made a noise.

"Excuse me," Jem said. "Did you just snort?"

"No. I mean, no, ma'am."

"Seth, this isn't funny."

The barest hint of dawn was visible through the windows. It illuminated the shadows and planes of his face. "Someday, we'll tell this story to our grandchildren. And we'll laugh."

Jem stared at him. "You must *want* to quarrel."

"No, no. Really, I don't." There was laughter in his voice. "Come, Jem, you knew we would have hardships."

"I've already had hardships. I *churned*."

"And a fine job you did."

"Your flattery comes much too late."

He rested his hands on her shoulders. "Jem, we're going to build a proper house. I promise. But first, we have to get a good crop of wheat to sell. And to do that, we need to focus our attention on getting it planted."

Jem handed him Charley and went to poke at the fire. "But you can't plant."

"No, not until things dry out. If I try to break sod in this, I'll just get bogged down. I could plant in the broken fields at least, but I've heard tell of seed rotting. We can't afford for that to happen."

A seedling of flame sprouted out of the hot coals, wavered uncertainly, then bloomed. Jem set kindling around it, careful not to smother it. "I'll put on the kettle so we can wash up."

"I ..." Seth drew out the word. "Darling, we may just have to resign ourselves to being muddy for a few days."

Jem rose and moved the kettle over the fire. "So I should just allow my child to remain filthy? Like a street urchin?"

"No, no. Not like a street urchin. Like a—a *farm* urchin. Excuse me," he added. "But was that a snort?"

"Of course not. I have very little to snort about this morning."

Seth sighed. "That's true."

Jem stopped working. She was able to make out more of his face in the dawning light, and there was no humor on it now. "It is?"

"It is. Jem, I'm sorry. I should have looked at the place before buying it, but I just didn't have time. I had to move quickly."

"Would you have bought it if you'd known there was no proper house?"

He hesitated. "Possibly. I don't know. This is excellent land, and that's the difference between success or failure out here. We had limited funds, and it was more important to get good farmland than a pretty house."

"You should have sold our old house yourself and kept the money. Father said you didn't have to sign it over to him."

"I can't keep property that was purchased with stolen money."

"He didn't—" she began, but Seth put his hand on her arm, halting her before the old quarrel could flare up.

"Let's not go over this again. The important thing is that we're here—all three of us together—embarking on a new life together. From here on out, anything we have, anything we accomplish, we do together."

She felt herself relax. "I like that. I want us to be a team."

He gathered her against him and kissed her forehead. Then he swiped his hand across his mouth. "Ugh. Mud. Disgusting."

She jerked backward, then hit him lightly in the chest. She inhaled deeply, breathing in the smell of damp earth. "Go ahead and laugh. It would serve you right, I'd say, if you got a whole mouthful of mud."

A splashing sound drew her attention. "Oh, Seth! You put him down. Charley, no-no. No splashing on the floor."

Seth laughed harder, so she hurried over to pick the child up. "Oh, for pity's sake! You're soaked. You'll get pneumonia."

Charley yelled his wordless protest and tried to thrust himself out of her arms, back to the floor.

Jem gave him to Seth. "Hold him," she ordered.

"He's already wet; he might as well—"

"*Hold him.*"

"Holding," Seth conceded. "But, Jem, until this rain ends, he's going to be muddy. We can't keep him off the floor all of the time. I guess I could rig something to hang him on the wall, but even there ..."

He trailed off. Jem waited, her hands on her hips.

"Do go on," she invited. But he shook his head and took a step backward, his arms securely around his wriggling son.

"Guess I'm done."

"Good. I would prefer that our son doesn't catch a life-threatening illness in his first weeks of prairie life. If it rains for a few days, we'll just have to take extraordinary measures to keep him dry."

The rain lasted for more than a few days. For weeks, it poured in a gray sheet, running in ropey rivulets over ground that was already saturated from melted snow. When Seth went to tend the oxen and their single cow, his boots squished into the grass so that water ran over the toes. He couldn't plow, couldn't repair the barn, couldn't build a proper chicken coop for the peeps. He did what repairs he could inside the barn or house and spent much of his time reading, preparing for the moment when he could begin farming in earnest.

When Jem went outside one morning her boot sank into the mud and wouldn't come out. She ended up unlacing it and limping in her stocking foot to find Seth in the barn. It took Seth 45 minutes to dig the boot out with a shovel, and it was never the same.

Jem learned to keep the lid on her kettle at all times, lest sodden globs of mud fall from the earthen ceiling into dinner. She washed clothes and hung them around the inside of the soddy to dry, but they never quite did, no matter how high she stoked the fire. Mildew grew on everything—their clothes, their quilts, their papers.

Susan's wedding gift for Jem and Seth had been the beautiful Joseph's Coat quilt that had been on the bed when they first arrived at the Caldwell's. Susan had wrapped it carefully in both tissue paper and a linen sheet. Folded inside was the matching quilt she'd made for Charley. Jem kept them wrapped, tucked deep into her trunk, where she prayed they wouldn't be damaged by the wet weather.

Susan's other gift was a book: *The American Frugal Housewife*. On the inside cover a message was penned in spidery handwriting: *To my Suzy: a good girl marrying a good man. Be a good wife and love the Lord and be happy. With all my heart I love you: Granny.*

Below that Susan had written in her much neater script: *And I pass this to you, my friend Jem, with all of my Granny's good wishes and more of my own—that you and Seth will have all the happiness life can offer. Your friend, Susan.*

Jem would have liked to keep the book in the trunk next to the quilt—safe and protected—but she found it too useful. She ended by keeping it handy on a shelf that was nailed onto the wall's supporting stud. She pulled it down 20 or more times a day, looking up everything from recipes to chicken care to preventative medicine. Although she tried to keep it back a little from the dirt wall, the edges of the pages still darkened from mildew. It took on a musty smell that she knew would never completely go away.

Jem fretted that one or all of them would develop pneumonia or diphtheria or some other deadly disease from the unhealthy conditions. The surface of her skin always felt cold, even in mild temperatures, because it was never dry for long. Bathing was futile; her scalp was gritty from dirt even an hour after washing her hair. The insides of her knees and elbows developed an itching, burning rash. Seth blew his nose into his handkerchief continually, and he developed a hacking cough that kept them both awake at night.

Charley's face was never clean but for around his mouth, where he licked his lips. Jem could scratch any part of his skin and come up with dirt under her nails. He removed his shoes as quickly as Jem replaced them, so mud caked between his toes and ran in streaks up his legs. He delighted in the earthworms that poked through the walls, stretching them until they popped free and landed in his grubby fist. Jem resigned herself to clearing the wriggling piles from his bed each day before putting him down for his nap—until the day he screeched in joy and held up his best specimen yet: a little brown snake, whipping furiously in his grip. Jem's screams had Seth coming from the barn at a dead run. "No more worms, son," Seth said sternly.

Charley wept bitterly—"'erms! 'erms!"—but finally settled for pointing out each worm to Jem as it appeared.

"He'll surely be sick," Jem told Seth. "He's filthy and nearly always wet. He'll catch pneumonia or some other horrible disease from the filth he plays with."

But Charley thrived. When the rain eased enough to allow him outdoors, he ran in the grass, chased after prairie dogs when they popped into view like jack-in-the-box toys, and had long, unintelligible conversations with the oxen. When he was trapped indoors, he amused himself by splashing in the puddles on the floor or drawing on every surface but the stove with muddy fingertips.

"I'm tempted to tie him up," Jem confessed to Seth when they had been there for a month. She ladled beans into Seth's supper bowl. "I can't get a minute's peace. Today while I was kneading the bread, he poured the water bucket on the floor to make his puddle bigger."

Seth winced. "I shouldn't have shown him how to float boats in it."

"Well, no, you shouldn't have, because he doesn't understand that he's only supposed to use bark from the firewood. I caught my hairbrush in the nick of time the other day."

Seth smiled at her. "You don't need a hairbrush. You look beautiful the way you are."

"Oh! I know what I look like. You don't need to make fun."

"I'm not," he said, and she couldn't find any teasing in his face. "We'll both be glad when we can feel clean and groomed again, but you do seem to be ... I don't know how to explain it. You're just more beautiful than ever."

"Well, there's a mystery that will never be solved, if you think I look beautiful." Jem felt a blush take over her face and wondered if he could even see it under the grime. With her scraggly hair, dirty skin, and ragged work dress, she was relieved that she had no mirror and that every reflective surface was dulled by mud or ash.

Now that she thought about it though, Seth really didn't seem to be troubled by it. She had looked up from her work several times lately, swiping her soiled sleeve across her sweaty brow, to see him paused in his work, just staring at her with a smile—as besotted as he'd been when he'd courted her. More, perhaps. If he had fallen out of love with her in Kansas, he'd fallen right back in Nebraska.

"It's different now," she said, realizing too late that she'd spoken out loud.

"What is?"

"Well, us. We are different."

Seth handed Charley a bit of cornbread that was greasy with the salt pork drippings they used as butter. "What do you mean?"

Jem tried to find the words but failed. "I guess I don't know what I mean."

He tried to help. "I imagine being out here has changed both of us."

"I suppose. But that's not what I—I mean, I guess that *we*—the two of us together—are different. It turned out that I'm not so … charming as you must have thought I was. And you aren't so …"

He grinned. "I'm afraid to hear the end of this sentence."

"I can't decide how to end it," she confessed. "I thought you were strong and gallant, and you are. I thought you were a hero, and I do still think that. But you aren't—"

A knock sounded sharply on the door, startling her badly enough tea sloshed over the edge of her cup. Charley jerked in surprise also and reached for Jem, crying.

Jem pressed her hand to her chest. "Goodness! I really have turned wild, if a knock on the door sends me into such a dither."

Seth didn't smile. "Let me see who it is. I don't know who would be clear out this way in this weather."

She thought he would take his rifle from its hook above the door, but instead he opened his small trunk and took out the pistol he had from his army days.

Jem stayed away from the door but heard a raspy voice without being able to hear the words. Seth responded, then glanced back. "Stay here. Latch the door until I come back."

"But, Seth—"

He lifted the lantern off the hook and stepped out. "Latch it," he repeated.

She did, then paced the tiny space of the soddy for a moment before putting her time to better use by clearing the table. The wash water was already warm on the stove, so she did the dishes. She heated fresh water and washed Charley's face and hands. She scrubbed his hair with the rag until he broke free.

He ran behind the wood box and pointed his chubby index finger at her—a stern warning. "No!"

Jem laughed before she thought, then rearranged her face into a frown. "No, you mustn't tell mama 'no.'"

Charley matched her frown. "No!"

"I see." She bit her lip and pondered the situation. "Well, now if I don't wipe your hair, you'll think that you are the boss. You'll think you can run away from me and do what you want."

Charley's scowl deepened, and she had another urge to laugh. He was really so cute. Such an interesting mixture of herself and Seth played across that little face.

"I wonder if you've gotten the worst of both of us. Your father's stubbornness and my … emotion."

"No!"

"Well, we can hope not. Meanwhile …" She eyed him keenly, then dove like a chicken hawk on a prairie dog, and snatched him up in her talons just before he broke for a hiding place under the bed.

He screamed and wriggled wildly, but she held fast. "My goodness, you're acting just like that snake you caught. How did you ever hold on to it?"

"'Erm?"

"That's right. The big, long 'erm with the fangs. Well, I didn't see fangs, but I'm sure it had them. And deadly poison, no doubt." She dipped her rag in the water and went after his hair again.

Then, in spite of his outrage, she gave his feet a good scrubbing too. Finally, she set him on the floor. He stood in place, wailing, looking strangely bald without his outer layer of dirt.

"Oh, now stop, Charley. You're fine. You should be proud. I do believe you're the only clean thing on the place."

The door rattled, making her jump again. "Jem?" It was Seth's voice. "It's me. What are you doing to that poor little fellow?"

She opened the door and grinned, knowing everything must be fine if he was teasing her. "The worst thing possible," she told him. "I'm afraid—I'm ashamed to admit it—but I'm afraid I cleaned him up."

Seth gave her a reproachful look and lifted his boy. Charley collapsed against him, his sobs renewed now that he had a sympathizer.

"Poor little fellow," murmured Seth. "I don't know what possessed her. We'll have to get some dirt and rub it on you—restore you to your natural healthy state. Although, I suppose we can count on you to handle that."

"Who was here?" Jem asked.

"A hobo."

"A what?"

"A hobo. A bum. They—there are fellows who travel all over the country, hopping freight trains and looking for work." Still holding Charley, he used one hand to open his trunk and put the pistol away.

"Oh. A tramp. Isn't he far from the train?"

"I think tramps ride the rails, but they don't work. Hobos work. I had no work to offer him—what with all the rain—but I said he could put up in the barn tonight."

"Seth, do you think it's safe? What if he's a—a *crazy* person or a mad killer or something? Really, you would have to be crazy to live like that—no home, no life really."

"Darling, some people could say that about us. The way we're living like—how did you put it? Moles?"

"I've changed it to 'erms. We're living like 'erms. Is he hungry? Shall I take him some food?"

"I'll take it to him. But, yes, fix him up some grub."

"I'm sorry? Some what?"

Seth grinned. While she made up a generous plate of cornbread and beans, he explained that the hobo had taken some work on a homestead some 40 miles south. Now he was traveling back to the train to resume his usual life. "A lot of these men were soldiers who didn't know where to go after the war. So they took to the nomadic life."

"The war was so long ago! Surely they could have found a better life by now."

"Some did. Anyway, this one is too young; he wasn't a soldier. Maybe he just likes the life—the open road, the scenery. No chains binding you to any one place or person ..."

Jem handed him the loaded plate and gave him a prim look. "Sounds as if you'd like to give it a try."

"Sure would. What do you say—you, me, and Charley, riding the rails? Cooking our food in tins over an open fire? Running from local sheriffs and dogs? And railroad authorities? Soot on our faces ..."

"We can be dirty right here at home and save ourselves the trouble of tying our belongings into a bundle each day."

"Or that. Do we have any bones or scraps? He has a dog. Several actually—a female and two or three half-grown pups."

"Oh, mercy. That's what we need—dogs running about the place." She huffed and went for the scrap bucket.

CHAPTER TEN

Jem heard the dogs bark a couple of times during the night but never actually saw their visitors until the next morning. The sun was out—pale and weakened after its prolonged absence, but present, glowing through the white sky with a dim hopefulness. Jem released the chicks—half-feathered now so they looked like they weren't sure what species they belonged to—into the yard and watched them pecking and muttering over the worms that had perished on the wet ground. Charley chased them, yelling admonishments, or perhaps instructions.

Jem caught movement in her peripheral vision and turned to see the hobo, standing a respectful 20 or so feet away from her. A gaunt hound leaned against his legs as if she needed the support to stand—or he did. He was shabbily dressed, his bright green eyes shining in his grimy face. She was shocked to see his age—surely he couldn't have been more than 18! He offered her a jerky nod when he saw her looking.

"Thank you, ma'am. It was a fine supper—better than I've had in a coon's age."

"Oh, well, you're very welcome, I'm sure. If you're leaving, let me pack you a bundle, will you?"

"That's awful kind, ma'am."

She picked up Charley, ignoring his protests, and went to make the man—boy, really—a lunch. She put in the last half-tray of cornbread, reasoning she still had mush she could fry for breakfast, wrapped a piece of salt pork in brown paper, and—just for good measure—poured dry beans into a paper and folded it shut.

"There!" she told Charley. "That should hold him to the train depot."

She held the bundle, ready to take it out. But her feet didn't move toward the door. There was a Bible verse in her head—one Seth had read at dinner a week, maybe two weeks ago. His readings were always short, since Charley had no patience at mealtimes. Jem usually let the words wash over her, enjoying sitting down and the sound of Seth's resonant voice. But now, one of the verses was circling in her mind, just out of reach. Something about parents?

Had it been from Matthew? The Sermon on the Mount? She strained to remember how it went. "Although my parents ... no. How did it go?"

The boy was waiting. She had to take the bundle out to him. But she couldn't. She just couldn't, until she remembered that verse. Was it from Deuteronomy? Something Moses had told his people?

"Proverbs!" She grabbed for Seth's big Bible, hating the musty smell that wafted to her nostrils when she flipped it open. "Proverbs ... Proverbs." She scanned the chapters, the words, hoping it would jump out at her. "Oh! There it is."

"Though my father and mother forsake me, the LORD will receive me." She let her head drop backward in disgust. "Oh, for heaven's sake, why did I need to remember that? This has nothing to do with this situation!" While her head was tipped backward, she went ahead and spoke upward, through the mud ceiling. "That has nothing to do with this situation. Maybe you wanted something about a wanderer? Or being hungry?"

The response she felt was a steady pressure, as if God were pressing his hand on her shoulder to restrain her words, her impatience. She sighed, relenting.

She tore a sheet out of the back of Seth's notepad and blotted his pen. She wrote the words, blew on them until she was sure they were dry, and folded the paper into the bundle. The satisfaction she felt came from beyond herself.

She went out to the boy and handed it over. "God bless you," she said.

"Uhhh ... yes, ma'am. Thank you, ma'am."

She went back inside to tend to her work. Seth came in later and gave her an odd look.

"What's wrong?" she asked.

"What did you tell him?"

"The hobo? Nothing. Why? I just packed him up some food."

"Huh," Seth said. "Well, he left you something."

He led her outside, where a little mess of bones and fur wiggled at the end of a rope.

"A puppy! Seth, I don't want a puppy! What will we do with it?"

"It's not a bad thing to have a dog out here. It's safer."

"They dig in gardens and carry fleas and track in mud ..."

Seth laughed. "Mud in the house? We can't have that!"

"Oh, well really, Seth. We won't always have a house made of mud. Catch up with the boy and tell him thank you, anyway."

"He's long gone. Anyway, he wanted you to have it. He could have sold it for good money, you know. This country is short on dogs."

"Great," Jem told him. "Well, keep it on that rope, will you? I don't want to trip over it." She stalked back into the soddy, making sure he heard her mutter about people repaying good with evil.

He laughed again and called Charley to come meet their new pet.

Seth led the prayer at breakfast, and even Charley was learning to press his little palms together and shout, "'Men!" at the end. But Jem's best prayers began when Seth was headed toward the barn and Charley was busy tormenting the puppy.

She put the dishpan on the kitchen table so she could watch the boy and dog while she washed up, and she used the time to pray. She asked for God to keep them safe in this wild land, to protect them from savage Indians, grasshoppers, and disease. She asked him to keep Sally healthy and to help her father resolve his mysterious legal problems soon. She asked him to give her the strength to succeed in this strange new life, and to protect their marriage.

I'm not asking to go home, you'll notice, she prayed, glancing upward. *You've given me every indication that you want us to stay.*

She thought about the hobo, as she often did, and prayed for him. *Is ... I think, something is hurting that boy, Lord. Please be with him. Keep him safe. I don't know what his situation is. But I know you do, so please take care of him.*

She stacked the dishes neatly on the shelf, took another peek at Charley, and then hurried to make the bed and tidy the house. It was Wednesday, but the mending would have to wait. She wanted to finish getting the garden in today.

She glanced around. Was there anything else she needed to do before she went outside? Anything else she needed to pray about?

Oh, just protect that poor boy, Lord. Give him—

She was stuck. She was always stuck when she prayed for the hobo. She didn't know his name, let alone what had driven him to live the way he did. They had barely exchanged 10 words, but she thought about him every day.

Of course, she had Zeke to remind her. Zeke was huge, and getting bigger every day. When he got off his rope—which was as often as Charley could untangle the knot—he chased the chickens, ran through the garden, and harassed the oxen.

"I have a great idea for meat," she'd told Seth one day after Zeke had helped Charley dig a giant hole right by the front door.

Seth shuddered. "Do you mind? That's disgusting."

"Some people eat dogs."

"Who?"

She gave him a sulky look. "That's not a fair question, and you know it. You probably know exactly who eats dogs, but you won't tell me."

"No, I won't. We don't eat dogs. That's practically cannibalism."

"Canni—isn't that when people eat people? Now, that's disgusting!"

"Well, the Donner Party—"

She raised her palm. "Enough! You win! We won't eat the dog. Just ... tie the knots tighter, will you? I really don't have time to watch him *and* Charley and get the garden in."

He rose from the table and kissed the top of her head. "Better if we train him to behave, I think."

"Do that, then."

But Seth was as busy as she was. He had sod to break, a barn to repair, and a chicken coop to build. So Zeke was under her feet, a constant reminder of his first owner.

And then, of course, there was the cat. A simple drawing of a cat was scratched and then burned into the post by the barn. It was charming in a comical way. She and Seth had puzzled over it.

"Had to be left by the hobo," Seth said. "Unless the dog did it."

"But what does it mean?"

He shook his head slowly. "No idea. I just don't know."

Remembering that, she glanced out the window. Charley and Zeke ran through the flock of chickens, scattering them in all directions. They ruffled their feathers and squawked in indignation, but soon resumed pecking and complaining in little disgusted asides to each other. They had become accustomed to the unruly pair.

Jem checked the fire, then went out to scold them. "No chasing chickens!"

Zeke hunched in ungainly embarrassment, but Charley grinned up at her. "Peep!" he yelled. "Peep!"

"I'm afraid they're not peeps anymore, Charley. They're chickens. Can you say chicken?"

"Peep!"

"Well, you mustn't chase the peeps. They won't want to give us eggs if you chase them."

"Ache!"

"That's right. You like eggs, don't you? If you scare the chickens, they won't want to give us eggs."

"Peep!" Charley threw in the last word before running off toward the barn, allowing Jem to laugh without fear of encouraging his back talk.

Charley had changed so much in their time on the prairie. He'd grown lean and brown, and his hair had grown and thickened into a sun-bleached mop that fell over his forehead no matter how Jem combed or greased it. His words still came in one syllable bursts or unintelligible streams of conversation, but he understood most of what Seth and Jem told him—even if he didn't choose to mind.

On the few occasions when Jem—tired or frustrated by the work—imagined returning to St. Paul, the thought stalled when she considered Charley. She couldn't imagine taking him away from the freedom he enjoyed on the farm. He loved the animals, the dirt, the sun—even the rain. Most of all, he loved being with his father.

He followed Seth everywhere, imitating his work, chattering nonsense, showing Seth the bugs, worms, and rocks he collected. He could hardly bear it when Seth left for a day to get supplies in town; how could he stand it if Seth had to go to work every day? Worse, what if Seth got another job where he had to travel for long periods?

Once the question occurred to Jem, she was shocked that she hadn't considered it before: How could Seth teach Charley to be a man if he was never with him?

"Charley!" She ran for him. "No! No throwing rocks at Zeke! You'll hurt him."

"Deek!"

She slung him under her arm. "To the garden. We have work to do!"

"No!"

"Come, you can help me plant."

She tied Zeke up and carried Charley to the garden. She engaged him by letting him dig at the end of a row of potatoes. She got the rest of the turnips in and most of the carrots before he began throwing fistfuls of dirt into the breeze.

The third time a spray of gritty dust hit her face, she rose to standing, hearing protesting creaks in her back. Sudden exhaustion ran through her veins like muddy water, making her legs shaky. A headache throbbed against the base of her skull.

"No, Charley. No throwing dirt." She reached to push her palms against her lower back. "Ouch."

Charley threw another handful of dirt and giggled. He darted away when she approached.

"Oh, no you don't!" She caught him. He screamed, but she nuzzled his sweaty neck until he giggled. "Are you hungry? Let's have dinner."

"Pa!"

"Not today. He's working too far away. He packed a dinner."

Charley understood well enough to start fussing. He twisted his dirty fists against his eyes. It was a beautiful sight to Jem; it meant that by the time dinner was over, he would be ready for a nap. She could tie her garden rope through his belt loop—a practice that offended him deeply—and put him on a quilt to sleep while she finished her work. It was a shame to have to tie him, but the prairie grasses were up to her waist in some places. If Charley wandered off, she wouldn't know where to look for him.

When they got to the house, Seth was coming from the other direction. He took Charley from her and kissed her lightly.

"You don't want to touch me," she told him. "I'm so filthy."

"Not filthy. This is good, clean, garden dirt."

"Yes. And good, clean, oxen patties. What brings you home? I thought you'd eat in the field today."

"A wagon's coming. From the north. I didn't recognize it."

"I should go wash up."

From his place by the barn, Zeke leapt to his feet and set to barking like he'd gone mad. Sure enough, a minute or two later a wagon came into sight, lumbering through the waving grass.

"Oh, dear," said Jem.

"You look fine, darling."

She huffed. The wagon pulled up. A big man jumped out and helped an elegantly dressed woman out the other side.

"How do?" the man said.

Seth nodded and stepped forward. "Welcome. I'm Seth Perkins. My wife, Jemima."

"Pleasure, ma'am," the man said. "My sister, Talli Griswald. They call me Grizz."

It was a good name for the man. He certainly did look like a grizzly bear. He was huge—maybe six and a half feet tall, with shaggy brown hair and brown eyes that didn't miss anything.

For a moment there was silence as they all took each other in. Then Charley squawked.

"Oh, dear," said Jem. "He's hungry. May I offer you something to drink? Will you join us for dinner?"

She mentally scrambled. She'd been too busy to cook during the days. She'd planned on having fried eggs and cold mush with Charley. Well, if the Griswalds chose to join them, it would have to be good enough for them as well.

"No, thank you, ma'am," Grizz said, then addressed Seth. "We're neighbors, Mr. Perkins. I've bought the place south of here. Southeast, actually. My sister has just arrived, and she needed some things from town. Thought we'd take a detour to come by and meet you all."

"Glad you did. It's pretty quiet out here this time of year—what with everyone so busy on their own places. How are you faring? You have everything you need?"

"So far. You? I could come back after I get Talli situated."

"So far. At least let us offer you a beverage."

In the end, Grizz consented to sit for a short spell. Seth pulled the short logs they used as kitchen chairs into the shade of the soddy. Talli sat, while the men propped against the edge of Grizz's wagon.

"I'm afraid it's not very fancy," Jem said, passing out cups of water and pieces of bread spread with jam. Charley clung to Seth's legs, whimpering until Seth picked him up. He stared at the strangers and ate his bread.

"I can't imagine how you're living like this," said Talli. She smiled when she said it, but Jem felt a flush rise on her cheeks.

"Well, we ... of course, it can be an adventure. But one day it will all be worth it." The words had a hollow sound to Jem's ears.

"But, my goodness! You're living right in the ground! You must feel like you're a groundhog."

Groundhog. Jem made a mental note. She hadn't used groundhog yet.

Grizz cleared his throat. "Talli's just arrived from New York. She's not used to the way things are out here yet."

Talli giggled. "I should say! Pigs right in the yard. And a dirt floor. My word! Of course, I told Grizz, that's the first order of business. Putting in a proper floor takes precedence over everything else. Just because we live among animals doesn't mean we have to *be* animals."

Seth raised his brows at Grizz, who grinned easily. "Guess I'll put my wheat in first."

Talli pouted. "No, Grizz, we discussed this. The wheat will hold. I *must* have a decent floor."

"Your dress is beautiful," Jem interrupted. She almost hated to say something nice, but the dress was beautiful—a heavy, navy-blue calico with pale blue flowers. Talli carried a matching reticule and wore a feathered cap that set it off beautifully. Jem glanced down at her own blue dress. Well, it had been blue. Heavy wear and harsh lye soap had reduced it to a sort of mottled gray.

Jem touched her hair, then flushed at the gesture. It was bad enough to look the way she did. No need to advertise it to this sharp-tongued woman.

"So," said Talli. "I plan on hiring a housekeeper while I'm in town. Where do you find your help?"

Jem held up her arms. "At the ends of my wrists mainly."

"Oh, but ..." Talli pulled a fan out of her reticule and waved it toward her face. "But I thought ... I was told that you were a Wilkinson. I thought your father was John Wilkinson? From St. Paul? That's one of the reasons I wanted to meet you. So many people here are ... well—"

"The West is the great equalizer," said Grizz.

Seth looked relieved at the change of topic. "It is. British lords farm right next to peasants, and everyone has the same chance at success or failure."

"We do have royalty in the neighborhood—an earl, I think he is," Grizz said. "Have you met him?"

Seth grinned. "In the neighborhood, huh? We really haven't met anyone yet. You're the first. We've only been here a couple of months, and all this blasted rain—"

"Seth—" Jem interrupted, and Seth flushed.

"I apologize, ma'am," he said to Talli. "I'm afraid that living out here has compromised my manners."

Talli fluttered her hand dismissively. "I suppose if I'm going to live out here in the wild, I'll have to get used to rough language." Then she wagged her finger at her brother. "But that doesn't mean I have to live like a roughneck."

Grizz grinned again. "Welcome to Nebraska, dear sister."

Talli pouted prettily and Seth laughed. Charley sagged on his father's shoulder. Jem went to take him.

"Will you excuse me? I think I need to put this little fellow down for a nap."

"Of course," Grizz said and added, "he's a fine little man. Sturdy."

Talli just smiled, a superior curl of her lips. Jem smiled back and nearly stumbled as she hurried into the soddy.

Seth found Jem there, sitting on the side of the bed and stroking Charley's back. "I wondered where you were. Our guests have left."

Then he saw her face. Her eyes were swollen and red rimmed, her face streaked with mud smears from the garden that hadn't yet been washed off. "Darling, what's the matter? Are you hurt?"

He knew he was in trouble when Jem gaped at him. "What's the matter? You have to ask what's the matter?"

He lowered himself to sit next to her, striving for a look of calm comfort while his mind scrambled frantically for what he was supposed to know. She wasn't physically hurt—that was clear now.

He glanced back at his son, utterly limp in sleep, his cheeks pink with health and sun, his thumb hanging loosely between his lips.

He looked back at Jem at a loss. Her eyes were wet, but she also looked annoyed.

"Maybe," she said, "if you had looked at me *even once* instead of being so fascinated with Talli, you'd have some idea."

"Now, wait a minute ..."

"Admit it! You were smitten with her." She bounced to her feet, waving her hands. "And why wouldn't you be? Why *shouldn't* you be? I've become one of those pitiful creatures the newspaper describes! My hair is stringy! My face is dirty! Even when it's clean, it's dirty, because the sun has so darkened my skin. I'm thin—and not in a good way!"

A drama, Seth thought and resigned himself to one of the usual conniption fits. But when she covered her face with her hands and began to sob in earnest, he thought again.

He went and wrapped his arms around her. "Jem, listen to me. Please." He tried to lift her chin, but she resisted.

"Don't look at me!"

So he held her, rocking her gently back and forth, until the storm of tears subsided. "Can we talk about this?"

She turned away. "There's nothing to talk about. I should get back to the garden. Are you going back out?"

"Y—yes. I'll work a little more. Tomorrow, I need to go into town and get a blade for the plow."

"It broke?"

"Not yet, but I can see it's about to go. This ground …"

He stopped. He doubted she was in a mood to hear his complaints about the tough prairie sod just now. But she nodded and used her apron to wipe her eyes.

"Well," she said, and her voice was steady. "You best get moving. I'll get a start on dinner and go back out when Charley wakes up."

She turned her back to him and sliced salt pork for bean porridge. Her hands were steady, her back straight.

He watched her for a minute. But then—not knowing what else to do—he went back out to his field.

Seth left for town early the next morning. The farm had an eerie emptiness when he was gone. The wind blowing through the grasses took on a vaguely haunting sound, and the sky seemed too big. Jem tended to Charley and the house quickly, then hesitated.

"I should be in the garden," she told Charley. "I still have more to plant, and I could add more fertilizer."

"No!" Charley answered. But he didn't look up from his self-assigned task of using a hard rock to pound a softer one to pieces. The resulting powder floated in the air, hanging suspended in the sunbeam coming through the window.

"It doesn't appeal, does it?" She looked out the window. The chickens pecked and strutted across the yard. They were still living in the lean-to attached to the house—what with spring planting, Seth had had no time to construct the chicken coop.

"Come, Charley. Let's go outside."

"Side!" He bounced to his feet, tossing the rocks aside, and they went out together.

The wood for the chicken coop was stacked next to the barn. Jem found the tools and nails in the barn. "I don't know how to build a chicken coop," she said.

"Peep!"

"Right." She tapped her chin thoughtfully. Seth had researched for months before embarking on farm life. He had talked to experienced farmers, taken notes, and read books. But in terms of practical experience, his farming days had begun exactly when hers had.

He'd never built a chicken coop before, so he did what he always did: He researched. Then, he drew out his plan.

And Jem had seen the plan.

She lifted the hammer and tested its weight in her hands. "Well, Charley, my days of been a lady are long gone. I suppose I'll have to make up for it in usefulness."

Charley smiled at her and held up a fistful of hay. "See?"

"I see. That's very nice hay. Charley, today we're going to build a chicken coop."

"Peep!"

"Exactly. Bring your hay and let's go."

CHAPTER ELEVEN

Warm weather and sunshine moved across the Great Plains, bringing forth growth of all kinds. Brown fields turned dark green with young crops. The woods around the river came alive with wildlife. Faltering communities—fed by sunshine and running trains—sprang to new life, creating towns seemingly overnight.

Back in Kansas, Susan Caldwell prepared to send her girls to school for the first time ever. She tugged at the strings on Lilly's bonnet. "Now don't let that hang down your back, miss. That sun is blazing out there."

"But, ma, it's too hot to wear a bonnet."

"You mind me, now."

Pansy's face was pale. "Ma, I don't want to go. Please don't make me."

Susan held the sides of her bonnet and pulled her forward for a kiss. "Don't be shy. It's a providence, finally having a school so near. You'll make new friends and learn so much."

"I don't need new friends. I have you and Pa and my sisters and Baby."

Daisy took her hand. "Come on, Sissy. We'll be together the whole time."

"Off you go then," Susan said, making her voice brisk. "Here's your lunch pail."

The three little girls held hands, their bodies close together as they set off up the path toward the schoolhouse. Susan stood at the window and waved cheerfully when they peeked back at her. She watched until they passed out of sight.

William's arms closed around her from behind. "You're not crying, are you?"

Susan had to swallow twice before she could control her voice. "Of course not. I have plenty to do here at home."

His chuckle tickled her ear. "I have an idea for how we can spend the time."

Susan turned her face up to him, and they had a minute to kiss—to actually kiss right there in their house in broad daylight. Then the baby began to wail.

The land around the Perkin's homestead was a hive of activity. Contrary to his sister's firm instructions, Grizz had his barn chores done before sunup and was out breaking sod as soon as he could make out the plow handle. Talli was just as bossy as he'd remembered, but it didn't matter—not this time of year. He hardly saw her. And by the time he came in and slumped at the dinner table, he was too tired to make sense of her ranting about wooden floors and people who knew how to live like civilized human beings.

The Hanson farm was off the far north corner of Grizz's property. Sometimes, when the sun was at the right angle, Grizz could actually see the waving grass and dark forms of

Mr. Hanson and his boys. No school for those children—nor for any of the boys hereabouts who were old enough to help. Not until planting was over and things slowed down.

⌒

Mr. Hanson rarely saw anyone but his wife, his two sons, and the occasional distant glimpse of Grizz. Because of the way the land fell away to the north, however, Mr. Teske—working with his boys Fred and Jakob—often saw both Mr. Hanson and the new man, Seth Perkins, behind their oxen on their farms. It gave Mr. Teske a sense of community, a feeling of being a part of something larger than himself. He and his family were part of the American dream. They were claiming and settling this broad, wild land. Just by being there, by plowing fields and sowing seeds, they were becoming part of its history.

He looked around as he worked, pointing out the neighbors to his boys. He talked to them—in English—about the dreams they were building, the freedom they tasted with each sweaty step through the tall grass. When his English failed him, he switched to Russian and told them again.

⌒

Seth had walked to town to spare the oxen the trouble and give them time to graze. The trip home seemed to take twice as long as the trip there. His bundle wasn't heavy, but his feet dragged on the rutted wagon trail that served as a road. He was fatigued, that was all. He hadn't worked this hard since his early days in the army, and maybe not even then. And he wasn't a 19-year-old man anymore.

He wiped his brow. The sun was going down, casting the waving grasses into hypnotic silhouettes. But heat rolled over him in waves. Sweat dripped into his eyes, making them burn. His foot landed on the edge of a mud rut gone dry and hard. He stumbled, regained his balance, and adjusted his bundle more securely on his shoulder.

He saw the barn before the soddy, a black form against the jewel blue darkness of the sunset. His knees went liquid at the sight, and he fell forward.

His face landed on a scratchy pad of felled prairie grass. He lay there for a minute.

"I could just rest here. Here in the grass."

Seth knew there was a rule against that, but his mind had gone hazy. "Keep moving," he remembered at last. "Don't fall asleep. You'll freeze to death."

He used his sleeve to wipe sweat off his face, and pushed himself to his feet. He staggered two steps sideways, then steadied. He started at a sound, then relaxed.

"Zeke. Come here, Zeke." His voice sounded weak, but the dog heard him. The barks became higher, coming at a frantic pace, but no closer. He was tied up.

Seth called him anyway. "Zeke. Come on, boy!"

He took a step forward, nearly went down again, but then managed another. "Here, Zeke."

"Seth!" Jem's voice came from beside him. He jolted, squinted to make her out in the darkness. "Seth! What's the matter? What's wrong?"

"Don't want to freeze to death."

"But it must be 70 degrees—"

Something cool pressed on his forehead and disappeared too soon.

"Oh, my goodness—you're burning up!"

"Do it again."

But she didn't. She forced his arm around her shoulders and started him toward the house.

"I bought you ... calico. For a dress," he told her. His tongue felt thick and clumsy.

"You bought what?"

"So you'll feel pretty. I want you to feel ..."

He didn't remember reaching the door.

"Man!"

It was a new word. Jem looked up from the potatoes she was slicing. "Man? Is that what you said, Charley?"

He stood on tiptoes so he could see out the mud-streaked window.

Jem wiped her hands on a rag and went to him. "Oh, my goodness."

A moan behind her made her turn. Seth sat on the side of the bed in his union suit, one hand pressed to the wall for balance. Jem hurried to him.

"Why are you up? You should lie down. You've gone white!"

She tried to guide him down, but he resisted.

"Is there someone outside? What's going on?"

"Yes. My goodness, someone is out there breaking our sod. It's either a good neighbor or a really nervy squatter."

She smiled at him. "See, Seth? God sent us help. We're going to be fine."

He fixed bleary gray eyes on her. "I shouldn't have brought you here. I can't take care of you. When I'm well, we're going home."

"Don't be silly. We are home."

He sighed, and this time he let her guide him back down to the straw-tick mattress. "We're leaving when I'm well."

"Well, whither thou goest, I'll go. But thou aren't goest-ing anywhere right now. Do you want more soup?"

He shook his head, and his eyes drifted shut.

Two weeks. Two weeks, Seth had been sick. It had started with a high fever. Jem sat with him day and night, sponging his hot, dry skin, spooning broth into him, putting her hands on him, and praying harder than she ever had in her life.

She knew that God was good, but she also knew that he had allowed others to die out here in the West. He had allowed other wives to be widowed, other little children to be orphaned. She promised God in her prayers that she would trust him no matter what, even if he took Seth. And then she prayed for the strength to keep that promise—she knew she wouldn't have it on her own. Even the thought of losing Seth was enough to make her angry at God. But she kept praying.

Finally, after four days, his fever broke. His skin returned to a normal temperature, and he swallowed broth and water more willingly.

"You're doing so much better," she told him and thanked God. But his strength was returning so slowly it was almost imperceptible. After only a couple minutes of sitting up, the color leached from his face, and he had to lie back down. He slept most of the time. It was almost harder when he was awake though. He didn't speak much, but she saw the fear in his eyes, and it broke her heart.

He was afraid he'd failed her and Charley. Afraid he'd brought them out here, made them vulnerable to the elements and the capriciousness of farming life, and now he was going to die and abandon them.

Once Jem was sure he was out of immediate danger, she set about keeping the farm going. She had taken Charley out each day to feed the oxen and the cow. But now that Seth was doing better, she stayed out for longer periods. She hauled water from the river and weeded and tended her garden. She planted wheat on the ground that Seth had already broken, weeded, and even tried to figure out how to harness the team to the plow. That proved to be too complicated.

A half-grown boy had come by a week or so ago, walking the wagon trail north. His name was Fred Teske, he said, and he was en route to town. His pa had sent him for a plow blade.

Jem looked out the window again, at the man criss-crossing their field with strange oxen. She'd told the boy about Seth's illness. Was that his pa out there? How could he afford to take the time away from his own fields?

Once she was sure Seth was asleep, she took Charley by the hand and walked out to meet him.

He took his hat off when he saw her, revealing a round, bald head. His face was red from the sun and heat, but his smile spread wide under his thick mustache. "Mrs. Perkins?"

"Oh, thank you so much! Thank you! Are you ... are you Mr. Teske?"

He bowed. He had a strange accent, heavy enough that she had to concentrate to separate his conversation into comprehensible words. "Mrs. Perkins, I'm sorry for your trouble. My wife, she prays for your husband. And I—I do also."

"Thank you so much. Will you come in, have some dinner?"

"Thank you, but no. We will visit, yes? But when the planting is done. You have wood to burn? You have food?"

"I do, thank you. Oh, dear, I'm so grateful. But what about your own fields?"

He waved his hand toward the south. "My boy works. I go home now. Then I come back. Then I go. You understand?"

Jem felt tears prickle behind her tired eyes. She could only thank him again, and then again and again. Before he left, she slipped a loaf of sourdough bread into his pack.

The next day, Mrs. Teske came with Mr. Teske. She was even shorter than her husband, a child-sized, plump woman with expressive black eyes. She spoke rapidly in a language Jem didn't recognize.

"She speaks only Russian," Mr. Teske explained. "She thanks you for the bread, and she—" He paused, listened to her for a minute. "Yes, yes. She thanks you, because we haven't had bread. No yeast. Cornbread only. It is a very big ... nice thing?"

"Treat?" Jem supplied, then flushed. She hadn't meant to boast on her own food; she just couldn't resist the temptation to supply a missing word. But Mr. Teske grinned widely.

"A treat! Yes. Yes, my love," he added to Mrs. Teske, and waited for her to finish speaking. "She is happy to have such a neighbor and wanted to meet and thank you in person."

Jem took both of the woman's hands in hers. They were calloused and hardened, but as tiny as a child's. "I'm so glad to have such neighbors! But I didn't use yeast—I used sourdough. Let me give you some starter."

Mr. Teske translated, and Mrs. Teske smiled widely in response, showing crooked teeth. Jem found herself grinning back.

"I don't know what it is about that woman," she told Seth later, as she spoon fed him soup. "She just radiates warmth. I wish you'd try a piece of bread, honey. The sooner you eat, the sooner you'll feel better."

"Dip it," he said. His voice was raspy.

"Does your throat hurt again?" Jem felt his forehead. "No fever, thank goodness." She dipped a piece of bread into the broth and handed it to him, cupping her other hand under to catch the soggy crumbs and drips of warm broth.

Seth raised his hand and touched her cheek lightly. "I love you."

She drew back a bit in surprise. "Oh. Thank you. I—I love you too."

His lips curled, a shadow of his boyish grin. "Obviously."

"Whither thou goest," she quoted, making her voice sound prim, and his grin widened more. "Anyway, you were right, Seth."

"No I wasn't. It wasn't in our vows; it's from Ruth, remember?"

"Oh, not about that. You know better." She frowned at him. "And you knew better all along. You want more bread?"

He shook his head. She started to dab at his mouth with the napkin, but he took it from her and did it himself. "What was I right about?"

"Nebraska. The prairie. This is the right place for us."

He looked away. "I wish I was still certain of that."

"I'm certain of it." She took his face in her hands so he had to look at her. "Seth, every time I prayed to go home to St. Paul—or anywhere else but here—I felt … I'm not good at talking about this like you are. But I just know I wasn't even supposed to ask for that. When I pray about staying here, making our life here, that's right. I can feel that that's what God wants us to do."

He studied her face for a long time. "It didn't used to be like that for you. With God."

"No, it wasn't. And that alone was a good enough reason to come here. I understand it now." She paused. "I don't understand *him.* Not at all. But I understand, well …"

"That you don't understand? That sounds about right."

"It does. I thought I understood the basic idea of Christianity. I went to Sunday school, knew some Bible stories. Sometimes I even listened to the sermon."

He snorted. She held in her smile and went on. "It wasn't until I started to need it—until it got real—that I realized I know nothing. It's all too big."

Seth leaned over the bowl she still held to give her a careful hug. His face was taking on that pasty look, so she set the bowl aside. "Come. You need to lie down again."

She settled him into the quilts and kissed his forehead.

When she started to rise, he took her hand and held her there for another minute.

"I'm having a really difficult time, right now," he said very quietly. "I'm actually … a little angry. At how this is all going. How hard it is. I feel like God has abandoned us."

Jem opened her mouth to reassure him, to remind him that God proved his love once and for all many years ago, to say that Seth just had to have faith. But then she closed her mouth again. He knew the facts far better than she did. This was a different kind of doubt—a heart sickness.

"It's a psalm," she said, and she kissed his forehead again.

"What do you mean?"

"In the Psalms, they feel abandoned. They cry, they hurt, they complain. They practically … why, they practically yell at God. But, at the end, they always remember that God is faithful. It's not that they forget during the beginning and middle. It's just that … they hurt."

"Yes," said Seth, and his face cleared a little. "Yes. But it helps. Having you be so sure. It's helping me get through the beginning and middle of my psalm."

"Well, I happen to be at the end of this particular psalm. I'm at the end of the 'why-am-I-living-in-the-prairie' psalm." She stroked his face, patting the soft beard that covered his chin now. "Sleep, Seth. Keep getting better. I have things to tend to."

His eyes drifted shut before she finished speaking.

Jem planted where Mr. Teske had plowed and eventually persuaded him to show her how to harness and drive the team. After a day of fighting her skirts, she hemmed and belted a pair of Seth's old pants. It was immodest—shocking, actually. A woman working in trousers like a man! But it was just her, Charley, and the fields.

She did her own chores and Seth's too, and finished the plowing and planting. By then, Seth was out of bed for hours at a time. With him minding Charley and preparing meals, she was able to accomplish even more. She fell into bed each night, her bones aching and her muscles screaming at the hours of abuse. But she slept peacefully, full of a confidence and certainty she'd never experienced before.

As May moved into June, the Teskes visited several times, bringing their children. Mr. Teske and Fred helped Jem put the finishing touches on her chicken coop, while Mrs. Teske played with Charley. The little Teske girls, Magdalena and Freni, chattered to Jem and Seth in English but delighted in teaching Charley Russian words. They pointed to an object and chanted the word in Russian until he accommodated them by attempting to repeat it. Jem knew he didn't understand the game, but she had to laugh at how he grinned when they praised and applauded him.

Seth seemed much cheered by these visits. He and Mr. Teske took manly stances, leaning against the barn or on the rail fence around the small paddock, chewing long blades of grasses and discussing the government, grasshoppers, and groundhogs.

It was his pleasure at these visits that gave Jem her good idea. "We'll have a picnic," she told Mrs. Teske. "For Independence Day. We'll invite all the neighbors."

She paused while Magdalena translated and again while Mrs. Teske answered.

"My ma can make pies," Magdalena reported. "Real American ones. Cherry, Ma? Will you make cherry?" Then the little girl remembered herself, giggled, and translated her own question to Russian.

CHAPTER TWELVE

Independence Day dawned hot and dry, but it was cool enough in the soddy. Jem flew from task to task, issuing rapid fire orders to Seth and even putting Charley to work. "Take the basket outside, Charley. Put it on the table."

Charley looked at the spot where the table was supposed to be and then at the door. His brow creased with concern. "Out," he said. "Out?"

"Yes, that's fine, Charley," Jem said, stacking squares of corn bread onto a plate. "Pa moved it outside so we can have a picnic. Won't that be fun?"

"He doesn't know what a picnic is," Seth said. "Darling, calm down. You have enough food to feed a cavalry troop."

"I still need to tidy the yard, and I wanted to rake the wood chips by the woodpile."

He gave her a look, but she waved him off. "I don't want to hear it. I want everything perfect and that's just the way it is. Take these outside."

She handed him the platter and he moved off. He still moved slowly; his gait had a drag to it, but Jem sent a prayer of thanks upward. He was going to be fine. They were all going to be just fine.

Jem's worst fear was that her guests would arrive early, before she had a chance to clean up. Seth saved the day by watching the clock and forcibly removing a bowl of preserves from her hand. "Go. If it isn't done now, it's not getting done. Go get ready."

She hadn't had time yet to sew up the fabric Seth had brought her, but she wore her pink lawn with the little red flowers. It was the finest dress she'd brought from St. Paul. And if it wasn't quite suitable for a picnic, so be it. She looked nice. Her skin was tanned but clean and healthy, and her hair was in a tidy bun on her head—at least for a few minutes. The heat soon drew tendrils out of the bun and freed them to lie in springy curls at the sides of her face. She was exasperated to realize it, until Seth took one of the tendrils between his fingers and tugged it gently. "Pretty."

The way he smiled at her, she had to believe him. And if he thought she looked pretty, what did she care for the opinion of a haughty eastern girl?

The Teskes arrived first, with Grizz and Talli riding up shortly after. Jem was meanly gratified to see that the girl had lost some of her polish, though it was difficult to define just what had changed. By noon, three single homesteaders and two other families had arrived, creating a large, merry party.

Seth and Mr. Teske propped boards between cut logs to serve as a buffet table. The makeshift table sagged under the weight of the food the women had prepared. Fred Teske organized a game of baseball among the children and eventually persuaded some of the grown men to join them. Seth laughed at the sight of Mr. Teske taking wild swings at the ball.

"You're out!" cried Jakob, his younger son. "That was three strikes."

Mr. Teske didn't relinquish the bat. "I am not out. Throw it again."

"But, Pa! That was your third strike."

"Throw it again, Jakob," Mr. Teske answered. "I am old, and I am Russian. I will try again."

Jakob rolled his eyes as the other men guffawed, but he threw it again. Mr. Teske connected with the ball with a crack that echoed through the barn yard, and he trotted around the bases with time to spare. The game was temporarily halted so the boys could search the tall grass for the ball.

"I have made a home run," Mr. Teske told Seth. He mopped his brow. His face was red, even from his slow trot, but his grin covered his face. "I am an American."

Seth pounded him on the back. "You are indeed. Pure-blooded! How about a drink?"

Jem waited until Seth was a little separate from their guests to approach him. He smiled when he saw her. "I feel fine," he said before she could ask. "Really fine."

She scrutinized his face and then relaxed. "I'm sorry you couldn't play baseball. Were you very disappointed?"

He shrugged. "There'll be other years. This was a great idea, Jem. I think everyone was ready for a little fun."

Warmth spread through her. "Thank you. Everyone seems to be having a good time. But this heat is sweltering, isn't it? Maybe you should go sit in the soddy, just for a little while."

"No. But I will sit out here in some shade."

Mr. Teske filled Jem's washtub at the river so the little ones could play in the water. The adults were glad to sit on whatever they'd brought with them—chairs, benches, or crates. They settled in the shade of the soddy or the little barn and compared notes.

Jem and the other women listened with rapt attention as Mrs. Teske explained, through Magdalena, how to grow potatoes in an old washtub. "When the grasshoppers came, we brought the washtubs inside." Magdalena added, "we had potatoes to eat all winter."

Mrs. Hatfield, who hailed from Boston, gave her recipe for baked beans. Mrs. Walton—who had more of a medical leaning—urged Jem to take action right away, lest Charley grow up to be a dunce.

Jem stopped fanning herself and blinked at the woman. "I beg your pardon?"

"His speech is delayed, dear." Mrs. Walton could only be a few years older than Jem, but she was very tall and had what Sally would have called a presence. "It's one of the dangers of bringing children up in such isolated circumstances. They develop nerve problems."

"Oh. Well, I really think he's just fine."

Charley, unaware that all of the women had turned to watch him, slapped the surface of the water in the washtub, making the other children squeal and giggle. "'Pash!" he yelled. "'Pash!"

Mrs. Walton nodded crisply. "Delayed speech. You should put him on Dr. Morse's Indian root pills, dear. Just as quickly as you can."

Mrs. Hanson patted her wispy blond hair and pursed her lips. "Oh, I'm frightened of some of those patent medicines—"

"Oh, nonsense," interrupted Mrs. Walton. "The Indian root pills aren't patent medicines—they're a genuine remedy."

Mrs. Hanson's pale eyes flashed. Jem hurried to intercept what might have become an argument. "I've never heard of the—the root pills before. They're a remedy for, um, nervous problems?"

Mrs. Walton sat up straighter and pivoted her body away from Mrs. Hanson, just enough to make a point. "Dear, they are *the* remedy. You should read the description of how Dr. Morse cured his father. And he was a breath away from death! They are the only medicine I give my family. Your husband should be taking at least two doses a day. He'll be back to his old self in no time—or better. They cure biliousness, dyspepsia, headache"—she glanced toward Mrs. Hanson—"constipation."

A gasp from Mrs. Hanson let Jem know that the arrow had hit the mark.

"Where do you buy it?" Jem asked hurriedly.

"Well, Mr. Bumgardner doesn't carry it in the grocery yet, although I certainly had words with him about it. I order mine from Chicago."

"My goodness," Jem said, rising. "All the way from Chicago. Mrs. Hanson, would you mind helping me clear the food? I'm afraid the flies are getting under the cloths."

She led the other woman away, hoping she wouldn't hear Mrs. Walton's parting shot, directed to the other women:

"I'm sure Mrs. Perkins will order Dr. Morse's cure. She's not the type to stand by and let her family suffer for lack of a box of 20 cent pills."

Although the "like some people" was unstated, it hung in the air. Mrs. Hanson's face was bright red by the time she and Jem got to the buffet table.

Jem checked the napkins spread over the bowls and platters, rearranging a few things. "My first cat fight in Nebraska," she said, offering a smile to Mrs. Hanson. "I feel as though I'm truly part of a community again."

The tension eased on Mrs. Hanson's face. "She's a piece of work. But, you're right. I'm so glad to see other women. I'm awful tired of seeing the same three faces every day."

Talli sauntered over. "Mrs. Perkins, I was terribly sorry to hear about your husband's illness. Will you be returning to St. Paul?"

Jem remembered Seth's worries and chose her words carefully. "We have no plans to return now. How are you enjoying life in Nebraska?"

She made a little pout and dusted her skirt. "It's not what I'm used to, of course. It's a fine adventure, but I look forward to returning to New York and proper company."

Jem's cheeks started to burn, and she caught a sympathetic look from Mrs. Hanson.

"I wasn't aware you planned on returning. Will you stay here through the summer?"

"I haven't decided yet. I must say, I admire your willingness to live under these conditions. I wouldn't be able to live for long underground as you do and with no amenities. You have such a hardy constitution. Well," she plucked her nearly empty basket of berries from the table, "thank you so much for your hospitality. I'm sure Grizz and I enjoyed it very much."

Her skirts swayed elegantly behind her as she took long strides back to her brother and tugged imperiously on his sleeve. Grizz broke his attention away from the man he was talking to and nodded at her words. When he started for his wagon, others took the cue and rose slowly to gather their belongings and children.

"Speaking of a piece of work," Mrs. Hanson whispered.

Jem widened her eyes and shook her head. "How does she do it? If you listen to her words, you think she's trying to be nice. But by the time she's done talking, you're ready to put your head in the fireplace."

"She's not going back to New York."

Jem had been about to go to Seth so they could see all their new friends off properly, but that halted her. She chewed her bottom lip. "You have ... gossip?"

Mrs. Hanson lowered her eyes modestly, raised them again so Jem could see the twinkle. "Of course not. Gossip is wrong. Reverend Hinkley just preached a whole sermon about that, you know."

Jem clutched Mrs. Hanson's thin arm, glancing right and left. "I don't have much time. Tell!"

Their heads pressed together as Mrs. Hanson whispered. "She's here to find a husband. Her guardian was considerably rich—or, at least, well off. But she came of age. And when she didn't find a husband in New York, he packed her off to her brother."

"Why wasn't the brother her guardian?"

"Oh, he's younger than she—by quite a lot. You can tell if you look close around her eyes. Her age shows. I think they have different mothers. In fact, there's some sort of scandal there, but I haven't been able to get the details."

Jem blew out a breath. "Oh, how are you getting your information? I never get to talk to anyone!"

Mrs. Hanson smiled smugly. "Church. Even during planting time, Mr. Hanson insists we go at least once a month."

Jem took a peek at Seth, standing near the soddy. He was holding Charley and watching her, waiting for her to join him. Jem took a step toward him and then spun back to Mrs. Hanson. "Quick—is there a certain week you go?"

"We try for the first Sunday of the month. More, once things slow down."

Jem threw her a fast wave of thanks and hurried to Seth, just in time to hug Mrs. Teske and insist that they come for dinner next Sunday.

When the last wagon rolled away, Seth let out a contented sigh. "You have a good time?"

"Very! Did you?"

"Very. I suppose we better get things closed down for the night."

Jem nodded. "But Seth, there is one thing."

"What?"

"I was talking to Mrs. Hanson, and she said they make a point of going to church at least once a month. I felt like such a heathen, having to admit we've never been yet. Don't you think we should be going?"

Seth looked thoughtful. "I suppose. It's some distance ..." Then, "No. I'm not going to think about the distance. God has blessed us. You're right, Jem. I should have thought of it myself."

He took her hand in his and they started toward the house. "You're so faithful." He smiled down at her. "What would I do without you to keep me on the straight and narrow?"

She smiled back and hardly felt guilty at all.

CHAPTER THIRTEEN

Seth, Jem, and Charley attended church twice that July, and once again in August. Jem didn't care for Reverend Hinkley's fire and brimstone style—so different from the sermons she'd heard at home—but the female companionship after church more than made up for her discomfort during the service.

Nearly all of the congregation packed dinners and picnicked in the church yard. Once the husbands and children were fed, the wives were free to circulate. Jem particularly loved to have long conversations with Mrs. Hanson and Mrs. Teske. Magdalena, only 10, was privileged to far too many adult themes, but the women regarded it as a necessary evil. Mrs. Teske must be included in Talli's history as it emerged, as well as speculation about the eldest Alcott girl, and the likeliness of each young person in town.

"Magdalena is an exceptionally bright child," Jem told Seth one Sunday as they made the long drive home.

"Oh, really? In what way?"

Too late she realized she couldn't explain her reasoning to Seth. Had the child reacted to the adult conversations with shock or even undue interest, they would have been forced to discharge her as the translator. As it was, she relayed the comments back and forth without inflection and with such a bland expression, they were able to pretend that she wasn't old enough to understand.

Seth was still waiting for an answer, so she fumbled for one.

"She just speaks so intelligently." She kept her eyes on Ole's ears as he plodded along, but she could feel Seth eyes on her. He knew there was an unspoken part, but he couldn't guess what.

⁓

The heat in late summer offered a new kind of misery. Jem's dresses were always damp, but now it was from relentless perspiration instead of relentless rain. There was no rain at all. Once planting was completed, she'd expected a respite from the long hours of physical work until harvest began. Instead, she and Seth spent hours lugging water from the river and pouring it on the parched crops.

"Why didn't they dig a well?" Jem lowered herself to sit on the ground between loads. "How could they live here for 15 years and not dig a well?"

Seth sat beside her, mopping his brow. "They dug three. One went dry. The other two were failures."

"Failures? So ... we could go through all the time and trouble to dig for water and not get any?"

"I'm afraid so."

Jem closed her eyes and let herself fall backward into the grass. "I have to check on Charley."

"I'll do it," Seth offered. But he didn't move either. They stayed collapsed in the thin shade of the barn, too worn out to move or talk or even have an opinion until they heard a screech from the soddy.

Jem opened one eye. "He's up."

Seth had either fallen asleep or decided to pretend so. She pushed herself off from the ground and went to get him.

"Side!"

Jem lifted the boy and tried to hug him, but he wriggled free.

"Pa!"

She set him down and he flew out the open door toward Seth. Jem could hear the grunt when Charley landed on his father's chest.

"That seems fair," she said out loud. "Since I had to come get him."

She hated to leave Charley alone in the soddy. "If only we had a crib for him!" she'd said to Seth. But Seth had just given her a look; he didn't trouble to point out that a crib would have taken up nearly half the floor space in the little house.

Since they had no crib, Jem tried to make the house as safe as a crib. There was no fire in the cookstove, of course. Not in this heat. She'd cook flapjacks for dinner again tonight. It was all she had the energy for after laboring so hard in the heat.

Seth put hooks high on the walls, out of Charley's reach, and they hung up any implement or tool that might be dangerous. They closed up containers tight, and kept buckets of water and milk in the lean-to.

If Charley woke from his naps while Seth and Jem were still down at the river, he couldn't find much mischief to get into inside the soddy, and he wasn't able to open the door to get out. They left Zeke inside with him, but it still felt neglectful to Jem.

However, they simply didn't have a choice—not if they wanted to have crops to harvest in a few weeks.

Jem stayed in the relative cool of the sod house for a few minutes, building up her sourdough and stirring the kettle where she was soaking clothes for the wash. A shadow appeared in the doorway—Seth with Charley slung under his arm.

"Thank you very much," Seth said. He gave her a disgusted look. "I feel like a musket hit my chest."

"He missed you."

"No, he didn't. His aim was dead on."

It would have been a quarrel, but neither one of them had the energy to take it up. Jem handed Seth a piece of buttered cornbread and a bowl of cold fried potatoes.

"Thanks."

She sat Charley on her seat at the table and fed him. But she, like Seth, ate standing up. Her legs were watery, her head hurt, and her eyes felt gritty and dry. She didn't dare be seduced by the cool, dimly lit cocoon of home.

"Could use some rain," Seth commented.

She gave him a wry smile. "Any signs of it happening, weather man?"

"I thought I saw a cloud earlier. Unfortunately, it was just a bird who'd partly melted in the heat and got glued to the sky."

Jem gave him an assessing look. "That wasn't bad."

"Thanks. I spent some time on it."

Their last Sunday at church, they'd met a new member. He was a Texan—bold, brash, and always ready with a laugh. The man and Seth couldn't have been more different, but they'd become friends right away—talking all through the picnic dinner and after. The Texan had introduced Seth to the concept of tall tales.

"So he tells lies? For fun?" Jem had asked.

"Not lies, darling. Stories. No one really believes that a man can ride a tornado or shoot all the stars out of a sky."

So in between loads of water, Seth practiced this new hobby. Some of his efforts had been terrible, in Jem's opinion.

What point was there to a story about the longest 'erm in the West? But Seth wasn't one to give up until he mastered a thing, and he was getting better. Charley was entertained by the stories at any rate. Especially ones with animal noises that he could imitate.

Jem wet a rag and wiped Charley's hands, then swiped it across the rough-hewn table. She picked him up, and he let her nuzzle him. "Well, I suppose we should get back out there."

Before Seth could answer, Zeke—who had been lying near the door in a panting heap of black fur—sprang to his feet and barked a warning.

Jem looked out the window. "A wagon."

"Stay inside." Seth took his pistol off its hook and slipped it into his pocket.

The visiting wagon came to a stop in such a way that Jem couldn't see the driver outside. But a minute later, she heard the familiar voice booming across the farmyard.

"Where is my little girl? What have you done, boy, to bring her to live in such abysmal circumstances? Why, this is a hovel!"

Jem's heart stopped. She set Charley down before she dropped him, and ran for the door. "Father! Oh, my goodness. What are you doing here?"

She threw herself at him for a hug, but he set her back with his hands on her shoulders. "Hold, child. My word, you're filthy! Have you no pride in yourself?" He glared at Seth. "You've dragged her down low. I never would have thought it."

Seth glared right back. "We're living an honest life, Colonel. There are plenty of things dirtier than hard work."

"Oh, stop! Stop!" Jem tried to get past her father's hands for a hug, but he didn't let go. She gave up. "Come in, Father. Come right in. I'll make you some dinner. Have you eaten?"

But John Wilkinson didn't move. "My dear, I certainly will not eat here. This is no place for man or beast. I've booked a room in the new hotel in town. You'll come back to town with me. Go and pack bags for you and the boy. You'll both stay with me until your husband can come up with appropriate accommodations."

"What? Father, no! Really, things aren't so bad here. It's just, we've been working really hard. The drought. We've had to haul water."

"Colonel Wilkinson," Seth's voice was chilly, "you are welcome to visit. But you won't insult me, or insult Jem by suggesting that she'd leave."

John turned on him, his cheeks ruddy. "She certainly won't stay here. I was appalled when I heard she was living in a shanty in Kansas—appalled! Now I find that you have her living underground, like a—a—"

"Groundhog," Jem provided automatically, earning a furious scowl from her husband. "Sorry."

"A groundhog! Yes, a groundhog. My daughter is not a groundhog. My grandson is most certainly not a groundhog. Go and pack your things, immediately! Nevermind—I'm sure you have nothing worth packing. I'll buy what you both need. Come!"

Jem stepped backward. "Father, please. Let's just … why don't we—"

Seth moved in front of her, his fists clenched, his jaw set. "They're not going anywhere. Get out, Colonel. Leave my home immediately."

"Oh, Seth!" wailed Jem. Charley, wide-eyed from the commotion, wailed with her. She moved forward and clutched at her father's arm. "Father! Seth! Please, can we all just calm down?"

John shook her off and bent to snatch Charley off the floor. The boy thrashed in protest and cried harder.

"Daughter, you can join me or not. But my grandson will not live in these conditions."

He stalked out the door and toward his wagon. Jem ran after him, but Seth pushed past her and yanked the boy out of John's arms. He spun to thrust Charley at Jem. She barely caught him before Seth released him.

Then Seth spun back, drew back his fist, and swung. His fist connected with the underside of John's jaw. Time froze for an instant in a terrible tableau—Seth thrust forward from his momentum, her father's stunned, furious expression. Then John's eyes rolled up into his head and he collapsed onto the dry grass.

Jem stared, fixated. "You hit my father."

"Go inside, Jem."

"You hit my father!"

Seth turned on her, and his expression made her flinch. "Take Charley and go inside!"

She opened her mouth to protest but then backed her way through the yard to the soddy door. She patted Charley's bare back under his overall straps. "It's fine, Charley. Everything's going to be fine. Pa and Grandfather just had a little ... Oh, dear. Oh, dear, what is your pa going to do?"

Her father sat on the ground in a very undignified way. His hands fluttered uncertainly, and he wagged his head like a horse trying to shake off a persistent fly.

Jem felt a rush of weepy relief when Seth extended his hand to help John up. But Seth continued the motion, using his father-in-law's momentum to heave him onto his wagon. He thrust the reins into his hands and slapped the horse's flank. The horse shot forward. John rocked in the seat, but didn't fall—at least not while Jem could make him out.

Seth came and took Charley. The boy wrapped his arms tightly around his father's neck and finally stopped crying. "He's not welcome here again, Jemima. I mean that."

"Seth, please. He's my father. I know you're angry, but—"

"Yes, I'm angry, but I'm not saying this out of anger. He just tried to abduct our son, Jem. That doesn't bother you?"

"Of course it bothers me! But he wouldn't have kept him! He was just angry."

Seth shook his head and pushed past her to go inside. "How can you say that? How can you defend him?"

She followed. "I'm not defending him. It was wrong of him to grab Charley. But you know how he is. He has an opinion about everything."

"Including my son."

"Well, yes. But, Seth—" She paused when his cold gray eyes fixed on her.

"Yes?"

"Seth, Charley *is* his grandson."

"He's my son. You're my wife. Maybe it's time for you to decide where your loyalties lie."

"M—my loyalties lie with you!" She went to him, touching his arm. The muscle under his shirt felt hard and unyielding. "Seth, I'm here, aren't I? Whither thou goest?"

She tried for a hopeful smile, but his face was granite.

"You can't hope to please us both, Jem. Not anymore. Your father is now my enemy."

She sucked in a horrified breath, but he jerked his head. "I mean it, Jem. He's a thief, a liar, and now an attempted kidnapper. He stole that money from the army—"

"No—"

"*Yes*. You'd rather believe me to be a liar than see him for what he is. But he stole that money. Then, he lied. Rather than confess what he did, he denied it. Rather than surrender the money from the sale of both houses, he kept it, and fled to the West. It's only a matter of time before the army catches up with him and puts him in jail. And that's exactly where he belongs."

"No! No, Seth, don't say that."

"I don't want him in my home. I don't want him around my son. We're trying to raise a child with values, and your father doesn't have any."

Jem fled. She'd cried in front of Seth many times. Sometimes—she had to admit—even intentionally. But these weren't tears for Seth. Her heart was breaking. She ran to the grass, fell on the hard ground, and sobbed. She didn't return to the house until her eyes were dry and tired and all the crying had been wrung completely out of her.

Seth was cooking flapjacks when she went back into the soddy. He gave her a long, searching look, but she kept her expression as neutral as she could. "Do you want me to take those over?"

"No, I'm almost done. You want to pour Charley some more milk?"

She did, and they fell into an uneasy conversation about the upcoming harvest. She made certain to show Seth no hostility in word or tone. But when he reached for her that night, she forced her muscles to relax in feigned sleep, and she didn't reach back.

CHAPTER FOURTEEN

They were still hauling water when it was time to harvest. Early in the morning, they traveled to the river, taking three or four slow trips with the wagon. Only the most parched fields got watered, but it was almost over.

Once the watering was done, Seth hitched the oxen to cut hay, and Jem headed into her garden, Charley in tow. She harvested beans and peppers and reseeded the ground for another crop of late beets. The next day, she did it all again, and made time for pickling and drying in the evening.

Seth and Jem didn't quarrel, or even have civil conversations. With the amount that they had to accomplish in a day, they were barely nodding acquaintances. But—remembering Seth's illness in the spring—she watched him closely for signs that his health was failing.

A couple of weeks into the heavy harvest work, she saw what she'd been watching for. His face had taken on a bony look, and his skin—while brown from the sun—had a sickly gray shade. She poured him coffee, then sat across from him.

"I wish you wouldn't work in the wheat today," she said. "I was hoping we could finish up the chicken coop—get it tight for winter. And I was hoping you could do some research in your books. I don't have a root cellar, and I wanted to know the best way to store the turnips, carrots, and potatoes when I dig them."

Seth swallowed the last of his coffee and dropped his napkin next to his plate. "I'll help you dig holes around the house, and we'll drop crates in for storage. Hopefully, I can dig a proper cellar next year."

"I don't understand why there isn't one already. How did those people live here for so many years and not have a cellar?"

"They did. You can see the remains of it just south of your garden. They had a lot of losses with the last big fire—the chicken coop, the pig sty, and the root cellar."

"How does a cellar burn?"

"The structure around it burned and collapsed. They also lost the beginning of their frame house. I think that was the last straw for him."

"Well, I guess we're blessed to have what they did leave— the soddy and the barn. Seth, do you think we could have a collapse here?"

He looked impatient. "Jem, the sun is coming up. I need to get the team hitched and get out to the wheat. The sooner I start, the sooner I'll finish."

"Yes, but with all the rain we've had ... don't you think it weakened the soddy roof?"

"I'm sure it's fine." He kissed Charley on the top of his head, grabbed his jug of water, and packed dinner. He was nearly out the door when he stopped. "I'm sorry."

"For what?"

He came back, set his things down, and sat at the table. "Can you sit down for a minute?"

Jem felt a flutter of apprehension. She wiped her hands on her apron and sat across from him. "What's wrong?"

"I'm wrong. When I answer you that way."

"I don't understand."

He shifted, speared his fingers through his hair. "Jemima, I brought you here without your consent."

"But—"

"Let me finish, please. I brought you here without your consent and put you into a lifestyle you never agreed to. I'm not sure what choice I had, and you weren't ... well, equipped, perhaps, to help me make a good decision. But you certainly are now. You've worked as hard as I have— harder, at times. You certainly are capable of planning and detecting potential problems on this farm. You have the right to expect me to listen to your concerns."

Jem felt a warmth that had nothing to do with the heat outside. She couldn't keep her big smile in, so she curled her fist against her lips to hide it. "My goodness. I don't know what to say."

Seth leaned toward her, clearly ready to give her all of his attention. "Now, tell me. What is your concern about the soddy's roof?"

She knew her cheeks were pink. But if Seth was going to treat her like an equal partner, she was going to rise to the occasion. She stood up. "May I show you?"

Three of the main support beams flaked under Seth's thumb when he prodded them. "You're right. They're rotten."

"I suppose it was all the rain."

"Probably. And this is an old house, as soddies go. I don't think it was the original, but it has to be at least six, seven years old."

"Can it be repaired?"

"Yes. Yes, it has to be. We'll get new beams on our next trip into town. This has to be taken care of before the snow comes."

He dusted his hands off, then smiled at her. "Good job, Jem. That would have been a disaster."

She smiled back.

It was their first warm exchange since her father's visit.

In early September, the farm was as demanding as it had ever been, but Seth decided they couldn't put off a trip into town any longer.

"I'm sure we have at least two more months of decent weather," he said. "But it doesn't pay to take chances. Not out here. We'll get all our supplies in for the winter, so make a list. I'll get the beams for the soddy and more plaster."

"Do you think the chickens will be warm enough in the coop? I was thinking of moving them back into the lean-to for the winter."

"I imagine they'll be fine. They have feathers."

Jem made her supply list, and Seth added it to his own.

She hadn't had a chance yet to make up her green dress, so she wore her least faded housedress and decided it would have to do. They took the wagon and took their time, stopping to chat with the Teskes along the way before moving on.

"Oh, I forgot to add lamp oil to the list."

Seth pulled the paper out of his pocket. "No, you did. It's here."

Jem knew that Seth was anxious about getting his work done, but he didn't rush her as she made her way through Bumgardner's Mercantile, holding Charley's hand. She admired the machine-made lace, the creams and perfumes, and the brand new sewing machine waiting for some lucky woman to snatch it up. Seth lingered at the counter, chatting with Mr. Bumgardner and a few other men in town.

"Should be a mild winter," one man said. "We're due, after last year."

"You never know here," Mr. Bumgardner said. His slight German accent made his words sound even more foreboding to Jem. "You may be planting in January or you may be digging tunnels through snow in June."

"We'll be ready, either way."

"Gentlemen."

Jem jolted at the voice and turned. Her father entered the store with the air of one who was granting a favor with his mere presence.

He was still here. She'd been certain he would have left the area after his confrontation with Seth. She'd written Sally for information of his whereabouts, but hadn't heard back yet. She wanted to rush to him, but saw Seth watching her. After a moment's indecision, she went to Seth instead.

"He's my father," she murmured. "I have to acknowledge him."

Seth thumbed through a catalog on the glass of the counter and answered her just as softly. "Has he acknowledged you?"

The question hurt. The catalog went blurry, and Jem turned her back on everyone in the store until her eyes dried again.

"I'm sorry," Seth said when she turned back. "But I'm firm on this, Jem. I know he's your father, but he'll only bring us trouble."

Seth was wrong. Jem was certain of that—didn't the Bible say to honor your father and mother? She remembered the rotting beams in the sod house and came to a decision. "May we talk outside?"

Seth nodded. He picked up Charley, offered a nod to Mr. Bumgardner, and led her to the door—right past her father, who didn't even glance her way.

Once they were outside, Jem watched the dust swirl across the plank boardwalk and thought.

"Yes?"

"I—I was going to discuss this with you. You were so—well—*respectful*, I suppose is a good word, about the beams that I thought you might listen to what I have to say about this situation as well."

"All right," Seth said. "Go ahead."

"That's the problem. I no longer agree with myself."

Seth lifted his brows. "Beg pardon?"

"Well, at least, I *think* I no longer agree with myself. I was going to tell you about honoring my father and mother, and all, but ..." She swallowed hard. "But, Seth, he just ignored me. I tried to smile when I passed him, to make eye contact, something. And he just looked through me like he'd never seen me before." She looked up at her husband and saw the sympathy in his eyes. "How could he do that, Seth? How could he do that to his own child? I would never do that to Charley!"

Seth drew her into his arms, hugged her until Charley, trapped between them, squealed in protest. "Up!"

"Down?" Jem wiped her eyes. "You want *down*, Charley?"

"Up!"

"I wonder if Mr. Bumgardner carries those Indian root pills yet. Mrs. Walton said she'd talked to him about it."

"You're not giving Charley root pills or any other kind of pills."

"But, Seth, he has delayed speech. Mrs. Walton said they would help."

"No. Just leave him be, Jem. Anyway, Mr. Bumgardner will never carry them or any kind of patent medicine. His brother is a doctor. He knows better."

She scoffed. "Oh, I know those doctors. I'm quite certain Dr. Bumgardner is very opposed to home remedies—he loses business when people can treat themselves."

"He is also very opposed to false claims and poisons that masquerade as cures. Leave him be."

Charley pounded his father's shoulder. "Up!"

Jem gave Seth a meaningful look, but he just grinned. "He's fine."

While Seth went to the hardware store, Jem returned to finish up in the mercantile. She was both relieved and disappointed to find her father gone. But when she stepped back out into the blinding heat of the day, she jumped when a hand closed around her upper arm.

"I'll have a word with you, daughter."

Before she could answer, she was pulled into the alley next to the store. There was shade there; she didn't have to squint as she looked at her father. She kept her arms snugly around Charley.

She knew there was no real harm in her father, but no point in taking chances. She couldn't imagine what Seth would have said if John managed to snatch Charley again.

"Father," she said. She was going for a formal tone, but her voice quavered, killing the effect. Charley hid his face against Jem's neck and stole peeks at his grandfather.

"I'm very disappointed. Very disappointed to see how my grandson is being brought up."

Shame curled in her belly. "But ... he's really fine, father. He's healthy and so happy. He loves living out here."

"Why shouldn't he be happy? He's being brought up as a little wild animal. No discipline, no training."

"It's not like that. Father, I wish you'd try to make up with Seth. He's so upset. I know you didn't mean any harm, but when you grabbed Charley like that—"

"I'm prepared to send you and the boy back to St. Paul. I'll purchase the train fare today. You'll be back in your proper environment. I'll hire Sophie back—or someone just as good. You'll have decent clothes to wear, decent food to eat. You won't be shaming yourself by living in filth like sewer rats."

"No. You don't understand. We're living a good life. I'm proud of the things we've accomplished. Please. Can you please try to work things out with Seth?"

"Child, you are a Wilkinson. You are expected to live to a certain standard. You've shamed our whole family by living this way. You have no right to put my grandson in these conditions. Live as you must, but give me the boy so I can have him brought up properly."

"Well ... no!"

John's face took on a dangerous look. "What did you say?"

"I said no, father. I'm not giving you my child. Please, you're not being reasonable. You can't really expect me to leave Seth or to give Charley to you!"

"I *expect* you to be respectful. I am still your father, and you have a duty to me."

Jem saw movement out of the corner of her eye. She stepped backward, but it was too late. Seth stood at the mouth of the alley, staring at her.

His face was unreadable. His voice, when he spoke, was flat. "It's time to go."

"Stand down, sir!" John commanded. "I am speaking to my daughter."

Jem looked from one to the other. "Oh, dear. Seth, could you come over here, please? Can we please talk? Please, can we act like a family and work this out?"

"Let's go, Jemima."

"Give me the boy," John urged, more quietly. "He deserves better. You know it's true; you know I'm right about this. This is no place for a child."

Jem stared at her father. Then she looked down at Charley, slid him around on her hip so he had to raise his head. Charley tried to scramble back around to hide against her, but Jem held him tight.

"No, Charley. Look. That's your grandfather. Can you say 'grandfather'?"

John Wilkinson extended his arms. "Give him to me. He's my grandson."

Jem gave her father a long look. "I just wanted him to see you," she said finally. "I know he's too little to remember. But I just wanted him to see you."

She turned her back on her father and walked to Seth. When Charley saw his father, he reached for him desperately. Jem handed him over and walked beside her husband to the wagon.

John yelled after her, "He'll die out here! This is no place for a child. Mark my words—he won't survive it!"

Jem didn't look back.

CHAPTER FIFTEEN

"**L**ook at all the eggs. Those hens are working overtime," Jem said, putting the basket on the table. "Are you hungry?"

Seth smelled of brisk autumn air and hay. He kicked his boots against the door frame to shake the dirt off and sat at the kitchen table. Jem took that as a yes.

She pulled the johnnycake out of the oven and cracked eggs into the skillet. They spit and bubbled, filling the room with their good scent. "I sure hope the chickens keep laying. It was smart of you to buy that grain. If they're well fed, I'm sure they'll produce all winter."

Outside, a bird chirped. A meadowlark? Jem thought it might be. Water dripped through the saturated mud ceiling of the soddy, plopping with maddening regularity onto the floor in the corner by the bed, creating a slowly growing mud puddle. The rain wasn't as persistent as it had been in the spring, but the tiny raindrops felt like sharp, cold teeth on bare skin. Winter was coming.

When Seth pushed his plate away, she took it and sighed. "Would you like anything else? More coffee?"

Seth stared at her like she was a stranger.

Jem set the dishes in the basin and went back to sit across from him. "Did you hear the geese fly over earlier? They put up such a racket. I guess they're headed south."

Seth turned his face away from her, toward the window. But his expression was blank. She didn't think he was looking for geese or seeing the mottled landscape where green was giving way to brown.

Well, he was tired.

She knew he was tired.

He'd worked nonstop for days in both his fields and others'. Harvesting wheat wasn't a one man job. Mr. Teske had two sturdy sons to help him, but Seth, Mr. Hanson, and Mr. Griswald had helped each other, working in a different field each day so each man had a fair chance of getting his wheat in before the weather changed.

Seth had also repaired the beams in the soddy, which had proven to be a much more difficult job than they had expected. Pulling the old beam out had actually precipitated the cave in that Jem had worried about. But it was a controlled situation: both she and the baby were outside, and all of their susceptible belongings were either covered or stored in the barn. Once the new beam was installed, Seth had to re-plaster the inside of the soddy before they moved everything back inside.

Then he spent a day digging holes around the house to serve as fruit cellars, and the next making repairs on the barn. Right as Seth finished that job, Ole the ox took ill. Thankfully, most of the wheat was harvested by then. After that, he built traps to catch fish in the river. He pulled their bed out of the soddy and modified it so Jem could use it as a drying rack for beans and peas. They'd been sleeping on quilts on the floor for over a week now, but the lean-to was filling with stores of food. Now, Seth was cutting hay, using a harness that he'd re-fashioned to work with Toby alone.

So Jem knew he was tired.

But Jem was also tired. She was so tired, she'd quit carrying Charley. Her knees had taken to buckling unexpectedly. She always caught herself, but she didn't want to be holding him the one time she fell.

Today, she had to make cheese, pick more beans and peas, and pickle beets and cucumbers. She'd been up before either Charley or Seth, starting the porridge. And she'd be on her feet until the fish Seth brought home were salted in the barrel, well after the sun went down.

Seth kept his face turned away from her, so she studied his profile. She slapped the table with her palm, rattling the remaining dishes. "It's so frustrating to speak and have no one answer. I don't know why I bother."

Nothing.

She rose and tied on her apron. "Well, I best get to work then. And so had you. If we're going to bring our child up in a silent, angry home, we should at least make sure he has food and shelter enough."

Seth clinked his spoon against the china cup. "Is there sugar?"

She got the sugar bowl for him. Her face felt hot, and her hands wanted to shake, but she didn't permit them.

It was so rude.

How foolish of her to think such a thing after all they'd been through. They'd come here with almost nothing and they'd be lucky if they'd break even when the harvest was complete. They'd be lucky, in fact, if they did have enough food to eat over the long prairie winter. She'd been coated in dirt of one form or another for almost nine months now. Seth had been dreadfully ill. She'd lost any hope of a relationship with a man she admired above all but Seth—her father.

And instead of being sympathetic over her loss, Seth was furious at her.

"You've made your choice, I see," Seth had said, after helping her into the wagon.

"What do you mean?"

"I told you to decide where your loyalties lie, and you have, obviously."

"What? Seth, I already told you, my loyalties lie with you!"

Seth huffed, but said nothing. He'd spoken to her only when necessary over the last two weeks.

But the thing that pushed her to the edge of reason was a matter of mere etiquette. It was just so *rude,* the way Seth refused to respond to her, day after day! It wasn't as if she had anyone else to talk to. Charley was no conversationalist, and there were no visits between farms this busy time of year.

Her heart pattered in her chest, shortening her breath. Before her anger could boil over to her mouth, she pushed away from the table. She stomped outside, letting the door drop behind her with a sharp crack of wood on wood. Seth didn't follow.

Jem spent her morning in the garden, well away from Seth. Charley played nearby, reliable enough now that she didn't have to tie him. She didn't listen to him playing, exactly, but the instant she *couldn't* hear him, she was on her feet and calling. He was up to no good, or he'd passed out of ear shot. In either case, it always earned him some time sitting on the grass, with Zeke hunched nearby, looking embarrassed and miserable.

After a chill, wet morning, the sun came out. It was warm enough that Jem was able to discard her shawl, but too cool for mosquitoes to be a nuisance. It was perfect weather for picking beans. She should have been happy.

Instead, she fumed. His words still echoed in her mind.

"Made my choice, indeed," Jem muttered, tossing a handful of beans into the bushel basket. "I'm here, aren't I? I'm picking beans and milking the cow ... I work as hard as you do—you said so yourself! Made my choice!"

She had been extremely patient with Seth. After all, he was probably embarrassed. He had said that John was now his enemy, and it was rare for him to make such an emotional overstatement. She'd been careful not to remind him of it.

She waited a couple of days for him to settle down, then recounted the details of her conversation with her father. She'd expected him to at least acknowledge that she hadn't betrayed him at all! If anything, she'd proven her loyalty by standing firm.

But Seth's face tightened when she pointed that out. He didn't say a word. Jem sat across from him at the table and took his hand in both of hers. His was limp and unresponsive.

"You know, Seth, we're partners now. Remember? You said so yourself. Don't you think we should talk about this and work it out?"

He pulled his hand away. "I'm trying to decide what to do."

"What do you mean?"

"Are you planning on going to live with your father?"

She screamed in frustration before answering. "You know that I'm not!"

"That's for the best. It's best if Charley has both of his parents. If you're planning on staying here, perhaps we can find a way to set up two households."

She stared at him. "You're not serious."

"Jem, you've made your position clear."

"No," she said. "I don't believe I have. So let me do so now. My position is: I married you, for better or worse. Till death do us part. And I know for a fact that we actually did say those vows. So unless I die of frustration, or you push me too far and I shove you under the plow, we will live in this house. Together."

She'd stalked away, although her exit was quite ruined when she tripped over Zeke and had to catch herself on the door frame.

Since then, Seth went about his business, and she went about hers. He only spoke to her when necessary. She only spoke to him when necessary, but she sometimes shouted at him when it wasn't strictly necessary.

She dropped the last handful of plump beans into her basket. She climbed to her feet and dusted herself off. "Come, Charley. Let's go in for dinner. I want to try to write a letter to your Aunty while you take a nap."

Dear Sally,

How is life at Aunt Mitzy's? I sure hope she's not making you sew samplers like she did before. It's so odd that Father left you there—for a brother and sister, I never sensed much affection between them.

Well, I have to say father's been in rare form since he arrived in Nebraska. I wouldn't know how to explain all that has gone on, but let me just say that Father and Seth are not on friendly terms.

I wish you'd come here for a visit—you could see what a true frontier woman I've become. You hinted in your last letter that I've left Seth to do all the work, which isn't true. Actually, Seth wasn't well for a while, so I was doing some of his work as well. We have good neighbors in that way also—everyone gives each other a hand. I don't know how else people could survive out here.

You wouldn't recognize Charley, he's so long and lean and brown. He still doesn't talk much, and on the advice of a local lady I wanted to buy him a remedy, but Seth dug his heels in and wouldn't let me dose him! Can you believe that? I don't know what's gotten into him. Anyhow, Charley picks up a new word here and there, so I suppose he'll come out all right in the end. Meanwhile, he has a good time. Seth did build him some toys, but he doesn't care for them. He spends all his time cavorting with his dog and playing with rocks and mud. Also, he follows his pa around as much as he can, aping him and trying to help.

I do wish you'd come and visit, although I can't offer much in the way of accommodations. I'd hoped we could start building our frame house in the spring, but we aren't getting near the harvest we'd hoped for. We got enough for us and seed, but not much to sell. We bought some coal, but we'll be burning straw this winter and buffalo chips if we can find them—a time-honored way of heating one's home in the West!

Well, I've preserved fish and vegetables and even raspberries that Charley and I picked down by the river. We have wheat, and we've stocked up plenty—salt pork and sugar and the like. At least, it looks like plenty to me. Seth doesn't think so, and he made some noises about going back to St. Paul. But no—we didn't work this hard to just walk away.

Anyway, I don't know what the future holds, but I do know that we've come through a lot with God's help. And I expect he'll get us through our first winter in Nebraska. Only I wish I didn't feel like he's preparing me for something hard. I wish I didn't, because I already went through thinking I was going to be a widow, and that's not the way I want things to go.

Well, I'd better finish this. The neighbor boy will be by soon to take this to town. I hope to hear from you soon, but don't be surprised if you don't hear from me much over the winter. I'll write plenty, but it's a hardship getting back and forth to town, and even when we do, sometimes the trains don't come. I heard last year the trains stopped altogether for days at a time. I expect it could happen this year too. It's the middle of October now and nice as it can be, but out here that could change anytime.

Write when you can. I love you, and tell Father I love him too if you hear from him. I don't know what's gotten into him.

Your loving sister,
Jem

Jem was surprised to find Seth at the house when she and Charley got there. He sat slumped at the table, but he straightened when he saw her.

"Are you feeling well?" she asked.

"I'm fine. I drank all my water, so I figured I'd eat at home and refill."

His cheeks were flushed, but the skin around them looked too pale. He jerked back when she pressed her palm to his forehead.

"I think you have a fever again."

"I'm fine. Can we eat, please? I need to get back to work."

Jem ladled warm water into a small pot and put it on the floor. "Here, Charley why don't you play boats until I have your dinner ready? Here's your boat." She gave him a bit of lye soap that she'd squeezed into a rough boat shape.

"Boat!" He grabbed the soap and squatted over the pot, splashing the soap into the water and giggling.

Seth's lip twitched the slightest bit, and she felt a rush of hope. Was he finally relenting? She took a chance.

"How's the hay coming?"

But he just shrugged.

"Are we going to have enough for the winter?"

He shrugged again, but then answered slowly. "I don't think we'll have enough hay. I don't think we have enough of anything."

Jem slid cold green beans and pork into the pot and put it on the stove. "What do you mean? The lean-to is just stuffed with wheat and beans and all, and we have all those little root cellars. I think we could survive two winters!"

"It looks like a lot more than it is. Between me getting sick and the drought, we didn't get near the harvest I was expecting."

Jem thought of the stories she'd heard from her neighbors on Independence Day. "At least we haven't had grasshoppers."

"Don't!" Seth snapped. "Don't even say that word."

"Why, Seth!"

He held up a hand, closed his eyes briefly. "I apologize. I apologize for speaking harshly. This isn't about … the other matter."

Jem sat down across from him. "Then what is it? What are you saying?"

He drew in a breath. "I heard from Mr. Teske that there are a number of newcomers in town looking for homesteads. This is good land, already set up with a barn, broken fields, and even food stores. I could get a good price for the place—probably more than I paid."

"Sell the farm? You want to sell the farm?"

"I don't know. I'm thinking about it. You know what winters can be like here; you've seen for yourself. We didn't have any major disasters—no fire, no grasshoppers, and we barely broke even. How can we think we'll do better next year?"

"Seth, I don't want to sell. We're building a life here. It's just taking us a little longer than we planned to get established, that's all!"

He didn't answer right away. The beans were bubbling. She rose, served them each a bowl, wiped the dirty water off Charley's hands, and gave his face a good swipe. She stepped around the mud puddle he'd created on her floor and got the sourdough bread.

Seth spread butter on Charley's slice and gave it to him. "Jemima, I can't force you to go with me or even to see my point of view on this. I've certainly learned that."

He raised his palm at her sharp sound of irritation. "But I *can* ensure that you and my son are in a dangerous situation. I have calculated what we need in the way of supplies and fuel to survive a typical winter here, and we barely have that."

"But we do have it."

"We have no guarantee that this will be a typical winter, though, do we? What if the weather continues into late spring, as it did in '81? What if the trains stop running altogether? And what is the point of bearing another difficult winter, if we are doomed to fail here anyway? Best we sell while the property is still perceived as having some value."

"We aren't doomed to fail. I think we did very well for our first year."

Seth fed Charley a bite of beans, then handed him his spoon. "Go ahead. Use your spoon, like a big fellow."

Jem ate her own dinner and waited for him to go on. He emptied his bowl and ate the last crumb of his bread before he did.

"As I said, I can't force you to do anything. But if I do decide to sell out and leave, Charley goes where I go."

"How can you be so cruel? How can you say that? When you said that before, it was because I was refusing to work. Obviously, that isn't the case now!"

"I won't give up my son," Seth said, and she saw a flash of real anger in his gray eyes. "I won't allow you to keep him in this godforsaken land, where anything could happen, and I won't allow your father to raise him to be as dishonest as he is."

There were still beans in Jem's bowl, but the knot in her throat wouldn't allow her to eat anymore. She looked at Seth's face, his beloved, handsome face, tight with anger, and she wanted to curl up and die. "You hate me that much."

"This isn't a matter of hatred. It's a matter of trust."

"So you don't trust me."

"No. You don't trust me."

"Oh, Seth, I had a bad moment! I never seriously thought that you were attracted to Talli Griswald!"

"Not that kind of trust." Seth stood up and touched Charley's head lightly. "You don't trust my judgment about our household as much as your father's. You didn't trust me when I told you what he did—you'd rather think I'm deluded or a liar. And you didn't trust me enough to listen when I said to stay away from him and keep Charley away from him."

Jem kept her voice low. "He's my father."

"I'm your husband."

"Which is why—"

"I'm not going to discuss this again." Seth filled his jug and put his hat back on his head. "I'll see where we are in a few days, and I'll decide what we're going to do. I'll see you at suppertime."

But Seth didn't show up for supper. Jem waited for an hour, then took Charley's hand and headed out to the fields.

She saw the oxen first, off to the side of the cleared grass, grazing idly. The wagon had tilted on a rut so hay spilled out sideways. She sped up her walk, then scooped Charley up and broke into a run.

Seth lay near the wagon, face down in the dirt.

"Seth!" She set Charley down and ran to crouch next to him. He was breathing in short gasps. His skin was hot and clammy. "Charley! Bring me Daddy's jug. That small one. Bring that to Mama!"

She stripped his shirt off him and ran water over his face and back. "Wake up, Seth. Come on, now."

He didn't open his eyes, nor even moan or stir. He lay so limp that his body rose and fell with the ruts and dips in the earth.

Jem ran to the wagon and jerked at the halter, pulling at Toby's big head until he consented to end his break. She got the wagon back onto even ground and next to Seth.

She hooked her arms around Seth's trunk and heaved, but he didn't move. She tugged at his arms, his legs. He was much thinner than he had been in the spring, but he was still far too heavy to lift.

"Oh, dear! Charley, how am I going to get your pa home?" She paced in a circle around Seth. Her heart was pounding so she thought she might collapse right next to him. But, no. She had to keep her head about her. She drew a bracing breath and gave the scene another look.

"Gee, Toby! Gee!" She led Toby a little away from Seth, opened the lip and jumped in, pushing the hay out as quickly as she could. It prickled at her hands and poked through her dress, scratching her. Charley jumped onto the hay pile. Jem ignored him, throwing armfuls of hay so they showered onto his head. He squealed and giggled.

When the hay was only a foot or so deep in the wagon, Jem led Toby so the lip of the wagon was open nearly to the ground where Seth lay, forming a kind of ramp. "Stay, Toby! Stay!"

Jem wasn't sure if the ox knew that particular command, but it seemed to work. Toby turned his head and blinked sleepily, but didn't move. She dropped to her knees and pushed, trying to roll Seth onto the open lip. "Come on, come on!"

Seth's muscles were warm and lax. When she pushed or pulled, that part of him moved, but the rest didn't follow. When she stopped pushing, he dropped back into place.

She thought she wasn't going to be able to move him. She could have wedged a board under him as a lever, but there were none handy and she wasn't willing to leave him to go back to the soddy.

She sat back, panting, then pushed again. "Move! Move!"

She pushed his shoulders part way around, and with a mighty heave, kept him going so he flipped onto his back. His arm flew outward. His hand struck the edge of the wagon with a painful-sounding thud. "Oh, I'm sorry! I'm sorry, Seth."

But, of course, Seth was unaware. She heaved him over again, pushing him up the lip, holding him securely while she caught her breath, and then heaving him over again.

Charley stood by, a worried expression on his little face. "Pa?"

Jem raised the lip and lifted Charley in next to his father. "Yes," she said. "Pa. Pa is sick. We've got to get him home."

In the heat, Toby moved even more slowly than usual. His hard hooves plodded on the ground with a steady rhythm that seemed to strike on Jem's very brain. She pushed him as hard as she could, promising him all the turnips he could eat if he would just hurry. When they finally got to the soddy, she left him standing in the heat of the yard and dropped the lip open again.

She rolled Seth to the door and dragged him inside by pulling him backward by his shoulders. She found the boards Seth had used for a buffet table and rested them on the edge of the bed so she could roll him into it.

When he finally flopped onto the quilt, she sagged with relief and exhaustion. She felt his forehead.

"Burning up. Again! Oh, Seth, what is wrong with you? What can I do?"

It was worse this time than it had been in the spring. For days, he thrashed in the quilts, calling out nonsense, or sank into a sleep so deep she had to stroke his throat to work bits of broth down. She bathed his face with cool, wet rags. His fever still went up, so she stripped and bathed him, letting the water run across his lean body and onto the quilt. When his skin finally cooled, she dried him off and pulled dry bedding from Charley's trundle bed over him. He started to shiver, then started burning up again, so she did it all again.

In the early hours of the sixth morning, Jem dozed off, sitting on the edge of the bed beside his pillow. She jolted awake sometime later. Her head was tipped uncomfortably back against the dirt wall. When she straightened her neck, a cold ache ran up her spine.

She wasn't sure what had awakened her until a sharp knock sounded on the door. She jumped to her feet, adrenaline surging through her. She looked around, muddled.

A window-shaped block of sunlight lit a block of floor near the woodpile, which meant it was the middle of the afternoon. Charley lay curled up on a blanket in the corner. His thumb was in his mouth; his fist was curled around the remains of a piece of crumbling cornbread.

Jem's chest clutched in remorse. She had slept through lunch. Her poor little boy had had to find his own food and put himself down for a nap. Then she remembered.

Seth. Seth was terribly ill. His form was motionless under the quilt. She wanted to check on him, but the knock sounded again, louder and more insistent, and she heard a muffled call.

Jakob Teske was at the door. "My pa said to check on you. He hasn't see Mr. Perkins out in the field. He said you all might need help."

Jem started to cry. "Oh, yes! Please! I need a doctor. How did he know? My husband is so sick. Please, Jakob, can you ask your pa to get the doctor?"

"Yes'm," Jakob said, and he took off running.

CHAPTER SIXTEEN

Dr. Bumgardner—brother to the grocer—was a young man, small in stature, with delicate features. Even his voice had a boyish quality to it. He was obviously too inexperienced to be able to help Seth, but he was Jem's only choice.

She paced the soddy behind him as he examined Seth. When he finished, he led her outside to talk.

"Has he complained about neck pain at all?"

"Neck pain? No. But, he's not one to complain. I only know he's sick if I catch him with a fever. Or lying nearly dead in a field."

Dr. Bumgardner nodded sympathetically. "You've had a hard time."

Jem felt tears rush to her eyes, which was silly. What difference did it make, whether the doctor understood how hard this was? It didn't change her circumstances at all. But the simple acknowledgment felt like a small release of tension.

"Is it ... What is it?"

The doctor hesitated the barest second, which told her more than words could have. "He has either influenza or meningitis. I'm inclined to think it's meningitis."

Questions flooded her mind, but she couldn't grasp one long enough to speak it out loud. The doctor went on.

"Your husband's condition is extremely serious. You've done the right thing by keeping him cool. Keep giving him broth when you can, and as much water as you can get down him."

"And ... what will you do, doctor? What will you do to make him better?"

Dr. Bumgardner's brown eyes were sympathetic. "There's nothing we can do. We can only wait."

"Perhaps someone else, someone with more experience ... I'm sorry. I don't mean to be rude."

But he didn't look offended. "Mrs. Perkins, there is no one else—not for miles. But I assure you, they wouldn't be able to do more than I have. Unfortunately, we simply have no way to treat an illness like this. I'm so sorry. I wish I had more to offer."

Jem lowered herself to sit on the side of a cut tree trunk near the wood pile. "I don't know what to do. I just ... I don't know how to fix this."

"You have to pray. It's in the hands of the Almighty, now. I also strongly recommend you send your little boy away. Is there someone he can stay with, for the time being?"

She jerked her head up. "Charley? You think he might become ill?"

"Meningitis is contagious. And deadly, particularly for children."

The cow lowed in the barn, and the chickens chatted quietly amongst themselves as they hunted for insects in the yard. Birds flew overhead, and groundhogs and other little creatures played in the tall grass. Life continued its rhythm, as steady as a heartbeat.

But Jem was done. She had milk instead of blood in her veins. Her faith had dissipated into wisps of remembered joy. She studied her hands—the calluses on her palms, the ragged nails with the dark half moons under each one.

Dr. Bumgardner's voice came from above her, but she didn't look up. "Have you rested at all?"

He sat beside her and waited for her to look at him. Authority mixed with concern showed on his face; she wondered that she'd questioned his ability. He was young, but he was born to be a doctor. "Mrs. Perkins, on my way home, I'll stop and ask Mrs. Teske to come and help you. You'll certainly fall ill yourself if you don't get some sleep."

"No! No, please, don't do that. I—I can't risk it. I don't want them to get sick. Just—will you take my boy to them? Please? I know they won't mind keeping him."

"Of course. Go and prepare his things and I'll get my bag."

Jem checked on Seth first. His condition hadn't changed. His face was ruddy from fever, his eyes half opened but sightless. His mouth hung open.

She packed Charley's clothes and a couple of the toys Seth had made for him out of scrap lumber. She didn't have time to bake or prepare any food to send with him.

"Well, when Seth is better, I'll deliver the Teskes a feast, that's all," she told herself.

"Beg pardon?" Dr. Bumgardner sat at the table nearby.

"Nothing." She looked around. "Oh, my goodness. He must be outside. He likes to play around the chickens."

She went out and scanned the barnyard, the chicken coop, the low grass before the wheat field. "Charley?"

As if her ears had suddenly grown sharper, she could hear everything. She heard the oxen shuffling their feet, the chickens pecking, the grasses swaying and rustling. "Charley? Charley!"

Dr. Bumgardner appeared. "He's missing? Where does he usually go?"

"Nowhere! I don't let him out of my sight!" Jem thrust away the panic that threatened to swamp her. "I have to think. The barn!"

She ran for it, but Charley wasn't inside. If he'd gotten into the chicken coop somehow, she would have seen him, but she checked anyway. Then she checked the soddy again, looking under the bed and in the corner of the woodpile.

She nearly collided with Dr. Bumgardner as she ran back out. "He's gone! I don't know where he is! Charley!" She ran toward the fields. "Charley!"

"Mrs. Perkins." The doctor's voice followed her, but she ignored him.

The prairie grass was as high as her waist. She ran into it, slapping it aside, stumbling over roots and stones. "Charley! Answer me! Where are you? Charley!"

"Mrs. Perkins!" The doctor's voice was sharp enough to make her turn.

"What?" Even her question was a scream.

He put a restraining hand on her arm. "You won't hear him answer. If you keep screaming, you won't hear him answer. You must calm down."

"Calm down! My child! My child is somewhere—lost. Where is he?" She pivoted, yelled again. "Charley! Charley, where are you?"

Dr. Bumgardner's hand tightened, almost painfully. "You *must* calm down."

"My baby. My baby is lost. He's lost on the prairie!" Her voice rose again, but the small part of her brain that was still able to comprehend such things knew that the doctor was right. She was hysterical; she wouldn't find Charley this way.

She gasped for air, and the rush of oxygen made her light-headed. The world seemed to shift. She stumbled sideways, but Dr. Bumgardner held firm.

"You need to sit down."

"No. No." She sucked for air. "I'm calm. I'm fine. I have to find Charley."

"Yes. Yes, we have to find Charley. And we won't find him this way."

A keening sound came from her throat, but he patted her. "We'll find him. He has to be lost in the grass, since he's not in the yard or any of the buildings. Let's be systematic."

"What? Systematic? No! No, we have to find him!" She made to run, but he tugged at her arm.

"Mrs. Perkins, if we just run wildly around, we could miss him completely."

He made her drink some water while he checked on Seth. Then they began to work their way in an ever-widening circle around the property. They called for Charley once a minute, both of them together, as loudly as they could. The rest of the time, they listened.

Jem slapped mosquitoes on her sweaty face and neck, and shoved sweaty strings of hair out of her face. She tripped and stumbled on the uneven ground, fell to her hands and knees, and rose again. Once, she actually stepped on a snake. When it twisted under her foot, she jumped back with a started scream; it sped away through the grass.

Snakes. Charley could have been bitten by a snake. Or eaten by a wolf. He could have been stolen by one of the drifters who wandered far from the train depot. He could have fallen into a hole. The prairie looked flat, but it was full of dips and hollows that were invisible until you were right on top of them. Could he be injured—unconscious, perhaps—and lying in one? Could he have wandered as far as the river and drowned?

Surely not—surely he couldn't have gone that far in the short time she'd had her eyes off him.

She listened hard for his voice, a whimper, or a rustle of grass. Any sound that would give her a clue where her boy was. She heard the insects buzzing, birds chirping. Sometimes, she could hear one of the chickens squawk. Zeke, tied back at the barn, barked.

She and Dr. Bumgardner made their circles in opposite directions. When they passed, he urged her to take a drink from the jug he carried. "We'll find him soon," he promised. "He's so small—he can't have gone far."

But an hour passed and then two. Supper time came and went. Jem refused to abandon the search for even a short time, so Dr. Bumgardner returned to the soddy alone. He tended to Seth, then returned to his circle. When he intercepted Jem the next time, he handed her a bundle of food.

"Stand here for a minute and eat. If you don't, I'll drag you back to your home myself."

She was desperate to continue searching, but now that she was standing still, wooziness washed across her mind like a muddy wave. Her back and legs screamed with pain. "Maybe for a minute."

She ate and drank from a jug. Once Dr. Bumgardner saw that she was complying, he resumed his search. His expression was composed, but his eyes were worried, and he didn't offer any more hopeful promises.

They searched until the sun went down, until it was so dark that they couldn't see the path of bent grass marking their endless circles. Then Dr. Bumgardner did drag her to the house.

"Let go of my arm," Jem said. Her chest hurt, and she wasn't sure if it was from terror or exhaustion. "I'll get a lantern and go back out."

"You won't." Dr. Bumgardner sounded a lot less boyish when he used that grim tone. "I'm sorry, Mrs. Perkins, but we'll have to search again tomorrow."

"I won't! I won't stop until I find him."

"I'm sorry," he repeated. "But if you take a lantern out, you could set the grass on fire. Then where would he be?"

Against her will, Jem imagined Charley, curled in terror against one of the all-consuming prairie fires that she'd heard so much about. "No!"

"We'll get an early start tomorrow, as soon as the sun comes up. Let me help you feed your stock, and I'll sleep on your floor."

Sobs welled up inside of Jem, but she pushed them back. Her Charley. She couldn't afford to cry now. She had to be strong. For Charley. For Seth.

It was too much. She knew she couldn't do it.

But she put one dragging foot in front of the other, and led Dr. Bumgardner to the barn.

They fed and watered Toby and Ole and the milch cow. She went to pour fresh water in Zeke's bowl. He squirmed against her legs, whimpered and moaned when she automatically reached down to pet him.

"You're worried too, aren't you?" she murmured and actually felt a stab of sympathy for the annoying beast.

She was nearly to the house when she stopped short.

"What's wrong?" asked Dr. Bumgardner.

"Just a minute." She went back and looked at Zeke. He thumped his heavy tail on the ground and perked his ears.

As soon as she went into petting range, he plastered himself against her again. But she fought her way through his adoration and thick fur to his leather collar. It took her a minute to untie the complicated, Charley-proof knot she'd tied in the rope. When she did, it was another minute before the dog realized he was free.

As soon as he did, he leapt past Jem and tore through the yard and into the darkness. She'd hoped to follow him, hoped he would be able to find Charley, but he was gone.

"Well," she said. No more words came to her, so she shrugged and dropped the rope in the dust.

They walked to the house. She went in first. The doctor followed her, closed the door, then opened it again.

"Listen," he said.

"I don't hear anything."

"Do you hear the dog?"

She went to the door and strained her ears. "Maybe ..." She went back outside and heard it. From far in the distance came a faint barking. She walked toward the sound.

"Mrs. Perkins."

She ignored him and kept walking. The grass rustled behind her as he followed. They walked straight toward the sound, through wheat or grass as it came.

In a few minutes, she could make out the sound better. "That's Zeke," she said. "I'm pretty sure that's Zeke. He's just ... why, he's just barking to split in two! Listen to him!"

She sped to a faster walk, a trot, and then a run. Dr. Bumgardner's steady footsteps pounded right behind her.

"Zeke! Zeke, come here, boy!"

"No!" Dr. Bumgardner panted between words. "Don't call him. What if he's with your son? If he comes to you, we won't know where the boy is."

At the sound of Jem's call, Zeke barked louder and faster. His bass canine voice took on a higher, frenzied note, but it came no closer.

They followed the sound all the way through the tall grass, to the edge of the woods by the river, to the moonlight clearing where the dog stood—nose to the moon—barking his fool head off.

And where Charley sat on the ground by his dog, looking tired and puzzled and dirty.

The next day, right after breakfast, Dr. Bumgardner took Charley gently from Jem's arms. Charley fussed and squirmed. But his cries turned to high, panicked screams when Dr. Bumgardner climbed into his wagon, tucked the boy next to him, and drove away.

Jem bit her knuckle to keep her own screams in. Her boy! She was sending her boy away with a stranger.

To be fair, the stranger had sacrificed a whole day and put up with a great deal of discomfort to save Charley's life, but Charley didn't understand that. What if he thought he was being punished for getting lost yesterday? What if he thought that she and Seth didn't want him anymore, didn't love him?

She took a step after the wagon, nearly broke into a run, but held back.

"Better a short separation than a permanent one," she said out loud. "I can't risk him catching meningitis from Seth."

Her only response was a whine from Zeke, tied next to her.

She looked down at him. "I'm sorry I had to tie you up. Believe me, I know you deserve better. But I can't have you following the doctor and Charley."

Zeke groaned anxiously and pawed at her. She stroked his big head.

"He'll be back. I promise." She sighed. "I'd better get back in to Seth."

It was another three days before Seth's fever subsided. He lay very still. His skin looked pale and fragile—like damp crepe paper. When his eyes were open, they were blank and uncomprehending, like a porcelain doll's. Jem sponged his face and fed him a spoonful or two of broth, but she figured his battle was nearly over.

She pulled a log up beside the bed and sat beside him. She intended to pray, but she couldn't think of a thing to say. For now, she wouldn't think of how she would manage without Seth. She wouldn't imagine Charley's life without his father, or try to decide whether she would keep the farm or start a new life elsewhere. For now, she bowed her head, and rested in God's presence.

She tried to keep a vigil all night. But at some point, she fell asleep, sitting up against the wall again. She awoke with the sun on her face. Jem blinked a couple of times, tilted her head to crack the stiffness, and looked around. She looked at the still form under the blankets, but dreaded checking. If he was gone, she didn't want to know.

But—of course—she didn't have the luxury of ignorance. What did she intend to do, after all? Just sit here until someone came by to pronounce her a widow?

She drew in a bracing breath and pressed her hand onto Seth. He was still warm. She could feel the shallow rise and fall of his chest, and—as she moved her hand upward—the beat of his heart against her palm.

She got to her feet and went to his head, tugging the quilts down.

Seth's face looked … normal! His color had returned, and his face was relaxed into a natural expression of peaceful slumber.

She stroked her finger down his cheek and he stirred, turning his face toward her touch.

"Seth?"

He stirred again, shook his head as if shaking off an irritant, then opened his eyes. They were vague and uncomprehending at first, then cleared with recognition.

"Jem." His voice was a sticky rasp. She gave him a sip of water and he nodded. "Thank you."

"You're welcome. Welcome back."

A line creased his forehead, so she explained. "You've been sick for a while. How are you feeling?"

"Like a goat ate my arms and legs."

Jem thought that over. "That must be a peculiar feeling." And—how could it be? His lips quirked the slightest bit. Her throat clogged, but she swallowed hard and tried to keep her voice steady. "Would you like another drink? Or some broth?"

"No." His eyes closed. She thought he'd fallen asleep, but he spoke. "Where's Charley?"

"He ... went to stay with the Teskes for a few days." No need to alarm him with the story of Charley's disappearance. That could wait until Seth felt better. "I wish you'd eat a little, Seth. I could make you a flapjack."

He lifted his hand slightly and let it drop back to the bed. "A few minutes, darling. Just give me a few minutes, and I promise I'll eat."

Jem relented, but sat back and watched his face as he drifted off to sleep again.

Alive. He was alive.

She prayed her gratitude silently and fervently.

Then—once she was certain Seth was sound asleep—she covered her face with her hands and sobbed until her stomach and chest hurt too much to continue.

CHAPTER SEVENTEEN

Two weeks after Seth's collapse, Dr. Bumgardner declared him on the road to recovery and no longer contagious. He stopped at the Teskes on the way home and let them know. Jem could hardly stand the wait, but—finally—the entire Teske family came to deliver Charley home.

Jem cried when she saw him and cried harder when she felt his chubby arms around her neck. "Oh, little fellow, I missed you so much!" Charley seemed none the worse for his travels, though he insisted on being held more than usual. Neither Jem nor Seth minded that at all.

By then, Seth could sit up for 10 or 20 minutes at a time. It was another few weeks before he could stand for any length of time. One of the Teskes stopped by every day or so to check on them. The boys checked Seth's traps and brought Jem the fish, and Mr. Teske finished mowing the straw. Jem could count on Mrs. Teske and Magdalena to show up two or three times a weeks, bearing baked goods and gossip from church.

Jem wished she could go to church one or two more times before winter set in, but Seth wasn't strong enough, and she was loath to leave him—although Mrs. Teske offered to stay with him.

"I'm glad enough to see you," Jem said through Magdalena. "You give me all the encouragement I need."

"My ma said you're her first true friend in America," Magdalena reported. "Mine too," the little girl added, her cheeks growing pink. "Ma'am."

Jem hugged each of them. "You are both so dear to me." Then she gasped. "I have the most marvelous idea! We'll celebrate Thanksgiving together! Oh, my goodness. You all come over, and we'll have a big Thanksgiving feast with all the fixings. I'll butcher a chicken—two of them! And we'll have stuffing with sage. Do you think Mr. Bumgardner carries sage? I certainly don't have any."

Jem paced the floor of her little home. Magdalena spoke in rapid Russian, trying to translate and hear Jem's next words at the same time.

Seth, seated on the edge of the bed, looked up from the book he was reading. "What's the fuss about?"

"Thanksgiving! Oh, Seth, it will be wonderful. We'll all have Thanksgiving together."

Seth glared at her. "We'll be gone before then. I told you. We're not staying."

"Oh, don't be silly. You're not well enough to travel, at any rate."

"At *any* rate," Seth said, "Thanksgiving would be out of the question. It's the last Thursday in November. We won't be traveling by then; not if this winter's anything like the last one."

Jem stopped pacing. "Oh. Oh, dear." She patted her palm on her lips. "I have to think about this."

"There's nothing to think about, Jemima. You aren't going to ask the Teskes to travel that late in the year—it'd be foolhardy."

Jem drew a breath to answer Seth, but Magdalena interrupted. "My ma says we should do it early."

"Early?" Jem threw open her palms. "Early! There you go! We'll just do it early, shall we?"

So they planned their Thanksgiving feast for the second of November. Jem dug the last of the carrots and potatoes, made mincemeat pie, and baked sourdough rolls. The soddy was full of the humid smell of rising sourdough. Jem consulted her homemaking book, then cut the heads off of her two rudest hens. She followed the directions for dipping the birds into boiling water before plucking them clean. But the book failed to mention that the smell of wet feathers and chicken innards would have her on her knees behind the soddy. She ate no more that day.

"Only two more days," she told Seth. "But we're nearly ready."

Seth rubbed his forehead. "You should be trying to figure out a way to get us out of here, instead of wasting time with this foolishness."

Jem set down her paring knife and potato and moved to sit beside him. "Seth, I know you're worried. But, sweetheart, I don't see how you can travel right now. Even if we pay for better accommodations on the train, it will be too much of a strain on you."

He turned his face away. "You don't want to leave."

"No, I don't. I don't think we've given this a fair chance yet. But if you say we're going, we're going."

Seth swiveled his head back to her and studied her face with more interest than he'd shown in months. "You mean that?"

"Of course I do."

"Leaving here means leaving your father."

"M—my father? Oh, for heaven's sake, Seth. My father? That's what you think this is about?"

He raised his brows. "You claim it isn't?"

She huffed out an exasperated breath. "It isn't. Yes, I do claim that. I never even see my father, do I?"

"Jem, you can't convince me that you've suddenly fallen in love with churning and digging in the dirt."

"Well, certainly not churning."

"You want your father. It's all you ever wanted. You want your papa to take care of you, and protect you, and make everything in your life perfect. I've never been anything more than an escort."

"What?"

He slapped his hands over his ears. "Please! Don't scream."

"Don't scream? Have you lost your mind? Has your illness decayed your brain?"

Seth closed his eyes and tilted onto his pillow, hands still on his ears.

"You actually still think that I am more loyal to my father than ... Seth? Are you all right?"

He rolled so his back was to her.

"Go plan your dinner, Jem."

"Seth, you can't just ... just fling accusations at me and expect ... Roll back over! That's not nice—to say something like that and then not talk about it!"

"I'm finished discussing this."

"Well, I'm not!"

But Seth was. And nothing she said could persuade him to continue the conversation.

The next day dawned bright and clear, but the chill of autumn was in the air. Jem went outdoors to complete the chores, then hastened back in to begin her final preparations. Her hands flew, snapping beans, peeling potatoes, and mixing batter. She was too occupied to look outside. So when the room went dark, she was momentarily disoriented. Then her hands fell idle for the first time that day.

She looked out the window to confirm what she already knew.

Winter had begun. There would be no Thanksgiving dinner with the Teskes.

The sky spread over the prairie like a wet, gray quilt. Cold rain blew sideways through the cracks around the windows and door. Jem stuffed the gaps with rags, but they hardly seemed to cut the wind. She kept Charley in his jacket and boots, even when he snuggled into bed with his father to hear stories or jabber about his toys.

Jem piled every quilt on the bed, fed the fire, and roasted the Thanksgiving chickens. "We'll have the fixings cold," she said. "We'll have enough food to see us through this storm, no doubt."

Only Zeke, sprawled on the floor beside the stove, lifted his head at her voice; Charley had dozed off in the big bed. Seth stretched beside him, reading. He didn't look up from his book.

"I hope the animals are all fine. It's dreadfully cold."

Seth sighed sharply—his way of saying that, yes, he heard her, but she was bothering him.

"Ole's been so sick. Maybe I should make him some chicken soup."

That bit of silliness didn't even earn her a sigh.

The smell of sage and cooking poultry filled the soddy. The fire in the cook stove burned at a steady rate, and the woodpile was stacked high against the wall. She'd fed the animals enough to see them through; she wouldn't need to go back outside today. The dishes were washed and everything was tidy.

She didn't know what to do. It was too cold to sit and knit. Seth had the lantern beside him, so it was too dim to read at the table. Her shawl was over her head and around her shoulders, but her fingers, toes, and nose were numb. She didn't realize that she'd sighed until Seth looked up.

"What?" His voice was cold.

"Nothing. I—I guess I'll go check on the chickens."

"I don't think so." His eyes drifted back to his book.

She wanted to yell, to wave her arms in the air and scream. But she just stood there, arms hanging at her sides. She was cold, tired, afraid of the winter, and—

Lonely.

"You used to be my friend."

Her words hung in the quiet room, sounding as hollow and lonely as she felt. After a minute, Seth closed his book and looked up at her again. When he spoke, his voice wasn't quite as hard. "What?"

"You used to be my friend. Not when we got married." She shook her head. "I mean, I loved you. And I know you loved me. But we weren't friends. Later. Here. That's when we became friends."

"Jem," Seth rubbed his brow with his fingertips. "Stop, will you? Just stop."

The howling wind outside rose to a higher pitch, and a piece of wood cracked in the fire. Zeke whimpered in his sleep, pedaling his feet over the dirt floor.

"Jem, what are you doing?"

"Nothing."

"Well, stop it." He pushed himself to a sitting position, set his book aside.

"What do you want me to do?"

He looked around the soddy. "I don't know. Relax. Read a book. Sew something. What do you like to do?"

"I don't know."

"Well, sit down, at least. You look like you're hanging on a clothesline or something."

So she perched on the cut log that served as her chair, folded her hands in her lap, and waited.

For spring.

CHAPTER EIGHTEEN

Temperatures across the plains of Kansas and Nebraska dropped to 35 degrees below zero and hovered there. Blizzards came and went. They weren't as frequent or as persistent as the ones in the previous year. But the wind and the cold were brutal. Even when the clouds weren't dropping feet of snow, whole fields were scoured into frozen, muddy ruts by the wind. The wind penetrated every building, every article of clothing, even the thick walls of the soddy.

Early each morning, Jem put on coffee and fried up flapjacks or potatoes. Then she sped through her household chores while Seth made his way to the barn. He had recovered enough to take back his chores, but they took him all morning. When he came back, Jem served beans or soup and corn bread for dinner. Then they all went to bed.

They stacked every quilt in the house—including the ones from Susan—on the big bed and huddled there together. Even Zeke climbed up to flop across their feet, and Jem never objected to the additional source of heat. Seth and Charley napped, and Jem read or dozed or wrote letters to Sally.

In December, Jem discovered two chickens frozen to death in the chicken coop. She thawed them and made soup, and moved the rest into the lean-to, where they pecked and muttered and lay eggs on bags of wheat and in buckets of beans.

Only two days later, Seth reported that Ole the ox appeared to be failing. He went back out to the barn after dinner. When Charley fell asleep for his nap, she went out to the barn to see for herself.

The ox's nose dripped thick mucus and his eyes looked cloudy.

Seth glared at her, hands on hips. "Well, Dr. Jemima? You're here. What do you intend to do about it?"

Jem stomped her feet against the cold. "Oh, really, Seth, don't be grumpy. I don't pretend to be an ... ox doctor. I just wanted to see. It's nice to be out of the soddy for a bit, even for something so disheartening."

But it wasn't nice on the walk back. She'd always felt that the barn was much too close to the soddy—the manure stench had wafted into her kitchen all summer long, and houseflies were thick on every surface. But on the walk back today, she realized the barn was actually too far away.

Seth had attached a rope to the door of the house and secured it tightly so they would have something to hold during the blinding blizzards. They'd heard too many stories of people getting lost and dying only feet from the safety of their front yards.

They didn't need the rope today though; the air was terribly still and clear, as if Jem's vision had improved to that of a bird of prey. But after a minute or two, the cold drew the energy out of her. Each step grew more difficult, and her lungs resisted taking in the air. Her eyes blurred, and her fingers and toes screamed in pain. When they finally made it to the door, Jem threw herself inside and sank down to sit right on the floor.

Seth crouched next to her. "Are you all right?"

"T—terribly cold. Oh, my! Terrible!"

"I told you." He pulled her to her feet and helped her take off her wraps. She wished he would enclose her in his arms, but he just turned to add more wood to the fire. "This kind of cold is dangerous, Jemima. Best if you go no farther than the lean-to. At least until this cold snap breaks."

She nodded her head in jerky agreement, and moved her log to sit as close to the fire as she dared.

The cold snap didn't break. Throughout December the temperature never rose above 25 below. On December 10, Ole died during the night, and Jem had to go out with Seth to deal with the 1,800 pound body. They heaved and pulled, but it didn't budge.

Jem dropped back to lean on the wall, gasping. "I don't understand. He's in here, isn't he? He must have fit through the door when he came in here."

Seth grunted. "He's half frozen." He sighed. "Go on back in the house."

"But what are you going to do?"

"Go inside, Jem."

It was hours before Seth came back inside. He was covered with filth. His face was white from exhaustion, and his eyes looked dazed.

"What did you—" Jem started, then thought better of it. "Sit down. Let me get you some hot coffee. Are you hungry?"

His hand shook so he could hardly hold the teacup to his lips. Jem touched his forehead, but it was cool. "Are you ill?"

"Just tired." His voice sounded reedy. "Done, though. Ole is butchered."

"Butchered!"

"Won't go hungry this winter," Seth said. Then he slid sideways to the floor in a heap.

Seth was unconscious for a day and a night. When he awakened, he didn't talk, didn't seem to remember how. When she held his right hand, he gripped her fingers with shaky pressure. But when she held his left, it didn't move. His face was different in a subtle way, as if the flesh on one side had shifted downward off his cheekbone.

There was nothing she could do. She didn't dare leave Seth or Charley to make the trip to the Teske's, and she certainly didn't dare take either one out.

Remembering Dr. Bumgardner's previous instruction, she made sure to give Seth plenty of water and broth. She propped him up on pillow to feed him soup and bread dipped in broth. She spooned the food in. At first, most of it fell out of his lax mouth and dripped onto the quilt. But she grew more adept at getting the food into the right side of his mouth. He seemed to chew and swallow better from that side.

Once—several days after his collapse—he tried to talk to her. The noises he made were those of an animal—bewildered, unintelligible cries.

"I don't understand," Jem said, hearing her own voice tremble. "I'm sorry, Seth. I can't understand what you're saying."

He clamped his mouth shut.

"Please," Jem said. "Please try again. I—I'll try harder."

But he turned his face to the wall and didn't make another sound.

Jem hated to do it, but she had to leave Charley and Seth untended once a day, for the amount of time it took to muck out Toby and the cow's stall, feed and water them, and then go to the lean-to and tend the chickens. No matter how many layers of clothes she piled on, the cold was paralyzing and painful.

She kept her mind off of the cold by worrying. When that began to seem counterproductive, she decided to keep her mind off the cold by praying.

Cold air whirled through the sod house, snatching all the heat from the fire and rustling the pages of Seth's books. The sound of the wind was muffled again with the slam of the door. Jem had gone out to do the chores.

Seth opened his eyes. Charley lay on his side in his trundle bed, sound asleep with his thumb between his parted lips. The air smelled of mildew, damp earth, and the potatoes Jem had fried for dinner.

Dinner. He put his tongue behind his upper teeth and tried it. "Du—u—n." *Er*, he added mentally. He still couldn't get that "R" sound.

Lying on his back, he stretched his legs out, and flexed and unflexed his feet. His right leg obeyed his commands, but his left was sluggish to obey and sloppy in execution. Still, he persisted. One hundred of those, and one hundred ankle rotations. Then he moved to his arms. He flexed, rotated, pushed, and lifted the book he kept beside his bed. He panted with exertion, fighting with the uncooperative parts of his left side. By the time he was done, drops of sweat ran like tears down the sides of his face.

He let his body rest and began to work on his speech. He was up to the 10th chapter of Proverbs: "The proverbs of Solomon. A wise son maketh a glad father: but a foolish son is the heaviness of his mother ..."

His "V" and "F" sounded like puffs of air, his "S" sounded like "shh," and his "L" and "R" didn't exist at all. He listened to the sound of his muddy speech in the quiet. Rage boiled up, but he pushed it back. He managed a sort of "S" sound in verse 10 and again in verse 12. Progress. He just had to keep trying, to keep practicing.

He stopped, pursed and relaxed his lips, moving his tongue in his mouth.

He'd awakened in a prison, unable to move or speak. Jem was there, always hovering above him, begging him to eat, chattering to him with desperate cheer. He thought—for a few minutes—that he'd pushed her too far, and she had him bound and gagged. But, no. He'd betrayed himself, this time. His body had failed him.

When Jem finally went out for chores, he'd experimented, testing his limbs, then his voice. The sounds he made didn't sound like words at all. He wanted to rage, to hurl things across the soddy, but even that luxury was denied him.

He couldn't stand it.

But what choice did he have? He lived, and this was the body he had to live in. So he tried, tried again, and then again, until he developed a regimen of exercise and speech practice. Was it helping?

He didn't know. At least he was no worse.

He'd thought about quitting. Begged God to take him. What was the point in living? His body was broken. He would never be the hearty, endlessly energetic man he'd once been. He was weak. He was frail.

He'd come to this place as a man, ready to take on this hard new life, protect and provide for his family. Now he'd be leaving an invalid, relying on his wife for his every need. The humiliation of it burned in his gut like hot coals.

He wouldn't quit. Jem—flighty, spoiled, and disloyal—was no quitter. And neither was he.

"Treasures of wickedness profit nothing: but righteousness delivereth from death ..."

He figured he could make himself understood now, if necessary. But he had no intention of allowing Jem to hear him speak like this—like a drunk man with the bottle still in his mouth. He'd practice more, harder. He'd get out of bed and walk. He'd push himself until—even if he wasn't the same—he could stand as the head of his house again.

Maybe Jem was too foolish to see what her father was, but Seth wasn't. He had to protect his wife and son, and he couldn't do it from a bed.

He finished the proverb, then listened. There were no sounds from the lean-to side of the house. Jem must still be working in the barn.

He drew in a bracing breath, stretched his legs out to their full length, and started the cycle again.

CHAPTER NINETEEN

Jem poured Seth coffee and slid a plate of flapjacks in front of him. "It's certainly nice to have you out of bed. You've made a wonderful recovery. You'll be back to normal and pushing the plow again before you know it."

She turned her back to him to pour more batter into the skillet. She knew he didn't like her to watch him when he spoke. He still had to work too hard to control his mouth, still twisted his face to work through the more difficult sounds.

"We are leaving," he said at last in rounded, measured tones.

Forgetting herself, she turned back. "Oh, Seth. You still want to leave."

"Your f—father is probably long gone. From here."

The sharp exhalation was out before she could control it. "You still think I want to stay because of my father."

"You never wanted to be here. You never wanted to work."

"Well, I have worked, haven't I?" She flipped the pancake.

"Ma?" Charley said, looking between her and Seth.

"Everything's fine, Charley. Your father just can't see his own nose before his face."

"Hey!"

"Yes, fine. I'm sorry. I'm sorry I criticized you to the baby. Your daddy's a good man, Charley. A fine, hard-working, strong man, and a hero. He's also—usually—very smart."

"I'm also loyal." Seth held his fork with his left hand while he used his right to cut his flapjack. The knuckles of his left hand were white from the effort of keeping that fork upright.

Jem slid the flapjack out of the skillet and onto Charley's plate. She cut it up and put it on the table. "Use your fork, Charley. Don't forget."

Instead of pouring another flapjack, she sat down at the table. "Seth, do you think I don't know what I was like? That I don't see?"

"What do you mean?"

"I mean, I was—well—spoiled. And selfish. I admit that. I see it now. And I know I'm not perfect. But I also see that I've changed. Why can't you see that?"

Seth scowled at his plate. "I s—see changes."

"Well, then why do you accuse me of being more loyal to my father than to you?"

He took a bite and took his time chewing before he answered. "Your father stole $150,000 from the army. He's a threat to our family in several different ways. Do you believe that?"

"Seth, one of the reasons that I fell in love with you is because you reminded me of my father. You had the same sense of honor, the same—"

"*Do you believe me?*"

Jem looked down at her twined fingers. "Just because I think you're mistaken about something doesn't mean I'm disloyal to you."

Seth pushed away from the table and grabbed the cane he'd shaped out of a long branch. He pushed up to his feet and went to the window.

"Seth, please. This has gone on for months. You can't be angry at me forever. It's just not reasonable. Our marriage comes first; you have to know I feel that way."

"Do the barn chores early today."

"W—what?"

"It's 25 degrees out there."

"Twenty-five below? That's a bit warmer than it was, isn't it?"

"Above. We'll get above freezing today."

Jem moved to stand beside him, put her hand on the glass. "Look how bright it is outside! And the glass is barely cold! Oh, I thought this cold snap would never end." She hugged him, even though he remained stiff and unresponsive. "Seth, do you think winter is ending? Do you think we're finally through the worst of it?"

"We're not done yet. It's only early January." He stared out at the sky for a long moment. "It feels bad."

"What do you mean?"

"The air feels bad. Do your chores early today. Don't go too far away from the house."

"Well, all right." She studied his face. Was he getting ill again? She considered checking his forehead, but knew he'd find it offensive. "Seth, it's really ... it's really lovely outside. I'm sure it's going to be pleasant all day."

He grunted and turned away. Then he stopped—his back to her, as if he couldn't let the conversation end without another comment. "Stay near the house."

Jem abandoned the breakfast dishes for later. Leaving Charley with Seth, she hurried outdoors. She wore her cloak, but left it unhooked at the neck. Fresh breezes, brisk and fragrant, danced around her face and into her nostrils. She couldn't help spinning a circle of joy on the hard packed snow. Zeke barked and plunged his body into a crouch, inviting her to play more, but she laughed and ruffled his ears.

"Maybe later, Zeke. Let's get Toby outside for some of this good, fresh air."

She propped open the lean-to door so the chickens could roam about. They pecked at the dirt and the frozen earth, muttering their displeasure at the lack of insects and worms, but at least they could enjoy the sun.

Toby's stake rope was hidden in a snowdrift. Jem found its source hook on the corner of the barn and pulled it out of the muddy snow until she reached the end. She led the ox out, slipped him a turnip from her dress pocket, and patted his big, hard head. "What do you think, Toby? Don't you think Seth is being foolish? This is fine weather—I'm sure we won't have snow for a day or two at least. Spring is on its way!"

Mucking out his stall was a dream. She could have gotten it done in half the usual time, with Toby out of her way. But she took her time, humming "The Oxen Song" and "True Lover's Farewell." After so many weeks of intolerable cold, she intended to make the most of the balmy temperature.

Across the plains, other winter-weary pioneers had the same idea. In Kansas, Susan and William sent their eldest daughters to school. For the first time in weeks, the girls joyfully shed their cloaks for knitted shawls and raced each other to the school house, only a half mile away.

Dr. Bumgardner took the opportunity to travel to some of the outlying farms in the area. He checked on two new babies, dosed an elderly man who was suffering from rheumatism, and provided skin cream to a dairy farmer who lived far north. The skin cream, of course, wasn't for the farmer, but for the dry, cracked udders of the cows. It was noon before the doctor started for home.

Mr. Teske had chores to do, and he could have used the help of his boys. Mrs. Teske, however, had other ideas. It was a beautiful day—the first in weeks and perhaps the last. The children would go to school. They would be spared a day's toil, see their friends, and perhaps even learn something. They would be children. She packed a single dinner pail for all: greased sourdough bread and cold potatoes. Then Fred, Jakob, and Magdalena were off. Little Freni cried when they left and wouldn't stop until her mother—at wit's end—scolded her and sent her to the loft to play.

Mr. Hanson wasn't as accommodating to his wife as Mr. Teske had been. He'd been in Nebraska long enough to accumulate quite a few head of cattle. Even after last winter's losses, he still had plenty to keep him and both his boys busy. "Time enough to see your friends later," he announced, without defining which part of a farmer's year would allow such a luxury. "We have work to do." They packed lunches to maximize their productivity, and were out the door before Mrs. Hanson could insist they carry their heavy winter wraps—just in case.

Now that Talli had run off and gotten married, Grizz was alone on his place. It was how he liked it. At least, that's what he told himself. He had his dog for companionship. But Bedbug was no conversationalist and no use at all in a game of checkers. Not to mention other, more companionable activities. Grizz went to the barn early and got to work. He'd lost three head of cattle in the latest bout of Texas fever. It was a bad business, but it did free up some stalls. He'd had enough of digging hay out of snowdrifts and hauling it to the barn. If this weather held, he was going to move every one of his haystacks into the barn.

Jem tried to lead the milch cow out, but she pushed her haunches against the back of her stall and wouldn't move. "Well, my goodness! Come on, Gertie. Don't you want some fresh air? It's beautiful out."

The cow lowed but wouldn't be led. Jem pulled and coaxed—even offered her a turnip. Gertie was nearly dry, anyway, so Jem supposed it wouldn't matter if the last of her milk had a bit of turnip flavor. Gertie took the turnip with a look of sulky gratitude, but still wouldn't be moved.

Jem finally gave her a light slap on the rear and gave up. "Your loss, you stubborn old thing. It serves you right to miss the one fine day we've had in months."

She waited to clean Gertie's stall, just in case the silly thing changed her mind later and made it an easier job. Instead, she cleared the ground along one side of the house and uncovered two crates of buried potatoes, carrots, and turnips. "Not frozen," she reported to Zeke. "These are just fine."

The dog flagged his tail in response. She lugged the crates indoors and checked on her men. Charley gripped two armlength sticks. "Rum!" he yelled to Jem, waving them above his head.

Jem looked to Seth, who had wood lengths arranged on the table. "Rum?"

"Drum. Are you done with the chores?"

"Pretty much. Toby and the chickens are out."

"You should put them away. I don't want you to have to go out if it storms."

"Oh, all right. It's really beautiful out, but I'll go do it in a minute." She sat across from him. "What are you working on?"

"A chair. I've had enough of sitting on logs."

"Oh, that's a good idea. A chair. That would be wonderful!"

Seth twisted his lip. "I might as well be good for something."

Jem didn't know what to say to that, so she thwapped his shoulder with the back of her hand, hard. Seth's head jerked up in surprise.

"Quit that!" Jem said.

"I beg your pardon. Did ... did you just hit me?"

She felt a flutter of nerves. He really could look so intimidating when he wanted to. But she kept her scowl on and stared back. "Yes."

"May I ask why?"

"Because you're feeling sorry for yourself."

His eyes were like frozen granite. He opened his mouth to respond, but that was the moment when the soddy went dark.

Charley shrieked. "Ma! Ma-ma!"

A thump and clatter sounded. Seth must have knocked some of his wood down, jumping to his feet.

Jem was momentarily blinded. She blinked a few times until her eyes adjusted, then hurried to Charley. She knelt to gather him into her arms. "Poor boy. Did that frighten you? It's just another bad old storm."

"Ma." Charley nestled into her and she picked him up.

"Seth?" His silhouette was barely visible in front of the dark gray light from the window. "Can you take him? I need to get the animals in."

Seth didn't reach for him. "You won't go out in this."

She chewed her lip and looked toward the window. "I'm sure it's not too bad yet."

"Hot," Charley said.

A deep chill was penetrating the sod house. Jem put him down and went to the stove. "I'll stoke this up before I go out. My goodness! I've never felt the temperature drop so fast."

"Did you leave the lean-to open?"

"Yes. So the chickens could go in and out."

"Get wrapped up and close it. Then come straight back in."

Jem straightened. He was so unreasonable these days, but she had to make him see reason this time. "Seth, I can't leave Toby out in this. He'll die! How would we manage without him?"

Seth's shadowy figure shifted as he turned to look out the window. Jem went to stand beside him.

Tension coiled in her stomach. She couldn't see any-thing—not the barn, not Toby, not even the thermometer, only eight inches away from the glass. "Oh, dear."

"We best forget about the lean-to door."

"No, Seth. No. I have to get my chickens in."

He was close enough for her to see his disbelieving look.

"All right," she said. "But I at least have to get Toby."

"We don't need Toby. Whoever buys the farm will have their own team."

"You don't understand." Tears tried to come to her eyes, but she fought them back. "You just don't understand."

"What don't I understand?"

She was almost too ashamed to say the words, but she got them out in a small voice. "I ... I like Toby."

Seth lowered his head. "I like him too. But, Jemima, you're worth more than an ox."

It was almost a compliment. It was the first nice thing he'd said to her in weeks. Maybe in months. She wanted to wrap her arms around him, to feel close to Seth after such a long distance.

But the wind howled. The cold deepened every minute. And she had a farm to tend to.

She took her cloak off the hook. "I'll go to the lean-to."

He watched her silently as she put on a second pair of socks, a hat, her cloak, and mittens.

"Only the lean-to," he said when her hand was on the latch. "Just close the lean-to door and come back."

"Maybe the chickens saw the cloud and went in of their own accord," she said. "We can hope."

It wasn't an assent, and he knew it. Their eyes locked for a long moment, then she pulled the latch and stepped outside.

CHAPTER TWENTY

All 10 chickens huddled in the corner of the lean-to. They glared at her when she fought her way inside and dragged the door shut, closing the worst of the wind and cold outside.

"I don't blame you for being upset," Jem told them when she had breath back to talk. "It's a wonder you didn't blow right away. It's a wonder *I* didn't. This is the worst storm I've ever seen."

She nudged the chickens with her toe until they broke their huddle. They squawked their outrage.

"Oh, settle down. I'm doing you a favor. I want to move these bags of wheat so you have some insulation on this side. Won't that be nice?"

They muttered and scraped at the frozen dirt floor.

"Well, I'm sorry. But, I insist."

The bags were heavy. When she lifted the first one, the wheat shifted inside. She lost hold of it and it fell to the ground with a plop. After another try, she pulled off her mittens so she could get a better grip. She built a low wall of bags, then built one on the other side and threw some boards over top. By then, stabbing pains were shooting up her fingertips, and the chickens were huddled in a miserable heap next to the drafty door.

She hefted bags onto the boards on top, creating a little cave, then pulled her mittens back on before moving the chickens to that end of the lean-to.

She slid her hand between their warm, feathered bodies to nudge them free of each other, but they resisted. She picked up two and put them in the cave, but they trotted back to the relative warmth of the flock.

"Oh, for mercy's sake! You're determined to die of stupidity!"

She used her hands and a nearly empty bag of dried beans to scatter the flock, then herded them to the other end of the lean-to. At last one, then another, settled into the cave. Finally, they were all secure. They peered at her with their reptilian eyes—muttering low—but she shook her finger at them.

"Say what you want about me, but just stay in there and keep each other warm."

Satisfied, she went to the door, braced herself, and opened it.

She was prepared for the slap—the sharp, cold blow against her face. She'd been in Nebraska long enough by now—had endured the past months of storms and arctic cold—to know what to expect. But this—this assault of iced needles driving into her eyes, her nostrils, her very skin—was instantly unbearable.

She hesitated, keeping her arm stretched behind her, hand gripping the leather strap that served as a door handle. Her eyes watered, and the tears froze instantly, scratching at the tender flesh above her cheekbones. She swiped at her face with her free hand and peered into the blowing white. The stable. Wasn't that the stable? She was sure she'd seen a darker form ... but, no. It was four o'clock in the afternoon, and she couldn't make out the barn.

Where was Toby? Was he suffering terribly? Was he looking for her, wondering why she didn't come to take care of him?

Foolish, perhaps, to an easterner. Foolish to herself, not long ago. Only last winter, she would have surely mocked anyone who would have left the comfort of her warm home—however unattractive and uncomfortable—to save the life of a beast of burden. Even a beast of burden who loved turnips and turned his big head inquiringly when he heard his name called.

She called it now, yelled it as loudly as she could, praying she would hear his answering bellow. "Toby! Toby, boy! Where are you?"

If she heard him, she could follow the sound and rescue him. But she heard nothing above the locomotive-scream of the wind. She barely heard herself.

She should go inside. Seth said to come back in after closing the door.

She looked back at the chickens. Between the dim light and her watering eyes, she couldn't really see them. "People die in storms like this, you know."

She listened again, prayed for a sound from Toby. A hint, even, that he was somehow still upright. He weighed something over 2,000 pounds. If he'd gone down, she'd be no help getting him back up. She'd have risked her life for nothing.

"I can't. I just can't let him die without even trying to save him."

She pushed herself forward into the wind, then halted. She was still clutching the door strap. "Let go," she said. For once, talking to herself seemed harmless enough. Any other fool out in this storm would surely be as blind and deaf as she'd become.

But her fingers didn't relax their grip. They felt frozen, even in woolen mittens. But it wasn't cold that held them fast. It was pure terror.

She could die out here. That's what people talked about, after church and at her picnic. They talked about Indians, grasshoppers, and blizzards. Mrs. Yusef's 32-year-old uncle had died in a blizzard like this one—only 10 feet from his barn. Russell Hatfield had lost two brothers and four toes in the Snow Winter of '81.

But plenty of other people did fine. You just had to be smart, take precautions, use the—

The rope.

"Oh, for pity's sake!" She'd almost forgotten the rope. She spun her head, checking to see if Seth had seen her stupidity. But, of course, Seth was in the house. He couldn't see her. She felt her way across the front of the soddy. She couldn't make out the rope, tied to a hook in the corner of the door frame, until her nose was nearly touching it. But there it was, looped over a peg. Insurance against a blizzard such as this.

She was able to release the door strap to the lean-to then. She flexed her fingers, already stiffening and numb. This cold was inhuman. She couldn't feel her feet, even in woolen stockings and boots. The air cut her throat and lungs with each breath. She had to get warm. She would go in the house, stoke the fire, and thaw before finding Toby.

She reached for the door latch. But stopped.

Surely, if she didn't get Toby into the stable soon, they would lose him. As awkward as it was to work with a single ox, half a team was better than none. If she went inside, Seth would not let her go back out.

She had to save Toby.

The heavy rope was iced to the peg, but she broke it free and began to back into the wind, dropping the rope, coil by coil. Before the third coil fell, Jem could no longer make out the dark shape of the door of the sod house.

William Caldwell had heard the phrase, "Couldn't see your hand before your face" many times, and had even experienced it a time or two. But he'd never seen a storm like this one. Within seconds of stepping out of his shanty, he felt sluggish and frozen. Every instinct told him to return home, but his heart forced him onward: His little girls were only a half mile away, in a schoolhouse with walls so poorly built you could stand outside the west wall and watch the sun come up in the east.

Only a half mile away, they were. Normally, a 10 minute walk, if he was taking his time. He'd been walking for at least 45 minutes. The storm rendered him blind and deaf, so he reached with his hands, feeling for the building—any building—to help him find his way. His hands felt like bricks on the ends of his wrists. But he had to trust that he'd feel the impact if he ran into something.

He prayed that he'd run into something soon.

Elliot Bumgardner knew he was in trouble almost from the first. He'd seen the cloud coming, moving like an evil, black presence across the sky. He looked around him to confirm what he already knew—there were no houses in view. It wasn't Elliot's first winter on the prairie, and he'd thought this through. He leapt out of his wagon and jerked at the harness to free his little mare. Her ears were flat on her head and her eyes were wild. When he slapped her flank, she took off so fast she sprayed icy mud and pebbles onto his legs.

"Good luck, sweetheart," he murmured.

The wind was already beginning its unearthly howl, and the temperature was dropping fast. He heaved his wagon upside down and dove under it, dragging his bag with him, pulling the lip closed.

He never left home in the winter without carrying provisions, so he had food, two quilts, and a jug of water. It was no guarantee of survival, but he'd done all he could think of to improve his odds.

"They will be fine, my love," Mr. Teske said.

Mrs. Teske paced her tidy little sod house, her white-knuckled hands clutched in front of her in supplication. "My babies," she said. It was all she seemed to be able to say. "Where are my babies?"

"In the schoolhouse. My love, I promise you. Our children are safe. Miss Piper will keep the children safe and warm. They have plenty of wood, and the building is tight. They're probably having a merry time, having a party with their friends."

Mrs. Teske smiled at that. "A party. Yes, they're having a party."

She smiled, and paced, and turned, and paced. "My babies," she said. Not to Mr. Teske, he knew. She wasn't talking to him. He wasn't sure she knew she was speaking at all.

"Oh, my Lord, where are my babies? What have you done?"

Mr. Hanson saw the cloud in time. His boy, Peter, was just outside the barn, shoveling hay. Peter was wiry, but small for his eight years. Mr. Hanson ran to the wide open door of the barn.

"To the house, boy!"

Peter's head spun toward him in. "P—pa? What, Pa?"

"Run to the house. Don't stop until you're inside."

While Peter was known for quibbling, he didn't now. He dropped his pitchfork and ran.

As soon as he did, Mr. Hanson ran for his horse. Samuel—only two years older than his brother—was somewhere between town and home, coming back with supplies they'd ordered.

The horse knew what was coming. He bucked and skittered sideways when Mr. Hanson tried to mount him. Mr. Hanson smacked him sharply and leapt on fast. He held the reins tight and spurred the horse into a dead run.

Straight into the storm.

⸺⸺

"This is one for the record books," Grizz said. Bedbug ran a few steps for the house, ran back to circle his legs, then ran toward the door again.

"Oh, I see it. Just sit tight for a minute." He tugged on the barn door to make sure it was closed fast, and grabbed the rope running from the barn to the house. The wind slapped at his coat, tried to steal his hat, so he held it on with one hand. "So much for moving the haystacks. I never did see it get so cold, so fast."

Getting to the house was slow business, even with the rope. But once he was there, he figured he was set. The animals were secure for a day or two, and he had plenty of provisions to see him through the storm. Bedbug shot into the shanty before him. He shut the door tight behind him, shook off his wet outerwear, and added some coal to the stove.

"Shame you can't play checkers," he said to Bedbug. "I guess I'll read a while."

Inside his house, all was peaceful and tidy—for a bachelor's place. The storm outside just made the inside seem cozier. He sat in the chair that he'd made for himself, propped his feet up, and—with Bedbug curled on his old quilt beside him—settled in to wait out the weather.

CHAPTER TWENTY-ONE

Jem held the rope as tightly as she could. Toby was staked about halfway along the length of the rope. All she had to do was walk the right distance and swing left of the barn, only 10 feet or so. Only 10 feet.

But she'd gone too far along the rope, or perhaps not far enough. A few times, she realized that she was actually stumbling through the fierce whiteness with her eyes closed.

It was too late for Toby. Her heart ached to give up, but she had to get back into the safety of the soddy. She fed the rope through her mittened hands, pulling herself against the wind, back toward home.

She forced herself to take a step and another. She reached her left hand forward to take the next step and missed. She swung her arm. Where was the rope?

She tugged backward with her right arm, to pull taut, but her arm flew backward without resistance. She lifted her hands to her eyes, but couldn't see her mittens nor anything but swirling white and gray. She pressed her palms together to confirm: She'd dropped the rope. Somehow, she'd dropped the rope. She tried to feel for it with her numb feet, then dropped to her hands and knees, groping blindly for it.

It was gone. How could the rope be gone? She'd just had it. She had to get back home. She pushed herself back to her feet, feeling as though she were lifting the weight of the gray sky as she went.

The rope was gone.

She'd go back home without it, that was all. She'd tried to save Toby, but couldn't. Now, she needed to get back home and take care of her family.

She counted 20 steps, swung her arms, but connected with nothing. She took five more—perhaps she'd miscounted. Nothing. The wind must have pushed her off course. She took five steps directly into the wind, then two more in the direction the house must surely be.

Nothing.

She turned slowly, peering with iced-over eyes, but she couldn't see anything. Nothing at all. Her eyes hurt. Her hands and feet and chest all hurt even worse. She needed to use the outhouse, but even if she could have found it, her hands were too numb to open her clothes. There was no direction here. There was no house or barn.

Perhaps there never had been.

Miss Millie Stark hailed from Topeka, Kansas. She was only 16 years old, just barely out of the classroom herself, but here she was, schoolmistress of eight young children—including the three oldest Caldwell children. Lily, Pansy, and Daisy were quiet little things, not given to the outcries or shenanigans of some of her other charges. They hadn't uttered a word when the storm dropped over them like a tornado, shaking the schoolhouse fit to bust. But she could see the terror in their pale faces and wide eyes.

"Everything is fine," she said. There was the slightest tremor in her voice. She could only hope they hadn't noticed. "We'll stay snug and tight here until the storm is over."

"But I want my mother," announced Ginny, and burst into tears. Now here was one who was prone to the melodrama.

Millie patted her shoulder, but made her voice as firm as she could. "Of course you do, but we mustn't go out in the storm. It isn't safe. We'll be fine here."

Jackie Meyer chewed his bottom lip. "But, Miss Stark, we haven't much more wood to burn."

Millie looked at the wood pile, then at the expensive desks the school board had purchased only last year. "We'll make do," she said.

Dr. Bumgardner was miserable. Even wrapped in his cocoon of quilts, out of the wind under his upturned wagon, his fingers and toes ached with the beginnings of frostbite. His muscles jerked and twitched in their effort to generate heat. It made him hungry and that was bad. He had provisions—a loaf of bread from Mrs. Yusef, a bit of pork, dried apples, and hardtack—but they had to last. He would be hungrier, he knew, before he could get home.

"Give thanks in everything," he reminded himself. He didn't want to. He felt a bit angry, actually. He'd been doing his duty, tending to the local people the best way he knew how. It was a ministry, he felt, in its own way. He could offer an encouraging word with a poultice for a torn ligament, a word of prayer with a mother whose children were suffering from ague. He tried to be more than a doctor; he tried to be an instrument of God's love.

"So here I was," he prayed. The tone was belligerent, and he strained to rein it in. "Here I was, Lord, doing my duty.

And I get punished for it with this storm. I know you have a good reason for everything, so ... well, I give thanks that you know what you're doing. Your ways are mysterious, after all. In the name of your Son, amen."

The prayer wasn't supposed to end there. He knew it the instant the word "amen" came out of his mouth. Thoughts of his flock enveloped him, as suddenly and completely as this dark-hearted storm. The Hansons, the Teskes, the Waltons. Young Mrs. Walker. The brave little Mrs. Perkins, with her ailing husband and little boy—that disappearing rascal. How were they all faring in the storm? Were they indoors by their fires, safe and secure? Or were they—

And that was when Dr. Bumgardner began to pray in earnest.

Mr. Teske couldn't stand it any longer. If his wife, his beloved little Trina, would only cry or perhaps yell at him. But she paced. Just paced, with a haunted look in her eyes. Murmured, "My babies. Oh, where are my babies?" in that hollow voice.

His beloved was in an agony of worry and despair. And the man in him—the same man who had courted in her the old country, not so very long ago, it felt—that man had to take action.

"Pack a dinner, my love," he said. "I'm going to get the children. They will no doubt be famished."

It was a small miracle, that Mr. Hanson even heard the high-pitched answering cry over the shrieking wind. But he heard it, and—more importantly—his horse heard it. As rattled as the animal was, it seemed to find new purpose in the distant sound of Samuel's voice. Blind, as Mr. Hanson himself was, the horse trudged forward.

"Help! Are you there?"

"Samuel!" Mr. Hanson had yelled until his voice was raw. Now it was barely a croak. But it was enough.

"Pa! Oh, Pa, I'm here!"

Mr. Hanson vibrated in the saddle when the small form collided with his leg. He wanted to slide off the horse to embrace his precious little one, but he knew his legs wouldn't hold him now. He hadn't *felt* so much as *sensed* his son's contact with his frozen flesh.

"Can you climb up? Can you get up here, boy?"

Samuel didn't waste energy with words. He climbed, with fumbling hands and feet, while Mr. Hanson pulled with hands that felt as useless as chunks of coal. At last, with his boy seated in front of him, he turned the horse toward what he hoped was home.

Mr. Hanson couldn't walk and wasn't sure where they were. His horse's steps grew heavier, and he stumbled every few minutes. "We'll ride until he falls," Mr. Hanson said. "Though the beast deserves better, God himself knows."

Samuel sagged back against his father's chest and didn't respond with word or movement.

Mr. Hanson wrapped himself around him as best he could, and let his head fall so it was pressed against Samuel's. I love you, boy. The words didn't come out of his swollen, frozen lips. He just had to hope that Samuel could hear them in his heart.

Grizz was ready for his third winter on the prairie. His shanty was small, made smaller by the double walls he'd constructed after shivering his way through the Blue Winter of '87. He'd stuffed the hollow between with straw, burlap bags, yellowed newspapers, denims that were past mending, and anything else he could find.

With the fire stoked high enough, and his lantern turned up, he was ... well, if not entirely in the lap of luxury, at least comfortable.

He was warm, full of his good buckwheat pancakes, and out of debt. What more could a man want?

"Something to do," he said out loud. Bedbug jerked his head up at the unexpected sound of his voice.

"I should have ordered more books," he explained. He'd read Victor Hugo and Jonathan Swift, Shakespeare and Twain. He'd read Emerson, though he found it didn't hold his attention, and even Mrs. Beeton's *Book of Household Management*, which had been included in his order by mistake. It had diverted him, for a few days, to read about cooking pheasant and screening ladies in waiting. But even that amusement had grown pale.

He supposed he would take a nap. He'd had a pre-dinner nap, but that didn't mean he couldn't take a post-supper nap as well. Maybe all this sleep would serve him, once spring finally came and he had to work 18 hour days.

He was drifting in his chair, hovering in the floating sensation that came just above real sleep, when Bedbug jerked him to full alert with shrill, hysterical barks. His arms flew open, the startle reflex of an infant, before he leapt to his feet, spun in a circle to find the threat.

"What? What is it?"

Bedbug hunched, head low in the direction of the western window. Grizz went to it, but, of course, he couldn't see anything but eddying swirls of darkness.

"What is it, Bug?"

Bedbug growled low, making Grizz draw back a little in surprise.

"Well, all right, old fellow. I believe you."

He looked out again. His haystack was out there somewhere, and, on the far side of that, the barn. Was someone out there?

"I can't see anything, and I can't hear anything."

The dog barked again and didn't break his gaze from the direction of the window. Although, unless he could see through the exterior wall, all he saw was wood.

Grizz shrugged. What could he do? Go out and wander in the storm himself until he either died or bumped into the intruder? If, indeed, there was an intruder.

He yawned and stretched. "Well, you've interrupted my nap. Now what am I supposed to do?"

As if in answer, it came. A voice, just a half note above the wind's endless howls. It rose and fell so Grizz thought it might be the wind, a new vocalization from this storm that felt like a living, evil being.

But, no. There it was again. Human. Female, he thought. Out there in the −35 degree cold and with zero visibility.

Grizz grabbed the extra rope he kept coiled on the hook near the door and ran for his coat.

⌒

The middle of the night? Early morning? Surely, the sun would rise soon. Some light would break through the whirling sky that stretched from ground to eternity. Some sunlight would heat the air.

Jem quit. She stood, leaning backward so the wind wouldn't topple her forward again. She'd fallen five times.

Six times.

No, five.

Maybe six.

She tried to stomp her feet to warm them, but they felt encased in thick mud, too heavy to lift. At least they didn't hurt the way they had. What had she —?

Five times.

Five times what?

She'd decided to quit.

When she fell the last time, she welcomed her collision with the ground. She would rest. She was tired. And this was just silly. Why should she fight the useless lumps that had been hands and feet? Why should she expend energy she no longer had, to try to get to—

Somewhere.

She'd allowed her cheek to rest on the ground and closed her eyes. But a sound had roused her. It was—a clang? Metal on metal? Perhaps there was a barn nearby. Perhaps a wash-tub was being battered by the wind so it connected with a shovel or pitchfork.

She listened, heard nothing, but got to her feet. And, when she heard the clang again, started walking.

She soon lost track of the sound in the scream of the wind. But she walked. One step, another, another. And now, here she stood. Upright, although at an angle.

CHAPTER TWENTY-TWO

Jem wished she would fall again. How had she done it before? She jiggled her legs, but her knees didn't buckle. Still standing.

Well, that was fine. Even if the wind didn't knock her down, that didn't mean she had to walk anymore. She would just stand here, in the dark, in the cold. She didn't have to take any more steps.

It was a relief, to give herself permission to stop. But the relief dissolved when she heard another clang, and then another and another. No clangs. Then three clangs.

Jem swayed. Would she fall now? Would she get to rest?

Three clangs.

No clangs.

Three clangs.

Washtub?

The wind.

No.

Jem sighed and gathered her strength. She wrenched her foot upward and took a wobbly step. She didn't get to rest. She had to go to the sound of the clanging.

Susan fed the baby and tucked him into the trundle bed next to Zinnia. She went to William, who stood staring out the window at the blackness.

"Our time could be better spent," she said.

William turned to her. His eyes were shadowed black, so they looked hollow, the skin pulled taut over the bones of his face. "Better spent?" His voice was raspy. "Better spent than waiting for our children?"

"Yes." Susan took his hand and led him away from the window. Her own heart was pounding so she could hardly breathe, but she folded a quilt and put it on the floor by the fire. She kept hold of his hand as she lowered herself to her knees. Yet another hard winter had left her weak and prone to fits of lightheadedness.

Then she released his hand and clasped both of hers in front of her, bowing her head. She began in her mind: *Our dear Father in Heaven.* But then she paused as she felt William take his place next to her. His big, calloused hands wrapped around hers, and he took the lead. "Father. Father, we're coming to Thee in fear. In helplessness ..."

The wind rocked the upturned wagon and slipped under the edges to tug at the quilt around Dr. Bumgardner's head and shoulders. He came back to himself and looked around at nothing. He was curled on his side in the narrow space, and his right side had gone numb. He was hungry and terribly thirsty, as bizarre as that seemed in this cold.

He cast his eyes upward. "I have more to discuss with you," he said out loud. "I'll take a short break and be right back with you."

He took a long drink of water from his canteen, letting the chips of ice melt on his tongue before swallowing them. Then he opened his pack. He couldn't know how long he'd be here, trapped in this little cave of survival in a wasteland of death. He'd eat half the loaf of bread, he decided, and save everything else for later. He broke a piece off and took a bite, and appetite overcame him. He shoved more bread into his mouth and then more, pausing to take sips of water so he didn't choke on it. Each bite seemed to leave him hungrier instead of more satisfied. He felt around the pack, thinking he must have dropped some. But, no, he'd eaten the whole loaf already.

And he felt he could eat another.

"Well, I suppose I'll get back to the matter at hand. That'll take my mind off my belly."

He adjusted the burlap sack on the ground, refolded the quilts on top of it, rapping his head smartly on the wood wagon bed a couple of times. Then he closed his eyes to resume prayer.

And heard a sound.

A cry? A calf perhaps or another small animal?

He listened hard but heard nothing else.

"Dear Lord," he began.

But there it was again.

He had to investigate.

Which meant unhooking the lip of the wagon and pushing it up. Letting the cold enter his cave unhindered. And risking losing the wagon altogether to the fiercely blowing wind.

A thousand times, he'd imagined his Nebraskan friends who might at that moment be wandering, lost and near death, while he was safe and warm. Well, if not warm, at least not freezing to death. Yet. But now he was going to put himself in that position. And for what? Some coyote pup who'd been separated from his pack?

He muttered, ashamed that he wanted to be selfish, but pushed the wagon lip up and gasped when the cold air hit him hard enough to knock the wind out of him. He lay on the hard ground for a few seconds and considered again the potential benefits of doing the selfish thing.

No one could blame him for not wanting to risk exposure.

Then he crawled out of the wagon and pushed himself to a standing position. He yelled, paused, yelled.

And a little form collided with him so hard that he cried out and fell backward.

Dr. Bumgardner couldn't decide later whether the boy didn't understand that he wanted him to go into the wagon cave or just couldn't manage his limbs well enough to comply. It seemed like hours passed before he got him inside and stretched beside him in the dark, and hours more before their combined body heat began to warm the air around them.

They didn't talk, and Dr. Bumgardner didn't pray anymore. At least, he didn't pray words. He pulled the little form as close as he could, wrapped him in so much quilt that he himself was half on the bare ground, and let his heart pour out wordless gratitude and praise.

This one, at least, would survive the storm.

It seemed to take half the night for Mr. Teske to make his way to the schoolhouse. He moved in short installments. His house to the barn. The barn to the plow on the edge of the field. He nearly missed that, but tripped over one of the edges and felt along it until he knew where he was.

Only 25 feet from there to the neighbor's barbed wire fence. He felt along that, and wondered whether the fence had been lengthened or reconfigured in some way. In the past, the fence had ended near the little row of trees that marked the edge of the Hanson property. But this fence was far, far too long. And shouldn't he have been able to make out the shadows of trees, even in the dark?

He considered crawling under the fence and bypassing it to figure out his mistake. He actually dropped to his knees to do this, but then pulled himself painfully back up. It was the cold talking. Anyone who walked without landmarks in this weather was taking a journey to certain death.

"The fence hasn't been moved," he mumbled. "It hasn't. It is the same."

So he followed it, snagging his gloves on the sharp wire and swiping at his sore eyes. And just when he decided once again to crawl under the fence, he reached his hand out and felt the corner.

"Ah! I am coming, children. I am almost to you! I bring you a fine dinner from your mother."

He made his way through the trees, down through a gully that ran the back of the schoolhouse property. And then, swinging his arms in front of him like a blind man, he set off to cross the small yard to the schoolhouse.

He hit the side of the building with a thump that reverberated through his body. He felt until he figured out where he was. Somehow he'd gotten turned around so he'd hit the building on the far side of where he'd began.

He chucked a disgusted sound, then shook his head. It didn't matter. He was here.

He made his way around to the door and pulled it open against the wind.

The schoolhouse was empty.

Mr. Hanson walked without remembering where he was going and held tight to the weight on his back without remembering why or what it was.

He walked, and kept walking, putting one wooden foot in front of the other—getting nowhere—when he hit a wall. He angled to the right and walked, staying pressed against the wall for support until hands pulled at him. A voice rattled in his ear like dry leaves in the wind.

He was drawn to someplace warm. The hands pulled at the weight on his back, but he resisted. No, he wanted to say, but couldn't. Can't let him go. Can't let him go.

The voice and hands were persistent. The weight was removed, leaving his back feeling naked and light. He tried to take a step—must keep walking—but his knees buckled.

He was given a drink of something warm. Wet clothes were peeled off of him, and a warm quilt was placed around him.

"Another drink," the voice insisted. "More broth, Josiah."

He didn't want to drink. He wanted to sleep. But the hands touched his face, pressed the teacup against his mouth. He was too tired to resist.

"Ava."

Her slim face, freckled even in January, came into view. She was weeping.

"Oh, Josiah. I thought I'd lost all of you. You're here, at least."

"Samuel."

She cried harder. "He'll be fine. He'll be fine, praise the Lord. We have Samuel."

"Lost the horse."

"The h—horse? The horse?" She looked almost angry. "The horse?"

Why did she keep repeating it? It was a horse. A good horse, but replaceable. The important thing was that they were here. All of them, safe and warm after such a near miss. Ava, and Samuel and—

"Where is Peter?"

"Peter?" She dabbed at his chin where some broth had dribbled.

He jerked his head away. "Yes, woman, Peter! You didn't let him go to the barn in this weather, did you?"

She stared at him, her pale blue eyes dry now. But, strange. They had such a strange look to them. "Peter? Peter was with you."

"No." His words came slowly now, his exasperation crystallizing into fear. "No. I sent him to the house. As soon as I saw the cloud—the storm—I sent him. I sent him. He ran! I saw him running to the house."

Ava lifted her hand as if to dab at him again, lowered it. Her lips trembled. "He was with you."

Grizz anchored the rope to his door frame and did a wide sweep of his yard. It wasn't long, at least by blizzard standards, before he heard the voice again and followed it to the wriggling shape in his haystack.

"Come!" he yelled. "I'll get you inside."

He couldn't hear his own voice, but the form rose, clutched at him, and he fought the wind for both of them until they got to the door. He could barely get it open, and then could barely get it closed, but they were finally inside.

Bedbug ran in frantic, joyful circles. He barked madly, then ran again, up over the bed, across the woodpile and through his legs.

"Enough," Grizz said sharply. He pulled his gloves off and wiped the ice off of his eyes.

Beside him, his companion seemed immobile.

"I know you're cold," he said. "But stay away from the fire till we see whether you've got frostbite. Where did you come from? How did you get so far out? I'm the last place for miles—if you'd missed me, you'd have been sore out of luck."

As he spoke, he unwrapped scarves and shawls, revealing a woman's pale face. He studied her closely in the lantern light. Her eyes were green and slanted like cat's. They caught his attention, so it was a minute before he took a proper look at the rest of her.

"I think you're okay. You were wrapped up good. You hurt anywhere?"

She shook her head.

"So you understand English, at least. All right, go on over by the fire and take your wet clothes off."

She started, gave him a wide eyed look. "I'm s—sorry?"

He grinned. "And you even talk." He extended his hand. "My name's Grizz."

She extended hers, looking bewildered.

"How do you do?" Her hand felt impossibly small and cold in his. He held onto it and led her to his chair. He knelt before her.

"Boots," he explained.

A little smile played over her lips. "Oh. I thought you'd decided to make me a proper offer."

"Boots first. I never propose marriage to a woman before getting a good look at her feet. What's your name, honey?"

Some faint color had come into her cheeks. She sat back against the chair, let out a deep breath, and closed her eyes. "Sally," she said without opening them. "Sally Wilkinson."

"Nice to meet you, Sally," Grizz said. He thought of a song he knew as a boy, "Sally in our Alley." He began to sing, "Of all the girls that are so smart, there's none like pretty Sally ..."

But she'd already drifted off to sleep.

CHAPTER TWENTY-THREE

Hazy sunlight shone over the glittering white world, making Jem squint and lift her hand to protect her eyes. Her gloved hand felt like a solid chunk of wood. She blinked, then blinked again, trying to get her bearings.

She was alive.

The thought fluttered through her mind, too elusive for her to grasp it.

She was alive.

Could she ... could she move? Could she go home?

She had thought to wake in heaven. She'd been so certain. So ... at peace, really, as her eyes drifted shut for what she'd thought was the last time. How could she be alive? Was she alive?

Surely she was dead or almost so. She tested her body and tried to move her legs, tried to roll to her feet and collided with something solid. A wall. She patted it with her wooden hand. Had she taken shelter against a wall?

After a minute she remembered.

Toby.

She'd stumbled against the animal and felt his fur over a body that felt frozen solid. But perhaps not. Perhaps his bulk had retained heat, keeping her alive through the night.

Her feet wouldn't move. She wrenched with her knees, trying to free her legs from the layer of ice that sealed her to Toby.

Poor Toby.

She rested, letting her eyes drift closed again, wishing the sun provided warmth as well as this eyeball-searing light.

Cold. Hungry. And, afraid, she realized. She'd spent the night sheltered next to Toby. She must be close to home.

Unless Toby had broken his flimsy tie-down and wandered, as helplessly lost in the blizzard as she? Had they somehow found each other, miles from home?

She needed to open her eyes again and look. She needed to stand, to walk home—whether it was 15 feet away or 10,000. She needed to check on Seth and Charley—they must be dreadfully worried and hungry by now! She'd spent the entire night on the prairie.

She rested.

It was impossible to gauge time as she lay there, part of the frozen landscape. Her heart was beating sluggishly, as if her blood was thick as maple syrup. Her breathing was irregular. Once, she tried to push off from the ground, but pain exploded through her limbs and into her chest, frightening her. She relaxed to the ground again. Perhaps she would die here, after all.

Her mind returned to the question: Was she truly alive? Was she in some sort of in-between state, no longer alive, waiting to be retrieved by angels and taken home?

But that was silly. The pain she felt, which had subsided but not disappeared completely, was evidence enough that she was still part of the fallen world. Pain. Pain in her chest and legs and arms—but not in her feet and hands. Perhaps she wasn't dead, but her hands and feet were.

The sun rode a little farther across the white sky. Finally, she felt stronger. Her breath was coming more regularly. She succeeded in rolling sideways. Panting, she rested again.

The sun was straight above before she stood up. She levered herself upward against Toby's frozen corpse. She took a step, lost her balance and collapsed part way, catching herself by twisting her fingers into the frozen spikes of his long fur. She couldn't feel her feet at all.

Stilts. Her legs were stilts.

She'd tried stilts once as a girl, when a colonel's son had been showing them off to friends. She strained to remember the feel of them now—the rigid wood jerking forward in precarious balance. She lurched her feet forward in a few successful steps, then paused, swaying, to look around.

Toby had died at his stake. She had wandered through the storm for hours, surely, but had somehow ended up only feet from her home. Relief surfaced, rose through the daggers of pain in her legs. Home.

In minutes she'd be in the dim light and warmth of the soddy, taking comfort from her husband and child. She would thaw her feet, submit to the pain, and then fix her family breakfast—a nice one, to celebrate the end of the dreadful blizzard. She glanced back at the frozen mound on the ground.

Poor Toby. He wouldn't be breakfast, but if her feet recovered in time, he'd serve as a hearty dinner.

She staggered forward, trying to ignore the pain and the fluttering of her heart. She knew she had to be cold, but she just couldn't feel it anymore.

Her eyes refused to focus properly—they must have been strained from the storm. She could barely make out the wooden door of the soddy, and she was very nearly on top of it before she made out the darker vertical line. What was—?

Was the door open?

It was open? Why would—?

She ran then, ungainly thrusts forward with feet that couldn't flex, knees that wouldn't bend. "Seth? Charley! Seth! Are you —?"

Seth lay in the doorway, his head nearly buried under drifts of snow. An icy tunnel ran through the snow in front of his mouth from where he was—or had been—breathing. Jem dropped to her knees beside him, barking out a harsh cry from the pain. "Seth! Seth, oh, no! Wake up! Seth!"

She shook him roughly and tried to lift his head between her useless hands. His head lolled back on his neck. He wasn't frozen then—not solid, anyway. She put her face against his, listening for breath. She wailed when she didn't hear any. But then she felt it—the slightest warmth against her cheek. If her scarf hadn't shifted, exposing unfrozen skin to his breath, she wouldn't have detected it at all.

"Seth! Oh, we have to get you warm. Oh!" She tried to push him out of the doorway. Failing, she pulled the door all the way open and tried to step over Seth into the house. Her feet got tangled up with his body and she fell forward onto him. Jagged shards of pain shot through her arms and legs and even into her feet, but she didn't take the time to reflect on what this newest pain might mean.

She rolled off of Seth onto the frozen ruts of the dirt floor and tugged her mittens off with her teeth. "We have to get you warm. We have to get you in bed. Oh, Seth!" She tried to hook her useless fingers around him, then wrapped her arms around him and pulled backward, landing on her seat. He slid three or four inches toward the bed, so she did it again, and again. One more time, and she would be able to close the door. Then she should build up the fire—that was even more important than getting him off the floor.

She sat beside him on the floor, panting for breath, planning. But alarm had begun to niggle at the edges of her befuddled, half-frozen brain. She looked around, trying to think.

The fire was out.

She had to get the fire going. The fire shouldn't be out—she needed to thaw herself and Seth, and it was bad for Charley. Charley already had a cold; he needed to be kept warm.

She looked back to Seth. Time to pull him back the rest of the way. She wrapped her arms around him, but didn't pull. She held herself against his cold torso, balanced, as the alarm in her mind grew louder. It crystallized at last into a single word:

"Charley!"

She let herself fall backward again, then pulled herself up the doorframe. "Charley! Are you here? Come to Mama!" She staggered to the bed, the trundle bed, the corner beside the stove. Was he hiding? In this little soddy? There was no place to hide.

She ran back to Seth, grabbing him again and pulling him backward the final few inches to clear the door. "What did you do?" She screamed at him. "What did you do? Where is my baby?"

Seth didn't move. She stumbled over him and back out the door into the sparkling white landscape. "Charley! Charley!" She realized she was screaming and tried to calm her voice. "Don't be frightened, honey. Mama's not angry. Just come to me, please. I don't know where you are. Come here, Charley!"

She repeated those sentences—fragments of them—until they were a nonsensical babble, as she staggered across the snow.

The wind had subsided, rendering the air less deadly. But it was still penetrating and painful. The cold drove Jem back inside the soddy after a few minutes. She hastily started the fire, crumpling precious pages of Seth's farming magazine and using them as tinder. The pain in her limbs made her gasp, but she didn't take the time to collect a bowl of snow to rub on her frozen skin. What did it matter?

Her child was missing—missing!—and her husband lay on the frozen dirt floor, dead—or close to it.

As soon as she could make her feet function, she wrapped herself up and made her way around Seth's motionless form and back out the door, closing it to retain the thin heat from her fire.

"Charley!" Her hoarse voice rang like a broken bell in the blinding white silence of the day. She searched the stable, the chicken lean-to, and every rise in the landscape.

He must have awakened and—finding his father unresponsive—gone outside to search for her. He'd probably left a minute or two before she got home. And now he was wandering around this blinding, frozen farm, looking for her. Poor little fellow! The wind had died down, but it was still so terribly cold. She needed to get him indoors and warm, before he caught his death.

She searched until she collapsed, exhausted, face down in a snowdrift. She tried to get up, but the blood pumping through her was too watery and weak to give her the strength. She rolled to her side and rested, closed her eyes. And floated. The drifted snow provided a soft cushion under her, and for some reason it didn't feel cold at all. She dozed, slipped into a dream—Seth spinning Charley in a circle, both of them laughing, until they collapsed into the tall prairie grass. Life was so much better now in Nebraska. They were a real family: Seth and her and Charley.

Charley.

Her eyes popped open. Charley. She wasn't in her bed—she was outside in the snow. And Charley was out here somewhere. She struggled to her feet, fell, then struggled up again.

She went into the soddy and added more braided straw to the fire. She dragged Seth closer to the stove, exchanged her wet gloves for his dry ones, and went back out.

She yelled, listened, and yelled again until—nearly a half mile from home—she heard a soft whimper.

"Charley!" She ran, stiff-legged, sobbing with pain and fear, toward a low rise in the snowy expanse, set among larger mounds that marked downed livestock. "Charley? Are you there? Answer me!"

She paddled snow off the mound with clumsy gloved hands, but then stilled. "Zeke," she breathed.

The dog whimpered, and tried to raise his head. Icicles hung from his muzzle, and crystals covered his eyes. He was curled in tight ball around something, but now he tried to pull himself free. He wiggled weakly, but then stopped with a pained moan.

Jem touched him tentatively. "Zeke? Can you get up? Come on, boy."

Zeke wriggled again. Ice crackled, startling Jem, making her jump back. Her heart was thumping in her chest, and she couldn't draw a full breath past the lump in her throat.

Zeke whined, then rested, laying his head on ...

She saw. She couldn't *not* see the crumpled ball of iced-over denim, the unnaturally white skin under a thin layer of white crystals. Charley was lying on his side in the snow, curled in fetal position. His eyes were matted by ice, completely invisible. His colorless lips were closed tight over his thumb. Zeke was curled in a half-circle around him, frozen to him by the snow that had melted from their body heat, and then re-frozen as their body temperatures dropped to match the ambient temperature.

Jem pulled off her gloves and held her hand near Charley's mouth. But there was no warmth. The snowflakes that had fallen on his lips, on his little curled fist, were undisturbed and intact. "No! No, Charley. You can't be ... no. No, you're not! You're cold, that's all. We have to get you inside, by the fire!"

She heard the hysteria in her own voice and sucked in a shaky breath. "I have to get you inside." Yes, her voice was calmer. She had to be calm. It was the difference between life and death in dangerous situations like this.

She pressed her bare hand to the junction between the dog and the boy, trying to separate them. She couldn't carry them both. "Try to stand up, Zeke. I need you out of the way."

The dog whimpered again but didn't move. Jem pressed her hand harder, praying her body heat was enough to melt the ice. "Up, Zeke. Get up!" Zeke groaned, then pedaled his forepaws. He found purchase against Charley's little body and pushed outward, but didn't break free.

It was so cold. Charley's body felt frozen solid—lifeless. She had to get him inside, had to get him warmed up, before it was too late. In desperation, she drove her fist downward, breaking the last of the connection between the two bodies. Zeke yelped and rolled away to his feet. His legs buckled under him, and he collapsed onto his belly. His eyes fixed on Jem, and she met his watchful gaze.

"You have to walk," she said.

Zeke stayed put, watching intently, as Jem pushed and pulled Charley's body, trying to free it from the ground. Jem was pulling when it came free. The momentum threw her backward, with Charley's stiff form still in her arms. Zeke sprang backward and paused a few feet away.

"You can walk," Jem said again to the dog. "You'll walk." Then, she pushed herself to her feet. Holding Charley, she started toward the soddy.

CHAPTER TWENTY-FOUR

Seth regained consciousness gradually. As blackness receded from his mind, red pain swirled in to fill the void. His muscles, his back, his fingers and toes. His nose, of all places—it hurt like the dickens. Was the fever back? He wanted to protest the idea, but his throat was too dry to make a sound. He needed a drink. Hot tea. He wanted tea. Where was Jem? A memory nudged at him, and he focused until it came to him—Jem. Out in the storm. The blizzard.

Jem.

He tried to sit up, but his muscles wouldn't oblige. But he opened his eyes, at least, turned his head and scanned the soddy. The stove was blazing hot—the door was actually tinged red from the fire, and flames licked tiny tongues through every opening. He must talk to Jem about that—there was no use in wasting fuel by burning such a hot fire.

And there she was. He breathed a slow sigh of relief. She wasn't out in the storm. It had been a dream. Or ... something. She was back, anyway. Safe. She'd pulled her log seat right up next to the stove and was sitting so close her knees nearly touched the hot metal. She was humming softly, a tune he couldn't recognize, and rocking a bundle in her arms.

Charley—was he sick? Surely he was too hot in that blanket, right next to the stove. Even if he had the chills, that couldn't be good for him.

"Jem?" His voice was gravelly, barely audible. But she raised her head and looked at him with a bright smile.

Too bright. "Hello. You're awake? How are you?"

"What's wrong with Charley?"

"He got too cold, poor boy. But we're warming him up, aren't we, Charley?" She rocked harder and hummed louder, while Seth studied the unnatural shape of the form in the blanket.

"Bring him here."

The strange light in her eyes frightened him. "I can't," Jem said. "I daren't take him away from the stove. He got so cold."

"How ... how did he get so cold?"

"Poor boy ... he was looking for Mama, wasn't he? I should never have left him. Everything's fine now, though. Mama will get you warm."

"Bring him here, Jemima!"

But she wouldn't.

It was an agonizing process, struggling his way to a sitting position, climbing to his feet. The whole time, he watched Jem, rocking harder, humming louder. The little form in the quilt didn't move. It was the wrong shape for a sleeping child. Jem looked ... why, she looked mad. Had she gone mad? Had she confused something else—some household object, perhaps—for her child? And, if so, where was Charley?

"Jem. Jemima, please. Bring him to me. I don't know if I can walk over there."

Jem hummed even louder, and the tune came to him: "Weary of Wandering from my God." It wasn't one of Charles Wesley's more rousing hymns, but she moved the tune like it was the third day of a Pentecostal revival, rocking to the rhythm. An unnatural smile lit her face. Seth used the wall to balance himself, but his legs were so weak he could hardly hold himself upright. He didn't know where his cane was. The twig broom hung on its nail beside the door. He flipped it broom-side-up and used it as a walking stick to cross the floor to Jem.

He braced on the broomstick and lowered into a crouch. "Let me see."

He tugged at the quilt, but she pulled it away. "Stop! He has to be covered. I have to warm him up!"

But Seth held firmly and drew the blanket back. Charley's fair hair lay in wet tendrils on his forehead. His face was still. Waxen. "No," Seth whispered.

"He's fine!" Jem's voice was shrill. "I just have to warm him up!"

"No! No, Jem." He tried to pull the bundle out of her arms. He could feel the give of Charley's thawing flesh over the still-frozen muscles. "He's not fine! He's not fine!"

They struggled for a minute, but when he realized Jem wouldn't let go, he did. He got back to his feet. He gasped for air, but couldn't catch his breath. "Not fine! Charley! Oh, Charley! How did this happen?"

"He's fine! He must have come looking for me, and he got too cold. I need to put more straw in the fire. He has to be kept warm."

Seth clung to his makeshift cane, but then his legs buckled, and he fell to his knees on the dirt floor. The broomstick clattered against the table and then fell to the floor next to him.

Jem frowned at him over the bundle of quilt. "Be quiet. You'll wake the baby."

Seth covered his face with his hands and began to sob.

It was early in the evening before Jem relinquished Charley. Seth pulled his trundle bed out and put it against the wall, as far from the stove as Jem would allow. They lay him there, still wrapped in the other damp quilt.

Now Jem sat by the stove, rocking, but no longer humming. Her face was expressionless. She didn't look up when a knock sounded.

It was Mr. Teske and Mr. Hanson.

"Come in and warm yourselves." Seth stood back.

They entered and hesitated, blinded in the dim light. Seth watched their faces as their eyes adjusted and scanned the soddy, resting first on Jem, and then on Charley's body.

Mr. Teske laid his calloused palm on Seth's shoulder. "Your little one," he said, his voice heavy.

"Yes," Seth said. "Your family? Are they all—?"

"I sent them to school," Mr. Teske interrupted. "Fred, Jakob, and Magdalena. Such a nice day, after such cold. Only my Freni, she stayed home."

There was a short silence in the room. Seth wondered. Had the children frozen on the walk home? Why hadn't the teacher kept them in the schoolhouse?

When Mr. Teske didn't finish, Mr. Hanson cleared his throat. "We're searching for them, now. I ... If it's a help to you, I'll come with my bobsled to take your son. This evening. I have ... my own boy. My Peter, I'm trying to find him as well."

"I'm very sorry. H—how many? How many children did we lose?" Then he regretted the question, because the fate of their children was still unknown.

Mr. Hanson shook his head. "Six, for certain, including yours. Mrs. Potter and her sister from the east—they were walking to town. No telling how many are missing. I never saw anything like it."

"It is a cursed place," Mr. Teske murmured and then patted Seth again. "I am sorry, my friend. So sorry." Then, he turned to Mr. Hanson. "Please. Please, we must go. We must find them."

Seth wrapped the last loaf of sourdough bread and sent it with them. Mr. Teske tucked it into his coat without raising polite objections.

"I'll be back tonight or tomorrow," Mr. Hanson said. "And tomorrow, I'll send my boy Samuel over. He'll help you with that ox."

The two men left. Seth went to Jem. "Let me check your feet again."

Was he imagining it or did her feet feel a little warmer? They were misshapen and swollen, already showing signs of flaking skin, but maybe she would be able to keep them.

"Do your feet hurt?"

Judging by how much his nose hurt, her feet had to be unbearable. But she didn't respond and didn't flinch or cry out when he touched her or manipulated her toes. Her eyes were open in the way of a blind man, or a dead man. Taking nothing in, communicating nothing.

Seth let his head fall forward for just a second, resting his forehead against her skirts. Then he pushed himself up and went to make dinner.

CHAPTER TWENTY-FIVE

Winter was nearly over.

Jem never felt warm, although she fed the fire constantly, going through straw at a dizzying rate. The skin on her hands, legs, and feet peeled—layer after layer—leaving raw red flesh exposed. The pain was muscle-deep and unbearable when she was sitting—worse when she moved around to make a meal or wash clothes. But Dr. Bumgardner hadn't had to amputate any of her limbs, not even a toe. Toby's remaining body warmth had been enough to keep her flesh alive. She tried to be grateful. If she'd been crippled, where would that have left them?

But she was sorely short on gratitude as she stood over spattering johnnycakes on the cookstove, listening to the breeze blow across the thawing land. It was the third Sunday in March and sunny. Finally, a sampling of springtime.

She'd thought about going to church that morning. She could leave Seth for that long, or even go by the Teske's, see if they were taking their wagon. If so, she knew they'd be glad to offer her and Seth a ride. She'd thought about it, but then let the idea slide through her fingers like cornmeal.

She didn't want to sit on a hard bench and listen to Reverend Hinkley preach about God's wisdom and love. God had permitted small children to wander lost in the blizzard, blinded by snowflakes as sharp as sewing needles. He'd allowed them to collapse in the snow, crying for their mothers, and to perish where they lay. God had allowed Charley to die, and was allowing him, still, to lie wrapped in the quilt made by Susan's loving hands in the undertaker's shed, beside nine other people, awaiting the full thaw and burial. What had she to say to a God like that? What had he to say to her?

Two, going on three months since the blizzard, she had no heart for keeping house, nor for tending Seth, nor for praying. It was coming time to put the peas in, but she had no heart for that either. Sometimes, when she went to the pantry for salt pork or dried beans, she'd tip the paper packet of seed peas into her hands. But then she put them back and closed the envelope up tight. Her heart felt like those shriveled green peas.

A rattle outside drew her attention and she listened. It was Seth coming in from the lean-to. Gathering the eggs was woman's work, but she'd put up no resistance when he started doing the chore each morning, leaning heavily on the sturdy stick he'd adopted as a cane. What else could he do? The cow was dry, so there was no milk. There was no team to tend. He could repair the stable where the snow's weight had caved it in, but only the mice would benefit.

Seth called, a sharp sound. She moved the skillet away from the heat and went out.

"Is something wrong?" she asked.

He looked at her as if she were a stranger, a peddler selling goods he had no use for and didn't quite approve of. "I can't open the door."

With his cane in one hand and the basket of eggs in the other, he usually used the toe of his boot to wedge the door open. But today the door had closed fast, no longer pressed out of the frame by built-up ice. He couldn't get his toe into the crack.

She let him in and he handed her the basket. "Lot of eggs," he said.

She felt the weight of the basket and tried to think of a reply. "Maybe I'll set a hen, after all. I figured we'd need the eggs more than the chicks." She went to finish making breakfast.

They sat across from each other, chewing, sipping coffee, listening to the birds and the gentle breeze.

"More coffee?"

Seth finished chewing and shook his head. "No, thanks."

The question hung over them like another presence at the breakfast table. They would have to decide soon. Whether to plant or to pack. Whether to sell or try again to build a life in this cruel place. They had to talk about it.

But they didn't know how to talk to each other anymore.

Zeke barked as a wagon rattled into the yard.

Seth glanced through the window. "Teskes."

He grabbed his cane and they went out front together.

Mr. Teske halted his wagon, offered a wave to them, then went to help Mrs. Teske out. Before her feet hit the ground, Freni rushed forward to Jem. Jem hugged her, loving the feel of the little body in her arms.

"Hello, little one," Jem said. Her heart hurt with the need to say more. To tell Freni how precious she was and what a comfort she was to her parents. But those words failed her.

She stood to greet Mrs. Teske instead. The little woman's cheeks were pale, and she'd lost all her plumpness. She opened her arms to Jem and enveloped her in a long, wordless hug. They were both crying when they withdrew.

Mrs. Teske took Jem's face between her small, calloused palms, and spoke to her at length in Russian. Her voice was rich in compassion and melancholy; Jem found herself nodding in agreement.

At last they linked arms to walk to the soddy. "Will you have some coffee?"

She quickly cleared away breakfast dishes and guided their guests to sit. They turned in their seats so they could see Seth, who had settled on the edge of the bed.

Mr. Teske took a single sip of coffee before getting down to business. "I have wheat for you. Seed wheat. Good. Good Russian red wheat—will do well, here in this land."

Seth shook his head. "I can't take your seed wheat."

"We are finished," Mr. Teske said, and Mrs. Teske nodded. "We go to Florida. My brother is there. We go to him."

"We're going back to St. Paul," Seth answered. Jem jolted, turning to stare at him. Had he decided, then? They weren't even going to discuss the issue? But he didn't turn her way.

"No." Mr. Teske answered, as if Seth had asked him a question. "No, you stay. You are young. You are strong. You stay and plant my wheat."

Seth made a dismissive sound and gestured toward his cane. "I can't farm now. We'll go back to St. Paul and start over."

"Doing what?"

He shrugged.

Mr. Teske drank his coffee and waited for a better answer. When one didn't come, he shrugged too. "I leave the wheat. You decide. I send you my team also, when we leave. You send payment to Florida when you can."

"No," Seth said.

"We'll take it," Jem said.

All heads pivoted to her. She felt her face flush. She hadn't even known she was going to speak, let alone openly defy her husband with company present. "I—I mean ..."

Seth's eyes burned her skin. "Jemima," he said, but then he stopped. His face was flushed.

This set off a flurry of rapid Russian between Mr. and Mrs. Teske. Mr. Teske looked from her to Seth and back. He nodded slowly. Mrs. Teske spoke again, her tone urgent. But he raised his palm to her. "We will see," he said. "We will see."

Seth returned his attention to them. His voice was quiet. "When are you leaving? We'll be sorry to see you go."

"We will go next week. My wife, she wants to wait until ... until the children are buried. But we must not."

Mrs. Teske must have realized what he was saying. Her expression grew blank, and she lowered her eyes to her coffee. There was a silence in the room. Jem wanted to break it—to offer comfort, but the lump in her throat blocked her words.

The boys had been found in their shirtsleeves, curled around Magdalena, who was wrapped in both of their coats. No one knew why they had left the schoolhouse, nor how they had become separated from their teacher—she had been found frozen to death in a haystack over a mile away.

"I'm so sorry," Seth said. "I'm so ... they were wonderful children. I don't know how you —"

"Blessings from God above," Mr. Teske said quietly. Then he added, "But—the Lord giveth and the Lord taketh away, yes? We have this one remaining. For this, we are blessed."

Mrs. Teske interjected a comment, and he looked pained. "Ah, forgive me. Forgive me, my friend. But, I trust that you, also, will see more blessings from God. In his time."

"Well," Seth said.

It was a short and solemn visit. Jem gave Mrs. Teske all but four of the eggs they'd gathered that day.

"Please," she said, when the woman tried to protest. "I'll have this many more tomorrow."

Little Freni translated, then translated her mother's thanks back to Jem. Jem felt Magdalena's absence more acutely as Freni tried to fill her place.

Outside, Mr. Teske stacked burlap bags of wheat against the wall of the stable. Seth shook his hand. "If I sell it, I'll send you the money. Send us your directions in Florida."

While Seth stepped back to exchange a few words with Mrs. Teske, Jem shook Mr. Teske's hand also. "Thank you so much. I'm just not sure what we're going to do."

"Good wheat. Russian red—made for this prairie."

"Yes. That's what Seth used to tell me."

His blue eyes studied her face. "Grief. It is ... it is broken glass. The heart is broken like glass. You will put the pieces together again. The cracks will stay, but your hearts will beat again."

For some reason, that made her want to cry again. She had the impulse to hug him, but—of course—she didn't. Instead she hugged Mrs. Teske, hugged Freni, and then hugged Mrs. Teske again. "I'm going to miss you so much!" And then she did cry.

"My friend," said Mrs. Teske, wiping Jem's tears away but letting her own run down her cheeks uninterrupted. "My friend."

They didn't see the Teskes again before they left. Seth and Jem only knew they'd gone when Peter Hanson, Mr. Hanson's younger boy, arrived a week later, driving Mr. Teske's team of oxen. Jem walked out to greet him. "How are you feeling, Peter? Are your feet well?"

"Yes'm. I didn't fare too badly. Ma said God intended for me to find the Doc that night. It was a miracle."

Jem heard many stories like his—people saved through either divine intervention or dumb luck. Back in Kansas, William and Susan's children had spent half the night shivering in the schoolhouse while their young teacher fed broken desks into the stove. When the roof blew off, she knew they couldn't survive there. She tied scarves to each child and herself, forming a long chain, and led them out into the storm. They were soon lost and headed for the open prairie, but the last child on the chain, Daisy, had connected with the corner of a homesteader's house, and they were saved.

Peter had been just as blessed. The boy had run for his house when his father saw the storm. But then he ran back to retrieve the book he'd secreted nearby, to read when his father wasn't looking. By the time he turned back for home, it was too late. He'd wandered for hours before coming across Dr. Bumgardner. The doctor had gotten him warm, fed him and gave him water, and he'd come through with nothing more than peeling skin on his ears and nose.

"It was a miracle," Jem agreed. She wanted to ask him—or perhaps walk over and ask Mrs. Hanson—why God hadn't made similar provision for her Charley. Had her child somehow been less deserving of God's providence? But instead she asked, "Are the oxen gentle?"

"Yes'm. They're like babies. This one here's Gosha and that's Yuri."

Jem moved slowly, reaching to stroke their damp velvet noses. "Hello, boys. Welcome to our farm."

"I'll put them up for you, ma'am."

"Thank you, Peter. Will you stake them by the stable? Now, don't you leave—I've got some eggs for your mother."

Peter shoved the mop of blond hair out of his eyes and grinned. "No, thank you. ma'am. It's no trouble, bringing the team by."

Jem smiled back. "She told you to say that, did she? Never mind. I'll be back in a jiffy."

When she handed him the basket, he peeked under the napkin with obvious relish. "Thank you, ma'am. I know my ma will be glad to have some eggs. She was down to three hens by last fall, and we had to eat 'em."

"Are you all staying on?"

He blinked. "Staying on? Oh, yes, ma'am. My pa has no plans to go anywhere. Ain't nowhere to go."

"I'm glad to hear it. I'm glad to keep such good neighbors nearby."

She saw him off with a wave and then went into the soddy.

Seth stood by the window, looking out. "I was afraid he'd do that."

"What? Peter Hanson?"

"No. Teske. I never agreed to buy that team."

Jem approached him slowly, and put her hand on his arm. They so rarely touched now, it felt like she was touching a stranger. "Seth, do you really want to go back to St. Paul? There's nothing there for us."

"There's nothing *here* for us, Jem. I can't drive a team. Look at me! I can barely walk!"

"You're getting stronger every day. And I'll help you. We'll work together."

He pulled away from her. "We'll sell the oxen and send Teske the money."

"Seth, please. Just come out and see them. Come out a see what a good, gentle pair they are. Why, they'll practically drive themselves."

The look he gave her chilled her. "You're so set on staying here. You want to stay here in this godforsaken land that killed our son."

"I—I want to. Seth, this is our home. Charley loved this place."

"Until it killed him. That doesn't trouble you though, does it?"

Pain and then anger surged through her like bile. "How dare you! How dare you say such a thing! I loved him! How could you even—" Words failed her, and before she knew what she was going to do, she opened her hands and shoved him, hard.

He was unprepared for the blow. It knocked him off balance. He landed hard on his backside on the soddy floor, stared up at her, mouth agape.

She shook her fist in his direction, her voice shrill. "This was my child! My baby! How *dare* you suggest that I don't care? What would it take, Seth? What would it take for you to believe that I loved our child? Shall I stop trying to live? Shall I die? Is that what you want?"

"I don't want you to die." His quiet voice severed her screams, creating a silence that rang in her ears.

He used the log seat to push himself to his feet. He'd lost a lot of weight over the winter—so had she—but he still had a good eight inches on her, and his forearms were still corded with muscles. She took a step backward.

She'd pushed Seth down? Oh, surely not! Oh, surely she hadn't—

She took another step backward, but he didn't make a move toward her. His face was unreadable, but his fists were clenched at his sides.

"No more, Jemima."

"You have no—"

"*Quiet*."

Seth's chest heaved. The tension hovered, leaching breathable air out of the room. They faced each other for a minute—more—before his face smoothed into that blank mask that she'd seen too often lately. "I apologize for raising my voice to you."

She knew she had to answer, to acknowledge his apology and give one of her own. But a storm of emotion had come up inside her, as black and deadly as that blizzard. She choked on whatever words she'd been trying to say. Then she turned her back on him and ran outside.

CHAPTER TWENTY-SIX

The sky was almost shocking in its piercing blue clarity. One cloud, as fluffy and harmless as a goose-down pillow, hovered in the east. Was that the sky they had watched fearfully all winter? Had it bulged with black ice storms? Was that the sky that had brought death to Charley?

She deliberately relaxed her arms at her sides, let her head fall back so the sun warmed her face. When she felt calmer, she straightened. She would go back inside and talk this out with Seth—like the mature, Christian woman that she was supposed to be.

She turned back toward the soddy, then stopped.

Seth was in there.

But Charley wasn't. Charley was gone.

This was Charley's farm. He'd run through this grass, chased those chickens, splashed in that mud. He'd spent hours staring at caterpillars and spiders. He'd run free like a little wild thing, grown strong and brown from the sun. And he had thrived.

She'd imagined him walking to school, working outdoors with his father. She'd imagined that he'd court a local girl, and marry—perhaps in this very yard. She could have had grandchildren—Charley's own babies—running through her yard, inventing the same mischief that Charley had.

Instead, her little boy had died here. Just on that field over there. Terrified. Miserable. Alone. Looking for her.

"Oh, Charley." The freshening breeze caught her whisper and danced it through the warm air. "I wanted this for you."

A spasm of pain grabbed her heart. It was the worst one yet—an agony that brought her to her knees on the cold earth. She curled her fingers into the mud, gasping for a breath. "Charley."

The razor edge sliced at her insides. She collapsed forward into the soggy slush. "I just want him back. Give him back!"

As if in response, she felt the presence gather around her.

"No! I don't want you." The sobs that claimed her were like none that had gone before. She screamed through them. "I want my boy. Give me my baby back! Oh, God, please, my Charley! Why did you take my baby? Give him back!"

The sobs racked her, clenching muscles and tearing across them. She struck her fists against the ground until they were raw. She raged—against the earth, against the sky, against God—until, at last, she was depleted. Her body deflated, went limp onto the ground. She lay with her eyes closed, becoming aware of her physical discomfort, but not resisting it, nor begrudging its place in her.

"Go away," she said.

"How did you know I was here?"

It was Seth's voice, right next to her. He must have been looking through the window when she collapsed. That wasn't surprising. It was surprising that he'd come out to her though.

"I wasn't talking to you," she said.

"Can I help you get up? It's not good for you to lie in the mud." How long had it been, since he'd spoken to her in such a gentle way?

Jem kept her eyes closed, savoring the gritty cool on her face. "No. I'll just stay here."

Around back of the place, Zeke barked once, probably sighting a groundhog or some other prey. A bird squawked, and a loose board on the stable creaked in the wind. She felt new warmth through the thin fabric of her dress—Seth was rubbing her back.

It made her sad. Her throat clogged and tightened. She fought it off; she didn't think she could withstand another bout of crying now. Instead, with a great effort, she pushed herself up onto her elbows and shifted sideways, so her upper body lay on Seth's lap.

"It was my fault." She whispered the words, but he heard her.

"No. No, Jem." Seth stroked her hair and back. "Not your fault. Nobody's fault."

When her tears came again—in a quiet storm this time— he patted her and wiped her tears with the corner of his shirt. And when she felt moisture drop onto her the bare skin of her arm, she rose to her knees, and held her husband while he cried.

They were quiet that evening, depleted by their tears. But they were no longer separated from each other by them.

She washed up the dinner dishes, then sat beside him at the table. He wasn't drinking coffee, nor reading, nor working on his chair. He just sat. When he noticed her, he patted her hand.

She waited a while before she spoke. "I loved him. I still love him."

His voice sounded tired. "Oh, Jem, I know that. How can we even measure … he was … that boy was my heart. And he was yours. I know that. He knew that."

"I don't think I want to leave."

He rubbed his forehead with his palm. "I'm … trying to make the best decision for our f—for us. For you and me."

"But, we have the wheat. You yourself said that Russian Red is the best kind for the prairie. It can tolerate the heat and the drought. We can work together—be partners, the way we were this summer. Remember how it was? We were so close!"

"We'll work together in St. Paul."

"No, we won't." She released his hand, stood to pace the short distance to the wall and back. "We didn't work together in St. Paul. We were barely married in St. Paul, Seth! I never saw you. You traveled all the time. I don't think—Why, I don't think we even knew each other until we came here. We were practically strangers!"

"Now, Jemima, you're exaggerating."

"Oh, really? Really?" She waved her hands and did another circuit. "Who were my friends in St. Paul?"

"What?"

"You heard me! Who were my friends?"

"Well … Sally, of course. She was your closest friend."

"Besides her!"

Seth turned his face away, as if protecting his face from a stiff breeze. "Please stop yelling."

"What did I do for leisure in St. Paul?"

"For—for leisure?"

"That's right! For fun!"

"Jemima, I just don't see what this has to do with—"

"You don't know, do you? Admit it! When we were in St. Paul, you didn't know anything about my life!" She threw her hands up. "Oh! Oh! You are just so—so—" She whirled on him and froze.

He smoothed his expression, but not quickly enough.

Jem stared at him. "Are you laughing at me?"

"Of course not."

"You are! You're laughing at me!"

He shook his head, his face severe. She approached him, feeling a bit like a cautious wild thing overcome by curiosity. She had to look close, but she saw it: the barest twinkle, the slightest twitch at the corner of his lips.

"Well, my goodness," Jem said softly. "I didn't even know you still knew how to do that."

The twinkle faded, but his face looked more relaxed. "I guess I didn't either."

He took her hand in his and held it to his lips. Her throat clogged at the familiar gesture.

"Jemima," he said. "Let's try to have a conversation."

"A conversation?"

He tugged on her hand until she sat down again. She waited for him to speak, but he was frowning at their joined hands. It was a long minute before he said, "This place feels alive."

Then he sighed sharply and shook his head at his words. "I sound mad."

Jem tightened her fingers on his. "If you are, than I am too. Sometimes I talk to the, well, the land, I guess. The prairie. It's like a ... child. A spoiled child."

He didn't lift his head, but just angled his chin so he could look at her. "A child?"

"Yes, a child. And we're its playthings. When it gets tired or cranky, the prairie has a fit—just stomps on us and throws us all over the playroom. Blizzards, droughts, grasshoppers—whatever it fancies. And there's nothing we can do about it."

"Yes. Well, I'm tired of being the plaything of a spoiled child. Let's go back to a place that is just a *place*, instead of an evil personality."

She kept her eyes downcast.

"Why, Jem? Why do you want to stay in the land that killed our son?"

Jem stood up, went to look out the window. Her eyes automatically scanned the horizon.

It was a harsh land. The summers were too hot, the winters, fatally cold. It wasn't a land for the faint-hearted or weak—they soon fled back east. If they lived long enough to book a fare. But for the strong ...

She looked around again, seeing their land as it could be. As it *should* be. She knew where the new barn would go—over there. And the house, when they built it, should be right against that hill, giving them a convenient cellar and shelter from the endless wind. And over there ... in her mind she saw the pasture filled with cattle and a few precious horses, all safely surrounded by the fence of barbed wire that Seth always talked about. She wanted a line of trees along the north and west lines of the property—that would help break the wind and provide better landmarks in storms. And a bigger garden with a fence around that as well. She drank in the color, the endless expanse, the open air. A person could breathe out here. A person could grow and never hit a boundary, never feel hemmed in.

"In St. Paul," she said at last, "we would have nothing."

"Here we have nothing."

"Here we have nothing." She put her hand against the cool glass, caressing the view. "No. Here we have no *things*. But we have something. We have our life. It's what Charley loved—this life we have here."

"It's what killed him."

"Perhaps ..." she had to swallow hard on the thought. It had been pressing on the edges of her mind, but she had refused it entry until now. "Perhaps he would have died in St. Paul."

When Seth said nothing, she turned. He still sat, watching her. His faced looked pale in the dim light.

"Do you understand, Seth?"

"No."

"Children die in St. Paul. Look at Katie's little girl. Look at the blizzard they had in the East, only a couple of weeks ago. In New York! Children died there. They die of pneumonia, diphtheria, smallpox. It's—it's terrible, but children die everywhere." She went to him and stroked his cheek lightly with her knuckles. His skin felt warm after the glass. "Charley lived here. He died here, but he *lived* here. I—I wish I knew how to say what I'm trying to say."

"Are you saying that you refuse to leave the homestead?"

He was so wrong that she actually chuckled. "No. Whither thou goest, Seth. I may not have understood that when we married—not really—but I do now. If you choose to go to St. Paul, I'll be by your side." She smiled into his eyes, marveling at both the strangeness and the familiarity of their closeness. "I'll probably complain the whole time, but I'll be there."

His return smile, scant as it was, eased the tightness in her chest.

She made her expression stern. "But I do refuse to go back to our old life."

His hands rose and rested on either side of her waist. "Oh, really? What does that mean, exactly?"

She put her hands over his and pressed them into place. "I'm afraid I'm just not cut out to be a ... decoration anymore. I want to set goals with you, work side by side, make decisions together. I want to be your partner. It will be harder to do that if we go back East, but I suppose we can find a way."

"But, you'd rather stay here."

Jem took her time answering. She thought about the hours hoeing in the garden, her skin burnt red, her head pounding. About the persistent mosquitoes, and the even more persistent rot on everything from food to clothing. About the fevers, the blizzards, the unspeakable loss.

"I would," she said.

"Let me think for a while. Would you please bring me my notebook?"

He began to figure on paper, and she went to her kitchen duties and left him to it.

"I can't see it," he said finally. "We have the seed and the team. Although we owe for both of those. But we don't have the labor, and we can't afford to pay for it."

"I can work."

He smiled at her. "Yes, you certainly can. But this just isn't a one-man, one-woman operation. And you have your own business to tend to. We can't live without those chickens and the garden, can we?"

"No. No, I guess not. We've been glad enough to have eggs, that's for sure."

"I'm thinking ..." he hesitated. "There are actually quite a few things I could do, even with my leg. I could hang a shingle out to practice law or become a merchant. I'd like that, actually. Finding new inventions and tools and recommending them to people."

"That would be wonderful!"

"Yes, but it takes time—and money—to set something like that up. And, meantime, we have no one to work the farm. You see? I'm trying. I really am, darling, but I can't see how we can manage it."

Jem wanted to argue with him or scratch out the numbers he'd written on the page. But she held the feeling in and nodded. "If we can't—well—then we can't. That's all. I just really feel like we're ... this will sound strange. But I feel like God wants us here."

Seth tapped his pencil on the table. "So do I, actually. Let's pray about it."

Jem stirred her soup a final time, then went to sit beside him. "Together?"

"You have a problem with praying with me?"

She knew she was blushing. "Of course not."

He tilted his head at her so she had to laugh.

"Well, a little. That's new for us, isn't it?"

A knock sounded on the door, making them both jump. "Saved by the bell," Jem said. But Seth didn't smile.

"Zeke didn't bark."

"What do you mean?"

It was a foolish question, and he didn't answer. He went to his trunk and took out his pistol. He held it loosely behind his leg as he unlatched the door. And then he laughed out loud.

"The one person Zeke wouldn't bark at," he said and stepped back. "Jem, come over here and say hello."

Jem joined them and felt herself smiling too. "Well, my goodness. The mystery of the cat on the post is about to be explained."

The boy had grown since last summer, but his face was still dirty, and his hair still hung in an untidy curtain in his face. His dog—just the mama now—leaned on his leg, looking worried and tired.

He shuffled his feet. "I didn't mean no harm, ma'am."

"No harm was done. Curiosity isn't quite as deadly as they say." She stepped back. "Come in."

"Oh, no ma'am. I don't want to intrude. I just ... came by. That's all."

"Came by?" Seth asked.

He shuffled his feet again. "Yessir."

Jem could see he'd grown pink, even under the grime on his face. Why was he embarrassed? "What's your name?"

"Levi." He cleared his throat.

Seth gave Jem a questioning look and she shrugged.

"So," Seth said. "The cat?"

"Oh, yessir. It means ... well, to people like me, it's our way of saying 'a kind lady lives here.' "

"It is?" Jem bit her bottom lip to keep in her smile. "That's what it means? That's so nice! Oh, Seth, did you hear that? A kind lady lives here."

"Well, it's surely true, ma'am. Anyhow," Levi added, as if he had more to say. But then he didn't go on.

"I wish you'd come in, Levi," Jem said. "Why, I feel like we're old friends."

She grabbed his arm and pulled him in before he could protest anymore. His dog whined but hung back outside. "Besides, I never got to thank you properly for Zeke. He's been a wonderful dog."

"Thank you, ma'am." Being indoors somehow made Levi seem even more gawky. "I ... went through town. I was awful sorry to hear"—he lowered his gaze, his voice went husky, soft—"about your boy. I'm awful sorry."

Jem put her hand on his arm. "Thank you. Come on and sit down now."

She fed him bread and beans and fried potatoes. It was a wonder how much food that boy could take in and still live. Seth sat with him, asking him about the places he'd been and the things he'd seen.

When Levi ate what had to be his last bite and sat back, Seth asked again. "So what brings you back this way? You have another job?"

Levi looked down, squirmed, but then looked up and met his eyes. "I'm here for you."

"For me?"

"For both of you. I ... I don't know how to explain it, no how. Because my ma used to drag me to revivals before she died, and I didn't get nothing out of them except free smokes from the bigger boys back behind the tent."

He rose. "I wish you'd sit down, ma'am. I hadn't oughtta be sitting when a lady's here."

Jem sat. "What happened to you, Levi?"

"Something. Something like, that piece of writing you gave me. It just, well, it just got me thinking that's all. I just started thinking, and, well ..." His cheeks had gone bright red. "That's all I want to say about that."

Seth sat back a little, looking thoughtful. "That's all, huh? And you came here to tell us that?"

"Nossir. I came to work here on this farm. That is, if you'll have me."

"Because ..." Seth prompted.

"'Cause that's what I'm gonna do."

"I can't afford to pay you, son."

Levi scowled at him. "I didn't ask you for no money. I just, why, I just have a need to work on this farm. So, here I am."

Jem opened her mouth to speak, then closed it again. This was for Seth to answer.

"Let me get you set up in the barn, boy," Seth said. "We'll have to talk all this over."

"I know my way," Levi said. "Thank you for the food, ma'am." He left the house with a quiet dignity that didn't match his appearance.

Seth looked from the closed door to her. "Just like that," he said. "We didn't even get the words of the prayer out, and he's here to work."

He lowered himself to his seat and raised his hand as if to say something else, then dropped it.

"You never know what to expect," Jem said. "Out here in the Wild and Wooly West. It's a never-ending adventure."

"I suppose you're right." He rubbed his chin with his knuckle, glanced out the window in the direction of the barn, and shook his head. "So you really want to stay? You've decided you like adventure?"

"I hate adventure," she said. "I want security and predictability."

"You won't find those here."

It had been so long, but seemed the most natural thing in the world, to sink down onto his leg, wrap her arms around his neck, and kiss his whiskered cheek.

"Then," she said, "we'll just have to *make* them here."